CU00656810

Truth is not Enough

Paul Runewood

paulrunewood.com

©2022 Paul Runewood

*Free thinkers don't find danger in another's words
– only possibility*

1. You're All Going to Die

"Millions of people will die. People you love, people from your family," frothed the prime minister from a lectern, freshly furnished with garish signage that read, 'Following rules saves lives.' The Downing Street media room was packed with all the big hitters from news organisations all across the globe.

Knuckles white, he gripped the edges of his podium as if the nature of his message was inducing vertigo. I knew him well enough to know when he was lying, like most politicians, it was usually ceded by the moving of the lips, but this wasn't his usual blustering exaggerations carried out on behalf of the PR department of his runaway ego. This felt different.

"We have consulted the science and if we don't act decisively the health service will become overwhelmed and many, many more people will die."

There was something insincere about his delivery that his swagger couldn't quite conceal. I spotted members of his backroom advisers looking on nervously. The PM was a maverick, a sharp mind encased in a fancy-dress buffoon's outfit, topped-off with clownish messy blonde wig. He was prone to regular self-destructive outbursts that gave his people nightmares but oddly increased his popularity. As risky as he could sometimes appear, he was still the front-runner in a field of political also-rans, so bland they could easily be mistaken for the wood panelling they stood before in Parliament's debating chamber.

A slick slideshow burst into life and we were danced through a tranche of graphs and images reinforcing the predicted death toll, with narration provided by Derek

Berkson from Royal College London. Always looking for the small print, I noted that none of it was based on real data.

"I am proposing a lockdown that will keep people in their homes until we have flattened the curve," said the PM. "Key workers will of course be expected to carry on regardless, but a mask mandate will be in place in shops, public transport and across essential services. We will review the situation again in three weeks' time."

At the short Q and A session that followed, I took the opportunity to dispute Mr Berkson's patchy record of predictions.

"Stig Fisher, Capital Post." I said, garnering the PM's attention. "Prime minister, Derek Berkson's forecasts for the previous major health scares have been so far off the mark, his name has become synonymous with disastrous predictions. 'Doing a Berkson' even became a catch phrase in a Television soap opera."

I could see Berkson's face flush with rage.

"Did he not predict a similar death toll of hundreds of thousands for the outbreak of Foot and Mouth? To date, the number of deaths for that remains in single figures," I said.

"Thank you, Stig, I have full confidence in Mr Berkson and his team at RCL. Next question," replied a visibly agitated PM, sweeping my prescient point aside.

"Do you think you could have locked down the country sooner?" asked Rachel Morrison, from the far-left Guardian newspaper.

The Prime minister took this as an invitation to position himself as a harbinger of measured and moderate policy, insisting that he had exhausted every other option as he knew how detrimental this temporary lockdown would be to the economy.

He continued ducking and swerving the questions, perhaps scared they might snare him, until he reached the finishing line of this aural obstacle course. Strangely, most journalists present gave him something of an easy ride. At the conclusion of the media session, he disappeared behind the curtain. He made the most striking statement of any serving prime minister since World War two but the substance he offered up as justification for it was thinner than Dickensian gruel. Our newspaper was the coat rack on which the Conservative party hung its hopes. We shone their PM's shoes while he was in office, occasionally raking them with a more abrasive brush when the owner felt the need to flex his inky black muscles in aid of vested interests. When sectors of industry, like oil and pharmaceuticals, spend millions in newspaper advertising, they are not paying for the fancy ads showcasing their products, their huge outlay secures influence over what is printed, or not printed in the pages in-between. As a political correspondent, it was something I frequently had to wrestle with.

The Capital Post hailed the PM as 'Captain Courageous' when he promised to tackle the recent spiral of inner-city homicides, and 'Captain Britain' when he bumped heads with the bureaucrats of the EU – unshackling the UK from the European Superstate. Tonight, his defeatism and economically paralysing policies would be better rewarded with the moniker 'Captain Bring-down.'

If there was indeed a looming pandemic, and I had no reason to believe that this wasn't the case, engulfing the public in a mood of fear and paranoia would be the exact thing you would wish to avoid if you were Head of State. For me, the press conference delivered more doubts than solutions. Back in the office, I sharpened up my copy, laced it with a series of pointed questions to the government and the wider scientific community and sent it to the editor.

It wasn't a hunch or any breakthrough evidence, I don't know why, but I had a sickening feeling in my gut that life was going to change for all of us. Whether that was to do with the government's relationship with the electorate, or just human connection in general, I wasn't sure.

I was lost in thought just gazing out of the sixth-floor newsroom window, overlooking London's Trafalgar Square. The colourful dots below me, puffing out hot breath into the cold spring air, resembled a swarm of animated cigarettes choreographed into intricate patterns. I studied the swish and swirl of a myriad of lives caught up in the motions of the cosmopolitan hustle and bustle. I was a news shepherd charged with corralling that flock.

The next morning, while perusing the papers, I was a little surprised that every edition had an identical take on the PM's declaration. From the neo-conservative Telegraph to the left-wing Guardian, via the lowest common denominator *Sun, Star* and *Mirror,* no-one was holding him to account. My own piece in the Capital Post, which was hardly revolutionary, had been softened and blunted to fit into the same mould as all the others. I was incensed. I was under no illusions about my pen being for hire, but I didn't appreciate my words being tampered with in such a manipulative fashion.

Clashing with Maxwell Silver, the newspaper's editor, was a regular pantomime at HQ. It played out like a game, but we were both aware of the seething undercurrent of mutual contempt. Unfortunately for me, he held all the aces.

Maxwell was an unpredictable, prickly swashbuckler with the habit of changing tact mid-sentence without skipping a beat.

My mentor at Scribe School, back in the nineties, was a fearless satirist by the name of Sonny McDonald. I adhered to his advice like some folk do the Bible. I used to record our meetings so I could listen over again to ensure I didn't miss a thing. "Perspicacity," he would say. "It's the currency universally accepted, even if sometimes begrudgingly."

I spent the rest of the day researching the pandemic, looking for an angle that was both sharp and original. Unusually, every parliamentary political party was dancing to the same tune, so there was no point scouring that area for shades of dark and light. The NHS had been overwhelmed for as long as I could remember. Regular austerity measures had stripped it bare. In winter it wasn't unusual to see trolley beds lining the corridors for lack of space. Those who spent their careers trashing the Tories for dismantling the National Health Service were strangely applauding the government's line about how they were protecting it.

I started with the World Health Foundation who seemed to be at the forefront of policy both in the UK and around the world. To add a counterweight, I made my way across the spectrum to the alternative voices of opposition.

A swift coffee and cake aided my journey into the zone. The only truly dissenting voices I could find belonged to a tranche of conspiracy theorists, led by Vernon Coleman, who actually made some very potent arguments against Lockdowns, revealing data that questioned the government's assessment of the severity of the virus. Dr Coleman discovered that deaths and hospitalisations were receding prior to the Lockdown announcement and that, seven days before the March 24 shut down, the state quietly reclassified the virus as less lethal than originally assumed, putting it on par with seasonal flu. The contradictions were written large.

I made a compelling and fair-minded piece that was head and shoulders above the strange mimicry I had found across the media in recent days. I sent my copy in and before hitting the sack uploaded a piece to camera for my online blog.

I awoke the following morning to an internet shit storm. I was being described as uncaring, ill-informed and dangerous, not just by online trolls but by my own colleagues. Even the populist journalists, who made a career out of playing devil's advocate, were assassinating me in print. My principal crime was to give air to Dr Vernon Coleman.

By the time I made it into HQ, both my online piece and video blog had been pulled.

"Stig," snapped Maxwell

I spun around and there he was in all his seedy glory. So shambolic in appearance, no matter how expensive his attire, the clothes always seemed to wear him and not the other way around.

"I warned you about the virus. Did I not?" He raved.

"There's nothing inaccurate about my-"

He interrupted. "You dropped a right pigging clanger."

"What's the big deal? I've got all the facts," I said.

"Facts, what have facts got to do with it? Why do you always do this to me, huh? I've got Ten Downing Street breathing down my neck, for fuck's sake," he ranted.

"Aren't we supposed to breathe down their necks?" I replied.

"I've got one word to say to you," said Maxwell.

"What?"

"Chicago," he said.

What the hell was he talking about? This confusion stole some of my ire.

He handed me a file. He was sending me to the Democrats national conference.

The file had Isaac Grossman's name scrubbed through and my name written atop in marker pen. Isaac was the international political correspondent and a real lightweight, at least I felt so. Underneath was another folder entitled 'Michigan.'

"Michigan?" I snorted.

"Oh, yeah," said Maxwell hardly containing his glee, "Two words. There's a little detour for the Sunday magazine."

I had been bumped off stories in the past, but Chicago? Somebody wanted me as far away from the gun cupboard as humanly possible.

Maxwell disappeared into his office.

"Hang on," I demanded. "I won't be silenced like this."

"Don't give me none of that '*Fearless pen*' bullshit," his parting words.

The heal of his left shoe connected with the door slamming it in my face. It wasn't like him, he normally relished our little clashes.

I motioned to follow him but was swiftly intercepted by deputy editor, Jason Benjamin.

"Stig," he said in a tone that was instructing me to back down. "Leave it. You can't win this one."

The *Fearless Pen* tag was the quip I received from the actor Mel Gibson when he praised me for being the only journo to print the facts about a trumped-up drink driving charge that hit the headlines some years back. My bosses hated it but eventually encouraged me to use it in the masthead of my blog.

A swift flick through the assorted photos and documents clarified exactly what kind of mission they were sending me on.

"Have you seen where he's sending me?"

"You've had worse."

"A nut in a hut? Oh, come on, that's not what I do," I protested. "And my blog was removed, what the hell, Jason? What the hell?"

"Word from above," said Jason.

"What's going on? Do we work for Pravda now?"

His smile was one of containment.

He could see from my expression that his words were bouncing off me.

"I mean it, Stig. Don't venture any further, this thing's got trip-wires all over it," he said.

"This is bullshit, Jason, and you know it," I said.

"You're the lucky one, you get out of here for a couple of weeks," he said. "When you get back it will be all over. Oh, and check out the Upcycle, there's a new directive. Make sure you're on point."

I slunk off to my desk to calm down. This had the Iraq war written all over it. I checked my e-mails and found the latest edition of *The Upcycle* which was a frequently revised companion piece to *The Knowledge*, an outline of strictures, faux pas and taboo avoidance for Capital Post journalists. *The Upcycle* was to the Knowledge what the Hadith is to the Koran.

I recalled a recent oversight in my story about the English philanthropist and slave trader, Edward Colston. My error had been caught prior to publication by a sub-editor. My crime was employing the term BAME (Black, Asian, Minority Ethnic) which I had been unaware was no longer in vogue, Ethnic minority being the preferred term once more. A few months ago, the reverse would be true but, regardless of this unnecessary minefield of constantly shifting monikers, it was considered poor form to challenge *The Upcycle*.

No man's land was where the real story lay, but if I dared to tread there, I knew I could be rewarded with my P45. This latest edition of *The Upcycle* however, was a whole new kettle of rotting fish. The paper had appointed *Sensitivity Editors*. We were having our hands held by the iron grip of censorship. We were being instructed not to deviate from the government's narrative with regards to their response to the virus. Such a broad brush was normally reserved for the greatest of whitewashes. We were now paddling in the shark-infested murky waters once haunted by Soviet media and the GDR. There had always been discreet nudges to go easy on one individual or another, but this was blatant censorship at a time where the truth really was a matter of life and death. Again, I could hear the voice of my mentor. 'Integrity might not pay the bills, but it beats the hell out of sleeping tablets.'

When I opened the door of our three-storey house on Clapham Common, Harley, my seven-year-old son, in his captain America jumpsuit, threw himself at me. His arms stuck to me like we were connecting strips of Velcro.

"Daddy," he said excitedly.

"Yes, soldier," I said.

I felt that wonderful rush of love, his little hands resting around my neck, like a cashmere scarf on a cold winter's day. I spun him around until he giggled uncontrollably.

"You'll make him sick," called my wife, Jasmine, who was flapping around in the kitchen in something of a tizz. I put Harley down and, arms out wide, he continued to twirl his way towards the sofa, crashing dizzyingly into its plump inviting cushions.

I didn't have long before I had to leave but would have to find a little time to spend with him. It seems crazy that we 'make time' for our children, when our moments with them are often the most emotionally rewarding times of our lives.

"I'm running late," Jasmine said, stylishly dressed in black, as she threw things in and out of her enormous handbag, that was a mix between a mobile tumble drier and a bug-out bag. No matter how flustered or over-stretched she was, she always appeared immaculately turned out and with a charm she could trigger at the flick of a switch.

"Did you hear about my blog being-"

"-I heard," she said, resisting unpacking that line of conversation.

"It's outrageous. Maxwell only just stopped short on asking me to lie."

"So, what's new?"

"They used to send people to Coventry to silence them, he's sending me to Chicago. I leave in the early hours," I said.

She didn't bat an eyelid and just informed me that our son, Iain, should have been home by now, as he was not supposed to be at his girlfriend Emma's house, because of the lockdown.

"I thought it was over between them?"

"So did I," she said with the raise of her eyebrows.

"Ah well, she's a sweet girl," I said.

"I know but we don't need him getting into any trouble." she said, as she prepared to hurry out of the door.

"He's supposed to get into trouble, he's sixteen," I said.

"Anyway, you're risking the wrath of *the Finger men* yourself, aren't you?"

"We're delivering food to old folk who aren't allowed to leave their homes, not marching on parliament with pitchforks," she said.

She hoisted her bag over her shoulder and unlocked the front door.

"Oh, 'bye then," I said a little deflated.

She stopped, and in a mechanical fashion, backtracked a few steps, gave me a smile and planted a kiss on my cheek.

"Call me when you get there, and pick up something nice for the boys," she said.

I watched as her flowing blonde hair disappeared into the night like a solo torch parade.

This whole charade wasn't unusual. If there were awards for being busy, me and Jasmine would have spent half our lives preparing acceptance speeches. In our circles, being busy was considered a virtue, a clarification of your status as an active participant in life. We were on a merry-go-round without any idea how to get off. I couldn't exactly point the finger at Jasmine, routine and journalism go together like oil and water and my little family had acclimatised themselves to my frequent absences.

I wanted to visit my dear old Mum in the care home before I left for the States, but that would not be possible under the new restrictions. As I contemplated how she might be struggling with this new sense of isolation, Harley grabbed my hand and insisted I follow him into his playroom.

"Daddy, I've got a surprise," he said.

I squeezed onto one of his child-sized red plastic chairs and covered my eyes with my hands.

"No, Daddy, it's not that kind of surprise, silly," he said.

I opened my eyes to see him standing in front of me, mimicking the stance his teacher took when reading out to his class at school.

"I made a poem for you," he said proudly.

I quickly grabbed my phone and set the video recorder going.

"Ready?" he said eagerly, a beaming smile on his face.

"Yes, my little angel, I'm ready," I said.

"My Daddy is my best friend,
We have lots of adventures,
He makes good stories and likes fun,
He likes books and banana sweets
My Daddy is number one,
He had a yellow dog when he was a boy
I miss my Daddy when he is at not home."

"That was the best ever," I said.

I should have been preparing to leave for the airport, but I spent the following two hours playing with Harley and his Lego Pirate ship.

"When I grow up, I think I'm going to be a Journo… or a Pirate," he said, brightly.

It was funny hearing him use the term Journo that he had picked up from me banding about my work lingo at home.

"One day we will both be pirates, Daddy," he said.

"Just don't make me to walk the plank. Not twice in one day, anyway," I said, mostly to myself.

2. This is Democracy

I hit the first snag before we had even left the tarmac at Heathrow airport. The captain announced that there would be a delay while the last remaining passenger was located. Everyone gave a communal groan and it dawned on me that whoever this inconsiderate oaf was, he or she would be sitting in the only vacant seat, next to me. Maybe it's just me, but at those moments I always imagine it's going to be a twenty-stone alcoholic with the kind of body odour that could strip paint.

About fifteen minutes later, a man carrying his duty-free bag in front of him like it was a protest, made the walk of shame down the aisle.

Just as he was half-way along, I heard the man behind me growl under his breath about what a selfish bastard he was, his wife pleading with him to 'just let it go.'

As he neared my seat, he pulled at his face mask and name checked me. My jaw dropped open as I recognised the villain of the hour. It was Dexter Harris, a journalist with a penchant for mischief. Dex was a livewire who previously worked with me at The Post.

Now the indignation reserved for the man who was holding us all up was directed at me.

Dex had the reputation of a cluster bomb, leaving wreckage wherever he went. After one lawsuit too many, he was shown the door. He had a tabloid demeanour, but that caricature often concealed a sharp mind and even sharper pen.

"Democrats?" he enquired, as he stuffed a trolley bag into the luggage compartment.

"Democrats," I confirmed.

"The bores in blue," he said taking his seat, oblivious to the distress he had caused.

"Who are you working for nowadays?" I said.

"RT are picking up the bar bill for this one," he said, with a cheeky grin

He unscrewed the bottle top from an expensive vat of gin and taking a neat swig before offering me the same.

I declined. Way too early to start that kind of shenanigans.

"Working for the Russians?" I said, in a faux James bond baddies voice.

"Don't knock 'em. I mean, sure, you can't have a pop at Uncle Vlad, but everyone else is fair game," he said.

Dexter was good company and had some pretty forthright views which, although often questionable, had a certain entertainment value.

In Dex country green energy wasn't green at all, oil companies were in the background raking in the dough.

"Climate change? Have none of those Bozos ever read a history book? Of course the climate is changing. It always has and always will," he raged, volume turned up to 11.

I caught a glimpse of the man behind as his face grew redder by the minute. Dex was riffling off his top ten outrages. International child protection agencies were a cover for human trafficking and child abuse, and we were heading for a switch where all money goes digital and the banks will be able to decide what you spend it on. It was like his mission in life was to seek out things that made him angry.

A flight attendant approached and asked him to adjust his face mask which was languishing on his chin. He complied but not before puncturing holes in it.

"These things are a joke. I'm not giving up breathing for nobody," he said.

Dex's real ire was reserved for the UK's virus response, which he referred to as *the Scamdemic*.

"Biggest fraud the world has ever seen," he said.

"What about all the deaths?" I said.

"Oh, man. The whole thing is based on the predictions of that lunatic Berkson. Come on, he couldn't predict snow in a blizzard," he said, taking another swig of booze.

"You slugging down a handful of conspiracy pills with that gin?" I replied, with a smile, even though I was with him on the Berkson analogy.

"I've seen the evidence. Classified government documents. They are putting people in a state of fear to control them. It's psychological warfare, man. Big Pharma, Big Tech, they're all in on the deal. Those self-righteous keyboard warriors are so easily coerced into slaying anyone who doesn't follow the rules. But none of them stop to ask if the rules make any sense."

He seemed convinced, but I wasn't buying the global conspiracy angle. I had concerns about the measure of state control within the narrative, but maybe if they failed to get the message across, the virus would run riot. I was sure there were plenty of dodgy deals being done under the cover of such a big health crisis, but a wholescale plot to deceive the entire population of the world. How the hell would you co-ordinate something like that? Dex had an answer for that too and suddenly I felt like I was no longer a passenger but a subject in his psychological experiment.

"What have Tony Blair, Keir Starmer, Angela Merkle and Emmanuel Macron got in common," he said, as if he was telling a bar room joke.

"Enlighten me," I said.

"They all went to the same school."

"What? How could they go to-"

"-They were all hand-picked to attend the *Future Leaders programme* run by the World Economic Forum. And that's just the tip of the iceberg," he said with relish.

Our conversation degenerated into one of Dexter's infamous rants and, when the air stewardess delivered the complimentary newspapers, it interrupted his flow, and I took the opportunity to lose myself in the pages of the Capital Post.

"I'll send you some info when we get back," he said, before he put his headphones on to indulge himself in a movie.

It was now my time to be riled. The whole newspaper had become one big editorial for the government. Page after page of dubious scare stories. The exasperation must have shown on my face. Dex flicked an ear free from the headphones.

"Told you, mate. I read it in the airport bar. It's all hokum," said Dex.

I just shrugged.

"Maxwell must have his nose out of joint now Barnard is running the show," he said with a snort.

Chris Barnard was chief adviser to the prime minister and Dex was right, the paper looked as if the Tory spin doctor had been appointed editor in chief. There wasn't one line of caution or critical debate.

When you've been regularly flying around the globe, like I have for the last two decades, the process of getting anywhere becomes so mechanised you can normally power-down your brain until you're hailing a taxi at the other end. It's interesting seeing different people and places but one hotel room looks much the same as any other, unless you're interviewing *the Egos*, as I call them. The big time Charlies of our era, so preposterously vain it's actually very entertaining.

The sheer decadence on offer in some of the presidential suites I've visited was part pantomime, part faux-satanic ritual – and it was your job to work out which was which. Many of *the Egos* flaunted their dangerous little perversions, knowing that a revelation could destroy their reputation but aware that as they were a protected species, I would never be permitted to dip my quill in that slimy ink well and live to tell the story.

The 2020 Democrats' convention was like a circus without the fun, all hot air and con tricks. I wasn't dazzled by the jaded razzamatazz on offer. Dexter's Chinese Rolex had more authenticity than this. The smiles on offer looked so fake, I imagined they would have needed a team of surgeons, post show, to extricate them.

Why they chose the running mate of the last Democrat President as their *numero uno* I couldn't for the life of me figure out. Joe Biden reminded me of my dear old Uncle Horace from Norfolk. Biden looked like a dementia patient who had slipped his nurse and wandered in, searching for clarity, only to find a theatre of confusion. No matter how many strings they attached, this puppet was uncontrollably stumbling from one gaffe to another, completely forgetting his place and, on one occasion, referring to black sportsmen as Negroes. I just wanted to give the old man a hug and lead him away to somewhere that he could enjoy a biscuit and a quiet cup of tea.

Unfortunately for my copy, I hadn't been sent here to write any of this. The Post was backing *Sleepy Joe* to topple the orange-faced firebrand currently inhabiting the Oval office.

I was sure that the distance between those on stage and the lesser beings in the audience could be measured in contempt, these restrictions had very little to do with virus protocol. They filled this enormous arena, but the organisers had everyone kept at arm's length and Joe Biden was wheeled in and out of the conference without so much as an off-stage nod to the faithful, many of whom had travelled from states all over the country.

There was no chance of me getting an interview with their *champion-in-waiting,* he didn't do any straight interviews or campaigning, bar the odd scripted video. I did manage to snag a chat with Hilary Clinton, who barged her way through a barrage of questions without really saying anything at all. She was a machine. Her eyes had the welcome of a cocked and loaded twelve-bore shotgun. I was one from only a handful of non-US approved agencies permitted to speak to anyone of any stature. As was sadly now custom with these events, my questions were vetted.

Although I wore a mask, I copied Dex by puncturing some small holes into the paper so I could breathe more easily. I was irritated at having to listen to people speak through their masks, it felt like an extension to my pet hate of people talking with their mouths full.

Sometimes, particularly when away from the family I would become depressed about my job. Things like the way my editor had altered my report on the prime minister's Lockdown speech would rile me to the point at which I considered throwing the towel in.

I saw Dex hustling some minor celebs and getting a few Democrat stalwarts hot under the collar with his bombastic approach to vox pops.

Dex ushered me into a corner like a schoolboy who had just found the keys to the tuck shop storeroom.

"I've got a story so hot, even RT will think twice about broadcasting it," he said excitedly.

I prepared myself to be underwhelmed.

"They… are… going.. to defraud… the election," he said.

"Who told you that?" I said dismissively.

"It's virtually an open secret. They have connections with the makers of the vote counting software," he said.

"You're going to need some hefty evidence if you're going to chalk that one up."

"That's why I'm telling you. I thought you could keep an ear open," he said.

"I'll give Hilary a call if you like," I said, before shaking my head and laughing.

"You'll see," he said.

The Democrats hatred for Trump was so visceral it overpowered any policy pledges of their own. It almost didn't matter who the contender was. This election was Trump versus anyone who wasn't Trump. It was a risky strategy.

The days in Chicago blended into one another, with the exception of a raucous night out with Dex. He thrived on walking on the edge and eventually got himself thrown out of the conference for referencing the contents of the leaked confidential emails of Hilary Clinton.

3. Pie in the Sky

I was standing in the reception area of the Old Dragon
Cross Hotel in Grand Rapids, Michigan adjusting my
face mask as I scanned the people around me.
"Fisher?" called out a beefcake in a baseball jacket.
I was told to look out for a man called Redeye, and this, I
assumed, must be him.
He was the photographer and contact for my mission
deep into the Michigan hills to meet a man who went by
the name of Baldur. Yet another joker in a long line of
snake oil salesmen propagating his status as modern-day
mythical prophet, no doubt picking up a pretty penny or
two on the way.
Baldur was known for predicting the 9-11 attack on New
York, although he said it was missiles and not
aeroplanes. He also foresaw the 2008 bank crash and
Donald Trump's 2016 presidential success, but I was
confident that enough probing would unravel the truth
about this Hollywood-style necromancer. I would chalk
him up as another weekend-wacko and then scuttle off
home to dear old Blighty.
Redeye held out a hand and without thought I reached
out and endorsed his greeting, which felt almost sinful,
considering the instruction to avoid human contact that
had become dictum since I arrived stateside ten days ago.
Redeye seemed immune to the heightened sense of
anxiety that I experienced at the Democrat convention.
He walked me to his four-wheel drive truck and, before
we got in, he stopped and looked over at me. He pointed
at my paper mask.

"You gonna look awful stupid wearing that thing on the mountain," he said.

"But it's law, isn't it?"

"Not where we're going, it ain't," he said.

I hated wearing the things but like most folk I had factored it in to my daily routine and felt a little sheepish as I removed it and shoved it my pocket,

We left the Hotel car park in his truck and ventured out into rural Michigan. Perhaps it was the nature in which I had acquired this assignment, but I reckoned I could probably write this article in my sleep. Ex-serviceman or disgruntled ex-policeman hiding out in the hills with a gaggle of Hicks hanging on his every word as, King James Bible in one hand, automatic rifle in the other, he predicts Armageddon from his homemade pulpit.

Refuses to pay his taxes, hates gays, yada, yada, yada.

"Know much about the great Baldur?" asked Redeye in a tone that made me feel that he had been party to my thoughts.

"Real name Myles E. Robertson. Some clever predictions and he has become something of a cult figure among some disgruntled people in these parts."

"Wikipedia," he chortled, shaking his head. "Oh, boy."

I suddenly felt a little awkward, like I had boasted a knowledge of Beethoven's mastery by describing the shoes he wore, so I resorted to a tactic I rarely used and shamelessly marked his card about the superior level of my journalistic prowess.

I wiped my brow and declared, "I've just done a week at the Democratic convention. Your Hilary, she's a wiry character; thirty questions and she ducked them all." I said, in a brash way of intellectually elevating myself from the boy scout adventure Maxwell had sent me on.

"She's not *my* Hilary," he said. "And she couldn't shoot straight even if you tied her am to a telegraph pole.

Those politicians, a dime a dozen. Blue or red; different roads to the same swamp."

"Is that what Baldur thinks too?"

He looked at his watch then back up at me, his face awash with a mischievous smile.

"I guess you ought to go ask him."

The Democrats convention had been so dull and mechanical, whatever this was going to be I was sure it would be a tad more entertaining. As we engaged in small talk, my thoughts drifted towards home. Iain coped well with my absence, he had the independence and confidence of his mother, but Harley was different. His vulnerability reminded me of my own at his age. I knew he needed me and at times like this it burned me. I would get this in the bag and get on tomorrow night's flight home.

Finally, we cut off the main route and bumped our way up a steep tree-lined dirt track, encountering guards with dogs at a century station. So far, so Hollywood. Still, I figured it would look good in the photos.

We drove on for about a mile, through a dense wood of pine trees, on a pothole road that had more dips than a rollercoaster. The path opened up to a large clearing where an enormous tree with five thick trunks shot up into the blue skies like a hand reaching out to the heavens. To the right of the tree was a large house which connected on to what looked to me like a church. I have to say, it was postcard perfect.

As Redeye pulled up and switched the engine off, he turned to me.

"You're not Jewish, are you?" he said.

"Would that be a problem?"

It didn't matter that I wasn't. The timing of his question made my heart drop at the thought of spending a day with a bunch of anti-Semites.

Redeye hopped out of the car and immediately started snapping pictures.

I spun around, slowly gazing at the magnificent scenery. The expansive view across Lake Michigan was stunning. As I swivelled my head back around, I encountered a giant blond-haired man with an outstretched hand. This must be the great Baldur. It was strangely impossible to fix an age on him, something that was also absent from his Wikipedia page.

"Welcome to Heimdall Falls," he said.

I took his hand to shake and he gripped it longer than felt comfortable, all the while his crystal-clear blue eyes felt like they were reading every intimate fear and thought I had ever experienced. A confidence trick perhaps. Hadn't Adolf Hitler possessed the same hypnotic powers? I quickly reminded myself why I was here. I wouldn't let the mesmerising charm of the place or any stage tricks get the better of me.

"Baldur, or is it Myles?" I said confidently.

He ignored the question, and I suddenly felt my impudent faux pas rebound, as he led us towards the church.

Affixed to the front of the building was a handmade wooden carving of a representation of the nuclear family, boy, girl, mum, dad and dog. It was pure American apple pie.

"Mr Fisher, allow me to show you around my… *hut*," he said with a wry smile.

The church, a beautiful wooden structure, its roof like the inside of an upside-down boat was devoid of the Christian paraphernalia I had expected to scream at me on entry.

Baldur turned and pressed a finger to his mouth. To our right was a group of about twenty young people receiving what sounded like a lesson on foraging.

Redeye was right, there were no masks on show, and it was apparent that social distancing was yet to reach these climbs.

"No hand sanitiser then?" I mumbled sarcastically to Redeye who had now re-joined us.

"Healthy people don't require the restrictions of a government who receive their medical advice from a banking institution, but if you would like to wash your hands there's a restroom to your left," said Baldur in a soft tone.

I now felt obliged to take up his offer and splashed water over my face and washed my hands in the bathroom. The figure that peered back at me in the mirror looked jaded. My repertoire was sounding clunky, I needed to sharpen up. If I could just press fast forward and find myself London-bound, feet up in business class, gin and tonic in hand, I would be a very happy man.

I followed the sound of Redeye's camera clicking away to an impressive looking library where Baldur offered us refreshments. I was hoping to top up my caffeine store with a strong black coffee, but the choice was herbal tea or… herbal tea. Baldur excused himself and left the room and I searched for defects in his floor-to-ceiling bookshelves. There were volumes on philosophy, history, poetry and eastern medicine. Just as I was about to concede, I spotted it, the fly in his ointment I was expecting to find. 'One born every minute,' the biography of the famous American fraudster Hungry Joel Arnstein.

I turned to find Redeye pointing his lens at me and Baldur returning with a tray of mugs.

"You're a fan of Hungry Joel Arnstein?" Asked Baldur.

"The godfather of fraud," I said

"A man's choice in books says a lot about him, wouldn't you say, Mister Fisher?" said Baldur.

"Indeed," I replied.

"It's interesting that you should be drawn to that book," he said.

He had completely turned it around at me. You don't get to be king of the mountain without being a bit light on your feet, I guess.

We were seated around a hand carved wooden coffee table as we sipped our tea. It had the aroma of pine trees, and a taste of watery nothingness.

"I can't seem to find anywhere that states your age, do you mind if I ask how old you are?"

"I am no more my age than you are your profession," he said.

Again, he batted me off with word play. I tried a different line of attack.

"A place like this must have cost a pretty penny to build," I said.

"It's beautiful but without the folk who come here it's just dirt and wood. If you look close enough, you'll find that humility is what grows tallest in these parts. I hope that doesn't make you feel uncomfortable," he said.

I started to wonder whether he had been trained to avoid straight answers by the Democrats.

"CNN tagged you as a fairground fortune teller without a fairground.' I wonder how you feel about that?"

"Nothing, Mister Fisher, I feel nothing about that. I wouldn't expect anything less. But the TV has an off button. People have been trained to fear the penetrating sound of their own thoughts that comes when the idiot box is unplugged."

"So, you don't have a television?"

"If the chair squeaks, you oil it or throw it on the fire. I have no use for such a defective device."

"Are you not just hiding away up a mountain, I mean, are you waiting for Armageddon?" I asked.

"We are not Monks or Hermits here, we do not *hide away* oblivious to what is going on in the world and we do not simply contribute from afar. As for Armageddon, Is it not already upon us?"

"Hardly," I said, trying not to smirk.

"Over half a million people were raped in this country last year, 25,000 people were murdered, nearly a million children reported child abuse, over 50 million people dependent on illegal drugs – over twice that on pharmaceuticals… It's been normalised. People of this country are already living in hell, we choose not to." Again, he'd trumped me.

Redeye and Baldur got to their feet, so I slurped back more of my tea and motioned to join them, but Baldur put out an arm and I realised he meant for me to remain in my seat.

Redeye raised his camera. "I'm just going to get you some shots of Baldur," he said.

"Okay, thanks," I said.

"Enjoy your tea," said Baldur, who placed the 'One born every minute' book in front of me before they disappeared out into the bright daylight.

I felt like I should be doing something, so I got to my feet, took another look at the bookshelves before returning to my seat. He had placed the Hungry Joel Arnstein book there for a reason, but I wanted to resist dancing to his tune. I didn't want him catching me reading the book, yet I thought it might lead to something, perhaps a better understanding of him.

To my surprise when I opened it, I found it didn't contain the famous swindler's book after all, but within its cover was placed a tome originally published over two thousand years ago in Ancient Greece. It was Nicomachean Ethics by Aristotle and it was there for a reason.

When Redeye returned, about thirty minutes later, I was informed that our time was up, and that Baldur was offering to reconvene the following day. I felt a little humiliated. In fact, inside I was furious, but rather than return to London empty handed, I knew I would have to commit to the extra day and get the better of Baldur and show Maxwell why I was so much more than a *Sunday-magster*. I was too long in the tooth to be treated like that, although I had to admit, it hadn't taken long for him to suss out my *modus operandi*.

As Redeye drove me to my hotel, I flicked through the photographs on the back of his DSLR. I hadn't gained so much as a paragraph but yet he had done a wonderful job of the pictures.

He dropped me off at the hotel and, before he sped off, he handed me a folder.

"Some reading material," he said.

"Is this from Baldur?"

"He likes you," said Redeye, to my surprise.

"Really, what makes you think that?"

"He don't never give no journalists two bites at the cherry."

When later that evening I opened the folder, rather than some in-depth pointers, flattering commentaries or manicured self-promotion, I found a collection of press cuttings I had written many years ago.

I was flabbergasted. I wanted to reject it. I wasn't comfortable with how he was leading proceedings. I was trying to unpick him while he was tying me up in knots. For the following four hours I did what I should have done originally and beavered away researching everything I could find on this enigma of a man. Most press reports were negative, this was tempered online by fanatical adulation from his supporters across the globe. The numbers on his YouTube blog, *From the Mountain's Eye*, ran into many thousands. I opened one at random and, unlike the presenters who green-screened a mystical vista behind themselves, Baldur was sitting on a throne-like carved wooden seat with the real deal in the background.

"The destruction of history and culture, both globally and personally, eradicates comparison. Comparison is the key component of justice and the mechanism that progress is measured by. Without the wisdom and culture of history there is only the here and now. The embodiment of the goldfish existence," he said.

I pondered his theorising and drifted off, flashes of my beloved Harley dancing through my dreams. I ached to be with my family.

I awoke and felt strangely uplifted, both emotionally and physically. I was fully prepped and would make the most of my time at Heimdall falls. If Baldur really was the fraud I had expected him to be, I would play his game and allow him to choke on his own words. Fraudsters can never resist the sound of their own importance. I was sure he would show his hand.

I still had a couple of hours before I would make my way to the mountain, so I switched on the TV news and saw the story of the year unravelling before my eyes. The virus had claimed thousands of lives globally and had now spread to every major city in the world to the extent that total lockdowns were being rolled out in Rome, Paris, Berlin and Madrid.

President Trump was on a rant about China, threatening what seemed like world war three. How did this great country, self-proclaimed leader of the free world appoint such a crass and indignant man? Back home, it was the 64-thousand-dollar unanswered question that everyone was asking. No-one in Britain drew such anger as the incumbent in Washington, six thousand miles away.

It was nearing 11am here in Michigan, way too early to call Jasmine. I had already secured a seat for my return on the night's flight to Heathrow. I would be back in England soon enough. I made a mental note to pick up some Nike's for Harley at the airport and maybe some fancy headphones for Iain.

I packed up my baggage, slung it in my hire car and signed out of the hotel.

4. Everything you've ever been told is a Lie

A sense of déjà vu ensued as I arrived at Heimdall falls and exited the car. The vista was simply stupendous. Again, as I slowly spun around, I found Baldur's outstretched hand.

"Welcome, Stig of London," said Baldur.

It was like a reshoot of yesterday's script, but hopefully this time I wouldn't flunk my lines.

"Why don't I show you around and we can talk along the way," he said.

I nodded and he led the way through the compound. It was about ten times bigger than I had assumed. We passed a shooting range, crossbow practice, people tending to a cow and an outside seating area that could probably cater for about a hundred people. Carefully integrated into their surroundings were pod-like wooden dwellings scattered around by the edges of the trees.

"So, tell me a little about yourself," I said tentatively, hoping his answers would be less cryptic than they had been the previous day.

"I was a war baby, born January 1945. My parents were good to me, they gave me nothing I didn't need," he said.

1945. That would make him seventy-five. I had him pinned at late fifties - early sixties.

"You witnessed war close at hand in Vietnam, highly distinguished by all accounts."

"They pin medals on you for killing another human being, yet you don't know why you killed him or what you were doing there in his back yard, thousands of miles from home," he said.

"So, you're anti-war?"

"It was kill or be killed, but we had no business being there."

"But your book, '*The brotherhood*,' was a homage to the US Army?"

"Is that what the publishers said?"

He smiled and placed an arm across my shoulder, which triggered a ripple of awkwardness in me. At last week's convention, I had been lambasted for absentmindedly offering to shake a senator's hand, such was the strict protocol of social distancing.

"It's okay Stig, it's not requisite to read my books to be able to talk with me. My squadron were some of the most decent and honest men I ever encountered. We were there to do a job, but any sense of honour I had was directed to them and not the American war machine. All that sensationalised garbage about drugs and prostitution you see in the movies bears no resemblance to my time in 'nam."

"But you were ruthless in combat," I said.

"Have you ever taken another man's life?"

I shook my head.

"It's a burden like no other and I will carry it to my grave and who knows, perhaps beyond. I will find out soon enough," he said.

"Is that one of your famous predictions? Your coming demise?"

"I'm an old man and this life will make way for the next. I don't fear death. The world outside this mountain is no longer mine," he said.

I perked up, sensing a thread to something that could resemble the story I needed to pack into my case for the flight home.

"Do you have a prediction for the current flux in the world?" I pressed.

"Last year I lost my dear wife."

"I'm sorry," I said.

"Death inspires. I miss her presence every second of the day, but I welcome my own death like a dear old friend."

"And the world?"

"That's a conundrum for you, not me," he said.

I took that to mean it was my generation's mess to clear up.

We stopped at a large wooden chair which I recognised from his daily blogs, and we took in the wild beauty of the panorama behind it. The picturesque waterfall and wide expanse heading out across the vast stretch of water towards Milwaukee made you feel you like were on top of the world.

His blogs were typical conspiracy stuff. Governments poisoning the water supply with chemicals to dumb us all down, 9-11 an inside job aided by agents from Tel Aviv and regular shark bating diatribes directed at prominent bankers and industrialists. Even though each video received a substantial number of views, in the main it was generally considered that he was rallying a toothless army of misfits, oddballs and fantasists. Irritation rather than insurrection.

To the right of us came an enormous thud as an arrow hit one of four target wheels. A dozen young men were lining up to let loose an arrow or two. An attractive middle-aged woman in a long white dress and cowboy boots was boldly issuing instructions.

"Just remember, everything happens for a reason," said Baldur. "Very little of life is random. You came here thinking you were going to find some low hand conjurer, but you found something else, you just haven't worked out what that is yet… But you will."

I could feel the blood flush across my face.

"Do you want to know my secret? What makes me tick?" he said with a smile.

"Sure," I replied.

"Instinct. It's like a finely crafted watch, you need to be in tune with yourself, seek to trust yourself. Only then you can measure the world around you with some confidence."

That was hardly ground-breaking and on paper it would look even less so, but there was something about the charisma with which he said it that incited a curiosity in me.

"And what about the name, Baldur, when did you acquire that?"

"Oh, I didn't find that name, it found me," he said.

We retired to the Library and I was pleased to see that Hungry Joe Arnstein's book had been returned to its place on the shelf. I took my seat while Baldur offered some refreshments.

"The drink you gave me yesterday worked wonders, what was in it?" I enquired.

"Pine needles."

"Oh," I said, a little underwhelmed.

"The magic ingredient is water."

"Yeah, we have water in England." I said, with a smile.

"You take yours with fluoride, ours comes directly from our natural springs, it purifies you."

He disappeared off to make the drinks and I took the opportunity to check my phone. No signal. I should have guessed. Being off the grid was frustrating. The views were nice, but I wouldn't fare well here, not without wi-fi.

"How many people reside here?"

"Thirty-two," he said.

"How much rent do you charge?"

"Their contributions aren't measured in that way."

"Okay. How do you maintain cohesion? I mean, there must be conflict from time to time?"

"Sure, but this is no hippy commune," he said. "We sort it out like men. You see, kindness comes from respect, you earn it. If you're disrespectful, you'll find goodwill thin on the ground."

"Does no-one ever yearn to go back to the modern world?"

"The folks here have worked out what's good in life and they dedicate themselves to living that way. We are not the anomaly. If our great-great-grandparents arrived today they'd recognise us as their modern descendants." he said. "If I took them into Milwaukee, they'd think the place had been invaded by aliens."

He reached out and took my cup and placed it on the wooden table before looking directly at me, his crystal blue eyes as clear as the conviction he placed in his words.

"Everything you have ever been told is a lie," he said, as his gaze penetrated through me.

It wasn't an aggressive act but felt more like a personal call to arms.

"Your mother's love, the pain you felt on your father's deathbed, the elation of your whirlwind romance with Jasmine Oaks and the birth of your children, they were all real, but like a gravedigger you just add layers of doubt and subterfuge to the casket of truth that's been buried beneath your feet by serpents of chaos."

He was going in for the kill. I wouldn't rebuke him like yesterday but would instead hold on to a clear mind. He had done his homework which unnerved me a little, but I wasn't an award-winning journalist for nothing. I could handle it.

"You are a writer, so who do you write for?" he said.

What did he mean? If he knew my wife's name, he would surely know the name of my employer.

"I write for the Capital Post," I said.

"Are you Stig Fisher who writes or are you a journalist for the Capital Post?"

"Both," I said.

"And when you write, are you motivated by truth, Stig?"

"Of course," I said.

I could see where he was heading, I wasn't naive, in my line of business truth was conditional and came with an Asterix and long list of provisos. It's just the way of the world. I was here to interview him and now he was turning the heat on me. I had to switch this around.

"And if you report that I am an intelligent healthy old man enjoying a wholesome existence among like-minded people in the picturesque hills of Michigan and your boss says you should change that to 'Crazy nut with dangerous ideas,' what then?" He said.

"You did say the US Government was poisoning the water and you're a vocal opponent to LGBT legislation and abortion rights for women. To a lot of people that would make your ideas crazy or even dangerous," I said.

"Free thinkers don't find danger in another man's words, only possibility. You will come to know this well, Stig Fisher of London. Right now, there is a ripple of rising deception that could become a tidal wave to change the world forever. That is what should demand your focus."

"You mean this savage virus?" I said.

"Is it savage?"

"Thousands are dying, hospitals can't cope, even stuck up here in the clouds you must be aware of it?"

"Which hospitals have *you* visited?" He said.

"Personally, I haven't visited any, but the story is everywhere," I said.

"Story, fable, fiction," he said.

He wasn't going to try and convince me that the whole planet was shutting down due to some corporate criminality. He's an interesting old man, and his tea is good, but I'm not having it.

"People are dying," I said, firmly.

"And many more will die. This is just the beginning and there will be choices and sacrifices to be considered. The decisions you take are going to impact what happens."

He really did seem to use the solitary *'you'*.

"Me?"

"Yes, you," he said.

"I have a decent readership, but I'm pretty certain the future of the world isn't dependent on what I do," I chuckled.

His face was calm and unmoved by my laughter which quickly died. If this empty flattery was part of some elaborate card trick, I was determined not to miss the switch.

Baldur was hard to pigeon-hole, and I guess he had crafted his persona with that objective in mind. I managed to get a few more questions in before my time was up. He said he had another blog to prepare for. There were probably worse things you could waste your time on than his pseudo philosophical musings, delivered with a dash of controversial politics to spice things up, but I wasn't signing up anytime soon. America was brim full of rent-a-gobs. As is sometimes the case with such characters, he wasn't lacking charisma and on reflection he had been gentlemanly throughout our encounter.

As I stood before the impressive oak, its finger-like trunks reaching into the ether, he told me he had named it the *Palm of the Gods*. There was indeed something wholesome about their existence here. But was it just a façade? An extended film set, perhaps. It would take more than a fleeting visit to ascertain that.

"Thank you for your time," I said. "You have a beautiful place here."

"Goodbye for now," he said.

We shook hands, which in the context of the virus paranoia actually felt pretty good. My senses and personal awareness had become heightened of late and I guess he was tapping into that. It was only as I passed the guardhouse and exited the dirt track out onto the main route back to Grand Rapids that, despite my professional suspicion about being duped by such a character, I couldn't help feeling a begrudging respect for him, if not for his politics. I had put up all kinds of safety barriers, yet I was left questioning my sense of self.

5. No Room at the inn

As I drove away from Baldur and his mountain, my
phone hit a signal and erupted into a chorus of 'bings'. I
pulled over into a roadside burger restaurant to retrieve
my messages and fill up on some of the American
diner's local delicacies.

Jasmine had left about twenty messages, so I called her.
Our joint bank account needed topping up. To help in the
fight against the virus, the school were demanding all
children be tested. Harley wailed for me when the
teacher pushed the swab way up his nose, causing it to
draw blood.

When she put Harley on the phone, I felt a flutter of guilt
that once more my *daddy duties* had been inadequate. I
wasn't there for him. His fragile little voice plucked at
my heart strings and that off-key resonance engulfed me
with home sickness.

Jasmine mentioned a flare-up at the museum at which
she was head curator. They were cancelling exhibitions
for the following six months.

"That doesn't make sense, the Lockdown is due to end
next week," I said.

"The hospitals can't cope, so the lockdown is being
extended," said Jasmine.

"Have *you* been to any hospitals?" I said, the words were not my own and had escaped my lips before I had a chance to proof-read them.

"What? No, I haven't," said Jasmine, with a hint of confusion. "Is that not the case?"

"How would I know, I've been up a mountain talking to the trees," I said, annoyed with myself.

"You alright?"

"Yeah, I'm fine. Just want to be home," I said.

When the call ended, I ventured into the restaurant and ordered a Coney dog and fries.

"Sir, where's your mask?" said the chubby young woman in a checked pinny that could have done with being a couple of sizes bigger.

I searched my pockets and realised that I hadn't one on me. I smiled and shrugged my shoulders but that just seemed to antagonise her.

"Sir, people are dying, the hospitals are-"

"-Full, yes I know." I said exasperated.

"You can pay up and someone will drop it at your car, please ensure you flip the trunk," she said, holding out a credit card reader.

Back in the car, I managed to connect with the wi-fi, and I skimmed through my remaining messages.

Maxwell had left a narky dispatch about a discrepancy with my expenses in Chicago. Everything surrounding the Democratic convention was extortionately priced, I imagined it was a policy to keep the ordinary folk from stinking up the place. It was par for the course. I had never cheated a penny or a dime out of expenses. The witch hunt had begun.

I checked the BBC website but found it was national bad news day so ditched the phone and

wolfed down the Coney dog and got busy on the article about Baldur. I shelved my preconceived ideas of Baldur as a narcissistic cult figure and turned it around on the reader, asking whether our fast-paced, rat-race lives would compare favourably with his rugged hillside existence. For it to become a viable alternative for the Fisher family, I light-heartedly declared that the installation of a few home comforts like a wide screen TV, wi-fi, a games console and a microwave oven would be essential.

I uploaded the story, while I tucked-in to some apple pie, before setting off for Chicago's O'Hare airport.

On arrival at the vehicle returns office, things started to go south. I got stung on the hire car because I had retained it twenty-four hours longer than originally agreed, the penalty of which was three times the daily rate. Entering the terminal building, I was grabbed and almost wrestled to the ground for not wearing a mask by an over-zealous security guard. The cherry on the cake was the news that my flight to London had been cancelled. No warning phone call, no text message, nothing.

It seemed that every man and his dog, who needed to leave the States, wanted to be on my flight home and had formed an orderly queue at the flight desk before I even had a chance to find out what was going on. I hadn't given the virus situation here too much consideration, spending time in the hills of Michigan had given me a false sense of security.

By the time I shuffled my way to the front of the queue at the airline's information desk, I was informed that the best deal, the jaded and heavily perspiring flight desk assistant could offer me, was an indirect flight via Berlin, in exactly one week's time.

"That's ridiculous. I need to get back to London today," I demanded.

Like a robot she just repeated what I heard her tell the people in front of me in the queue. "Due to the upsurge in virus cases here, the UK are not accepting direct passenger flights from the US. You can fly via other countries, but on-board capacity has been reduced by half to incorporate the new social distancing measures, the number of scheduled international departures have been reduced."

"That's crazy," I said.

"Sir, I appreciate your frustration at the inconvenience, but people are dying and the hospitals-"

"-Hospitals are full up, yes I know."

"Sir, if you are going to be aggressive, I will be forced to call security to escort you out of the terminal," she said, without a modicum of emotion.

Perhaps Artificial Intelligence was more advanced than I thought, and I had been conversing with one of Elon Musk's Androids.

I phoned the Post, but again the unprecedented nature of the situation rendered any leverage the newspaper sometimes had in such circumstances, null and void. I was informed that there were journalists stranded all over the globe. I relayed the bad news to Jasmine on a cell phone recording.

As if things weren't bad enough, the young chap at the hotel reservation desk informed me that nearby hotels were refusing new bookings. All strangers were considered *persona non grata*. He advised me that my best bet was to return to the hotel I had vacated earlier. First, I would have to retrace my steps to the hire-car company that had so recently fleeced me, and begrudgingly request another car.

A small part of me was relieved to get out of the madness and chaos of O'Hare airport, as I took the return journey to Grand Rapids, Michigan. I pondered on the sight of the giant rollercoaster I passed on the motorway and thought it a perfect symbol of the last month of my life.

When I arrived at the Dragon Cross Hotel there were police officers on the door. It looked like a scene from any random US cop show.

The manager was explaining to a couple in front of me that, due to a guest testing positive for the virus, they were prevented from taking any new bookings. In an attempt to extend my previous stint there, I contemplated telling her that I had just vacated my room earlier that day. She informed us that all current residents were locked in isolation and would not be permitted to leave for 14 days. As she was relaying this, I got the impression she had recognised me and was tipping me the wink to escape what would, for the next two weeks, become a sealed-off quarantine facility. The dingy little hotel rooms had become jail cells for the paying customers at this particular guesthouse.

I called Redeye who said he heard that all hotels were limited to serving current residents only.

"What am I supposed to do, sleep in my car?" I railed, before apologising for my outburst.

"Normally, I would ring around, and someone would offer up a sofa or a spare room, but everyone with a TV is gripped with fear. Not for all the popcorn in North Carolina would you get them to open their doors to a stranger. No siree. I only got a bedsitter, so the only place spare is my bath and I got to thinking that you don't gonna want to share it with a six-foot python."

"No, I think I'll pass on that one, all the same."

He chuckled.

"You could try the Marlowe Motel, two blocks down from where you are now, they most likely bend the rules, might cost ya, though," he said.

"I'll give them a go then, thank you," I said.

"We passed it on our way to see Baldur, Sorry I can't be no more help."

"Okay, thanks," I said.

I was about to hang up when he continued talking.

"You know it's a felony to sleep in your own car, but if you get stuck you might try your luck at the Mountain."

"Baldur?"

"He liked you. I mean, he ain't never had no journalist back a second time, 'specially after you pulled that stunt with the book an' all," he laughed.

I sought out the Marlowe Motel but, tired and flustered, I made the fatal error of letting it be known that I had been a recent guest at the Dragon Cross. This all but got me slung out into the street.

Eventually, after some deliberation, I reluctantly found myself careering up the dusty track at Heimdall falls, cursing my fate. I was surprised that, on my approach to the gatehouse, the barrier was lifted and a bald man in his fifties ushered me through.

"Go on up, we've been expecting you, Mr Fisher," said the guard.

Redeye must have phoned ahead and explained my predicament, either way it was bitterly cold outside, and this was the best and probably the only chance of shelter I was going to get.

I awoke with what felt like an industrial sized blue light burning into my eyes. I sat up and realised the cabin I had slept in possessed no curtains and what I was squinting at was an uninterrupted view of the sun-kissed hills and valleys lofting over the famous lake. It was mesmerising.

The sound of a thud on wood had me scrabbling to get dressed. As I opened the door, I was hit by a gust of ice-cold wind. I just caught the sight of a middle-aged man with ginger hair walking towards the centre of the compound.

"Hello," I called out.

"You're wanted in the hall for 8 o'clock," he said in a monotone drawl, without turning to face me.

I looked at my watch to see I had about five minutes to sort myself out.

At the grand hall, I was greeted warmly by Baldur. I thanked him for helping me out at such short notice. It was at that point that I was relieved about the tact I had used while writing the Heimdall Falls article. Should he ever see it, he would maybe appreciate it being non-confrontational and not of the snipey fashion he was probably used to.

I dug into my wallet and offered him some money, but he waved it away.

"We would like you to be our guest while you are here," he said. "If you are prepared to roll your sleeves up, join in and get your hands dirty. You can, of course, hole yourself up in your cabin and eat at a local diner, if you can find one that is open. It's your choice."

I didn't have anything to lose and who knows it could lead to something more interesting than the article I had already submitted to the Post.

"Thanks, I appreciate it," I said, not at all sure of what I was signing up for.

"Embrace it. Turn your prejudices down to zero and breathe. And at the end of your stay, if you want to write that we are a band of blockheads, then so be it. We have never given a member of the press an offer like this. But I believe Stig Fisher is more than his job title."

He put an arm around my shoulder and squeezed.

There were about twenty-five people, of all ages, with a ratio of two males to each female. Everyone took their places in near choreographed rhythm. Baldur introduced me to a tall bulky looking guy.

"This is Dylo, he'll show you the ropes," said Baldur. Baldur left the hall and I tried to ingratiate myself with Dylo.

"Name's Stig," I said, holding out a hand.

"The Hack," he said, without extending his.

A hush rippled through the hall and suddenly it felt like all eyes were on me. For a moment I imagined that I had been parachuted naked into a pack of baying Wolves.

"Folks here aren't too keen on you media types, you know," said Dylo, in a matter-of-fact way.

"'cause you breathe lies as other folks breathes air," said an old woman with a grievance painted on her face.

Her comment was met with a chorus of murmured approval.

I realised the man opposite was the same guy with ginger hair who had banged on my door. "There are some people we like even less," he said.

"Well, I guess that's something," I said, trying to find the olive branch in middle of this burning bush.

"Yep, we ain't keen on paedophiles neither," he continued.

Baldur reappeared at the head of the hall. A woman with long braided blonde hair led the deep breathing instructions which drew everyone's undivided attention for the next ten minutes. We breathed intensely in and out then exhaled and held that position for as long as we could. I was surprised that I was able to hold out for as long as I did before gasping for air.

Once the blood was flowing, she started making shapes that were based on old pagan runes, it was then that I realised I had enlisted in some kind of Yoga session. I was standing at the back doing my best not to fall over as I reached out and extended my body.

After the stretches I joined everyone sitting on the floor in meditation for what seemed like hours and like a silly kid I couldn't help thinking of funny TV sketches featuring Rowan Atkinson. Back in London I could imagine myself at dinner parties recanting stories of this crazy club for flat earthers.

At breakfast, I helped myself to some bread, ham and boiled eggs and took a seat on a church pew alongside a rectangle wooden table that could sit over twenty.
All eyes shot around at the sight of Baldur getting to his feet. He was at the high table flanked by four other people. Without invitation, everyone began rising to their feet and, after three taps of a wooden cane against a table, they burst into song.

"Be as the bird,
Who floats upon wings,
Be as the sun
Whose warmth she brings
Be as the friend
Of peasants and kings
Be as the maiden
Of nature's blessings
Be as my love
Oh, beautiful things
Be as the belle
Who works as she sings
Be as the man
Who works as he sings"

No-one mumbled, as so many self-consciously do in the stiff atmosphere of the churches back home in England. Instead, they bellowed it out at the top of their lungs and the acoustics of the great hall leant it a fullness that conjured up a majestic sound of a choir of thousands.
"The world simmers into a never-ending sludge of immorality, don't be distracted by the ill-woven words of the serpent's tongue, let nothing wrongfoot your march of progress, our march of progress," said Baldur.
He held up his glass of what looked like milk. "Make this glorious day belong to you, own it," he said.

Baldur's words drew a communal response. "Thy day will be mine."

It was all a touch melodramatic.

Everyone split up into four lines. Feeling like a Chelsea fan in the Tottenham end, I joined the nearest column. The man who had been sitting opposite me barracked me about being in the wrong line.

"Over here," called Dylo.

He pointed to a register of names on a chalk board sitting on an A frame. There at the bottom of the second list was my name at which someone had scribbled 'The Hack'. There were queues for work in the kitchen, cleaning and the stores. I was in the crew of diggers, and after the frosty reception I had been given from some of the inhabitants, I wondered if it wasn't my own grave we would be shovelling.

I would have felt more comfortable to pay my way, but I was clearly meant to work for my keep, like all the others. I thought back to how long ago it was that I got my hands dirty doing manual labour. It must have been well over thirty years, helping out my brother and his decorating business, and even then, the most I was shunting around was a few cans of eggshell, now, Dylo informed me, I was part of the chain gang tasked with digging out the foundations of a new chalet.

By lunchtime I ached all over and my hands were sore from the bitter cold and jarred from the digging. My attempts to indulge in small talk fell on deaf ears. All bar Dylo were demonstratively selective with the information they offered up in front of me. It seemed strange and a little awkward for me, but the intimacy of the songs we sang grew on me and once I figured out the words, it really helped pass the time.

After lunch, instead of resuming the house building, we all filed into an auditorium, to listen to Baldur. Here, I witnessed the man really come into his own. The philosopher turned rabble rouser, or perhaps it was the other way around.

"The world that has sprung up around us is like a casino, one of those glitzy establishments that offers you free drinks while it delves into your pockets and rips out your soul," he roared. "These shiny distractions, be it social media computer programmes, the smash and crash of Hollywood's sick debauchery or the sleaze-laden products of the music industry, they are fit for nothing but the garbage can. They have been designed to consume *you*. They take every precious moment that you happily surrender, in your pursuit of what amounts to a hollow jackpot of self-delusion. If you ask young people today what they most aspire to, they'll probably say *fame* or *entertainment* is their dream. It's the pinnacle of life for these misguided children, and I'm talking about infantile losers in their twenties, thirties and older. Folks that have yet to find the path to adulthood."

I had heard this kind of rhetoric before of course, usually accompanied by brightly coloured flags baring emblems derived from the ancient book of scapegoating. There was none of those fascistic trappings of uniforms, jackboots and slogans on show, but I kept coming back to Redeye questioning me about whether or not I was Jewish.

"You are all here for a reason, not the circumstances that brought you here but the purpose of what will propel you along the path to greater things. Some of you have yet to realise this. Most of you at some point will leave our community, but please be assured that, for as long as you carry goodness in your heart, the community will never leave you."

It was all very inspiring, and as Baldur's eyes met those before him, I could see that he held a genuine connection with them. I had to keep reasserting my own prudence. I would be open-minded but would not allow my guard to drop.

Everyone dispersed slowly, clusters of friends conversing. I gravitated to Dylo.

"You got your angle yet?" said Dylo.

"What?"

"D'ya get your story?"

"Oh, my report, yeah. It's more a reflection on modern life than anything else really," I said, passively wishing to avoid confrontation with the one fellow, other than Baldur, who had extended the hand of courtesy.

"Don't be fooled by Baldur's demeanour. I see Baldur grab a reporter by the scruff of his chicken neck and frog-march him down the mountain," he said, as if he had read my mind.

"What triggered him? I mean I would kind of fancy avoiding that sort of treatment, at least not until the day of my flight," I said with a smile that failed to lighten our dialogue.

"Oh, he don't care what you ask or what you write. The guy in question, he was trying to pay some young 'uns to make a Hitler salute for the camera. Folks here was for lynching him. When Baldur kicked him down the hill, he probably saved his life."

"Well, I can assure you, that's not the angle I'm going for," I said.

"Come to think of it, that asshole was from England, working for your BBC."

"Bad apple, huh?"

"If you ask me, them barrels get infected mighty easy. Your presence has got a lot of folks questioning Baldur," he said.

Lost for an appropriate answer, I shrugged my shoulders.

"Me? I know better than to do that," he said.

He left a hole in the conversation that he clearly wanted me to fill.

"I can't deny that this place is impressive," I said.
"And his words?"
"I can see he genuinely believes in what he's saying," I said with a dash of diplomacy.
"What about you? What do you believe in?" said Dylo.
"I'm a journalist, I am naturally curious about what interesting people have got to say."
"You mind if I gives you a bit of advice, Stig?" he said.
I nodded.
"If you spent a lifetime here as a journalist, you'd still fail to get it. You gotta take that hat off, and then you just might see what I see. You ain't gunna meet no timeshare salesmen, nobody's gonna fleece you of your hard-earned money. You get out what you put in."
As if right on cue, Baldur made an appearance and offered me the use of his office to be able to contact London.
I was astonished at how sophisticated Baldur's office was. The tech was good quality and he had three computers, which I guessed he must use to produce and upload his video blogs.
I called the office but was told they hadn't made any headway on getting me out of the States any sooner. I could get a private jet out of here but they weren't willing to stump up the thousands to fly me back and it jolted my thoughts to the reason I had been sent here in the first place. The situation would suit Maxwell down to the ground.
I spoke to Jasmine who was as busy as ever. When I was away, she rarely had the time or inclination to engage in lengthy conversations. She sounded stressed and tetchy. Jasmine begged me not to have any close contact with anyone. She had heard that the USA was in virus meltdown, even worse than London. We ended the call and I stood in thought for a moment or two. I needed to

be at home not halfway up a mountain in Rebel county, USA.

"I'm sorry, Stig. I couldn't help but notice, you called your office before you called your family," said Baldur.

"They're pissed off with me," I said.

"Your family or your job?"

"Both, I guess."

He raised his eyebrows as if drawing a line under the point he had made. It was like conversing with the Riddler.

"Normally magazine pieces are written weeks before publication, but they've moved it to the main body of the newspaper, should be hitting the newsstands tomorrow morning," I said.

"I had better put some extra guards on at the gatehouse," he said. "For the long line of new recruits."

"Don't worry, it's no hatchet job," I said.

"Ah, come on, Stig," he said, smiling. "Do I look like a man who is worried?"

6. Understanding

Sunday morning arrived like a cake at a child's birthday party. I slept like a king and was full of the joys of spring. At meditation, it seemed like my previous frosty reception had thawed a little. After breakfast, and the breathing and singing rituals, Baldur delivered a lecture on ancient history, where he declared that 'We were all children of the ice and snow.' European civilisation had not grown from the south and spread northwards but the complete reverse.

In the library, I helped Dylo carry a large pile of books to his cabin. He opened up a little and talked about his old life outside the compound. There was a potent streak of sadness about this middle-aged loner, a raw but likeable vulnerability.

"My younger life was chaotic. My grandparents were the only stability I had. They were so steeped in Catholicism, I was sure the Pope used to call up my grandpa to get advice. Every moment with them was a moment I didn't have to spend with my own messed up parents, God bless 'em. I couldn't tell you which Saints did what, but I never forgot that sense of right and wrong and the love that ran through everything they did."

I had expected his cabin to be army-like tidy, but it was a mess of newspapers and books. There were lots of wooden statues and ornaments and a mini workshop covered in shavings. He tried to subtly roll a bottle of gin under some clothes, but I figured he knew that I had seen it.

"When the Cardinals started hiding sex abuse in the church, that was the last straw. I mean, do you know how many children go missing each year?"

I shook my head. I didn't know, but I guessed the number was unacceptably high.

"It runs into thousands, but where's the outcry? I mean, you work for the media, why does nobody speak out?" He said.

I didn't have an answer for him. Not one that would easily satisfy his righteous anger. In the past I might have just written him off as a self-appointed puritan, here to make our complicated and capricious lives an unnecessary misery, but he had shown me kindness and I had to remember I was a guest here. If they hadn't taken me in, I would probably be freezing my arse off in a car right now.

"Is it a big issue in the States?" I asked.

"It's world-wide. You have it in England."

"We are not completely blind to it," I said. "There was a problem in some of our northern towns, I did a big piece on that."

"Stig, we all know about your grooming gangs, it took you over twenty years to face up to that one."

He moved some clutter around to make way for the extra books, they were mostly tomes on famous philosophers including Kant, Nietzsche, Jung and Marx. He took the pile I was carrying and looked me dead in the eye.

"You seem like a sure-fire guy, Baldur likes you, but I have to ask you, why didn't people speak out?"

The grooming scandal was a stain of great shame on England and I would never argue that there wasn't an invisible pressure on journalists to bury it. The inexcusable policy of censoring it created a vacuum into which doubt of our multi-racial society was allowed to grow. Everyone knew the racist tag could be the death knell to your career, yet this judgement alone impaired the justice denied to those poor girls, and there were thousands of them. It was their anguish that kept me awake at night and prompted me to break cover and address some inconvenient truths.

"I admit that these were the darkest days of my time as a journalist, I pressed and pressed and took a lot of flak. It's not difficult to stifle debate these days. People will trawl the wastepaper basket of your history and find some throwaway comment, take it out of context and magnify it. Suddenly, you find everyone painting you as the bad guy," I said.

"Well, I commend you for speaking out," he said.

"For what it's worth, I tried."

"You have children, right?" he said.

"I have two kids," I said.

"No, you don't," he said.

What the hell was he talking about?

"Stig, you have two children. Kids are young goats."

"I stand corrected," I said.

Freezing in the back of a hire car was starting to become a little more appealing.

"At the end of the day, I'm just a reporter, I don't make the news, I relate the news," I said.

"Until the moment that every man of influence refuses to blur the lines between good and evil, he will never see things straight."

I had experienced this simplistic view of life many times before and, if it wasn't for the conviction in his eyes, I would have dismissed it.

"Fair enough," I said.

"Take Baldur, you're sure smart enough to realise that it's often the words he doesn't say that you really oughta catch," he said.

"What lead you to him?" I said, attempting to temper his rant.

"I drifted for a while before I ended up here. Now, I would follow him into the fire, no question," he said.

"For one man to have that power, is that not dangerous?" I asked.

"Not if he's a good man. He let me into his life, he's not some crumb-bum politician with a hidden agenda or a crook with an eye for the next bribe. He's a great man."

I pondered the assortment of things he had on his shelves, ornaments and picture frames. There was a photo of a boy, probably mid-teens. The resemblance was uncanny.

"My son," he said, following my gaze.

"He's a chip off the old-"

"-He took his own life," he said, interrupting me as if any misunderstanding had to be pre-empted with haste.

"Eight years ago," he said.

The gravity of his previous comments hit me like a freight train.

"I'm sorry," I said meekly.

He picked up the bottle of booze he had tried to hide earlier and looked at me.

"I struggle," he said.

"Any father would," I said.

"Baldur can't know," he said, pain alive in his eyes.

There was a knock at the door, forcing Dylo to flinch and quickly stash the bottle.

"Dylo? Stig?" It was Baldur. "We're meeting at the auditorium at two."

"We'll be there," said Dylo, unable to conceal the fluster in his voice.

Baldur left and I could hear him knocking on the next cabin, continuing on his rounds.

"Your secret's safe with me," I said.

He flashed me a look of gratitude before his gaze moved to the floor.

"I'll just get the shack in order. I'll see you down there," he said.

I returned to my cabin and flaked out on the bed, chewing over my conversation with Dylo. I could have dismissed him as one of life's aimless wanderers but there was something intrinsically good about him.

I checked my watch and decided I would sneak out to the diner. No-one had said I wasn't free to come and go as I pleased. I could feel my journalistic cynicism waning and I wanted a circuit breaker to convince myself that I wasn't getting drawn into the clutches of Baldur's mind games. I had seen nothing untoward so far, and a lot of what they discussed was on the money, but I needed to get some perspective, not from Maxwell or anyone from work, but from Jasmine. She had the knack of knowing the right moments to keep my feet rooted to the ground, dousing my ego or de-fogging my lofty vision.

At the diner, it was take-away food only. Sitting in my car chomping a greasy burger down, I got to work clearing my twitter feed and backlog of emails.

I called the airport on the off chance they had found a way for me to fly to London. No such luck.

Jasmine had taken a breather from her usual state of perpetual rush. I told her about the lack of flights before waxing lyrical about Heimdall falls, Baldur and Dylo. As I talked, I completely forgot about the preconceived ideas I had originally conjured up about the place.

"That's wonderful, pray tell, when are they coming around for tea?" asked Jasmine.

"I know, I know, it's crazy but I really like them," I said.

"They haven't, you know… made you do things, have they?" said Jasmine.

There was silence and then we both burst out laughing. It was so refreshing to feel our strong bond over the phone.

"What's that racket in the background?" I asked.

"Harley's here, half the school have been sent home as a precaution because a boy coughed in assembly. He's just watching a movie."

"Give him a hug for me," I said.

"Of course I will," she said.

"What's the film?"

"Some Russel Crowe thing, *The good guys* or *the nice guys*, something like that," she said.

"He's only seven, honey," I said.

"It's ok," she said, a little narked by my concerns.

"Have you seen it?" I pressed.

"I'm only in the next room. Anyway, you know that his brother will only show him when I'm not around," she replied.

"It's pornographic," I raged.

"No, it's not."

It was one of the film choices on the flight here and from what I saw in the opening few minutes it definitely wasn't for 7-year-olds. I realised I was dictating to her from the other side of the world. I took a deep breath and calmed myself.

"Okay honey, I better get back to the compound," I said.

"Have fun with your new friends," she said, chuckling.

In the Heimdall falls auditorium, Baldur was dressed in a white doctor's coat, resplendent with pens and stethoscope.

"If you have a Television, you're in the middle of a deadly pandemic, if you don't it's Thursday," said Baldur, to a chorus of chuckles.

From the outside, the compound looked very much like an old-fashioned settlement and on first sight I half expected to see Amish folks ride by in their traditional black garb. Dylo said that what Baldur wanted to build here was the best of both worlds. Community, hard work and education with minimal technology, all at one with nature. Great brochure talk, perhaps.

"Well over ninety-nine percent of people who catch the virus survive, so why the lockdowns?" he demanded, as slides of information backing up his claims filled the screen behind him.

"This has been in the planning for years, in fact just last October they had a pandemic simulation at a preparedness conference they called Event 201. My kinfolk, this is the biggest scam the world has ever seen," said Baldur.

"But you don't have to believe me because I have one of these on, I'm not a doctor."

He started to take the white coat off.

"But then, neither is he," continued Baldur, as he pointed to the screen where a picture of the Tech billionaire, Gill Baits flashed up. Baits was standing next to the infamous paedophile Jeffrey Epstein.

"This man wants to vaccinate every man, woman and child on the planet. He funds the media, the scientists, the pharmaceuticals, government advisers and almost every other organisation that has skin in the game. He also patented the tracking chip technology that is being touted as a future health passport to be used to control where you go, what you can and cannot do and whether you get state assistance and medical care. No question. He is the most dangerous man on the planet."

I watched the faces of those around me and wondered if it was loyalty earned and justified or simply blind adherence to the chief of this particular clan.

Similar rhetoric was spouted by Vernon Coleman, and whilst there was a strong argument against lockdowns, I still believed that doing nothing was not an option any credible government could ever consider. As for Baits, I think he was fair game, I don't doubt that he has used his obscene personal wealth and connections to put himself at the forefront of this global reaction – you could tell from interviews that he enjoyed playing God. The idea that he was a 'humble guy who built a tech empire from his garage' was also manufactured bullshit. His father was a multi-millionaire with very powerful friends.

"What we have here in our community is the blueprint of a future where loyalty, dignity and hard work are the foundations of a rewarding life," he continued.

"Corruption has destroyed everything that was once good about this country. My kinfolk, it is time to celebrate beauty and wonder and smash the stranglehold of the young from the chains of the incessant grip of their tricknology."

Rapturous applause greeted Baldur's words.

"I am an old man and whilst the mind is as sharp as ever, I know the body will let go at some point."

"You gunna live forever, Baldur," hollered a bearded man in his forties.

"Ay-men to that," chirped another.

"No-one can defeat nature. But I believe we all have the power to alter the future of our lives on this planet. There is a broadmindedness required in the exchange of ideas, concessions in companionship, but there can be no compromise of the core principles that permeate the very beats of our hearts, because to forego one… is to surrender them all."

More applause followed, then he caught my breath with his next announcement.

"Tomorrow, our newest guest, Stig Fisher, will address the hall."

"Media snake," grumbled someone in the audience.

"You might have seen him about, please give him the courtesy of your time, Mr Fisher will give a talk on the media," reiterated Baldur to another negative murmur in the hall.

I caught up with Baldur at the end and made it known that I was usually pre-warned about any speaking engagements.

"I spoke with your agent," he pointed to the sky. "And he agreed to waive the fee," he said, with a smile.

He reasoned that I might prefer a morning preparing my talk in the comfort of my cabin than breaking up the ground with the chain gang.

"In regard to my talk, what angle are you looking for?" I said.

"Angle? We're looking for the truth."

"You want to hear my truth," I said, sounding a little too *new agey* for even my own comfort.

"*The* Truth. The truth of who you are, Stig. Tell us about your journey. Where did your journalistic instinct begin?"

"My instinct?"

"You can tune your body through exercise and nutrition and still die, nothing is guaranteed in this life, but you know you can experience the peak of existence if you breathe the air, respect the land and love your fellow man. The same is true of the mind. An intelligent man like yourself has to stretch his intellect beyond his prejudices and preconceptions. So, you read, you listen, you engage, and you explore. To achieve that you must cultivate your intuition. Train it, enrich it and then trust in it. As children we are programmed by the state to the extent that our instinct becomes blunted, but young people, those not distracted by violent games, cheap toys and the nihilistic desires for vacant materialism, can be very astute, we should listen to their instinct."

Nothing he had said was particularly revolutionary, but I liked this sense of self-empowerment that he projected. You couldn't help warm to his passion and commitment. "If you don't believe me, just think of how the infantile masses have responded to this so-called health crisis. Forced to stay home, volunteer for pointless tests, wear masks, distance themselves from their loved ones, welcoming every infringement on their lives without so much as a rational question to themselves."

The Post would consider that statement an example of ill-informed conspiracy bluster, but he made his point convincingly.

Before going to sleep I played the video of Harley's 'Daddy poem' and I drifted off into the cosy thoughts of all the happy little adventures we would enjoy upon my return to England.

7. Read all about it

"We each have our prejudices, our desires and our fears but let it be said that fidelity is the true measure of a man," said Baldur, on the stage that had been carefully lit and constructed, with me in one chair and Baldur opposite me in the other. The numbers in the room swelled to about forty and my nerves were jangling. I reminded myself that I had been in worse spots than this. As a cub reporter, I spent a nerve-wracking weekend with the Windsor chapter of the Hells Angels, but they never asked me to give a lecture.

"To rebuke the beast, first you must understand it. However, you should not underestimate every agent who serves that beast. I understand that many of you mistrust the presence of a mainstream media journalist in our midst."

"He's got no right being here," shouted the ginger-haired man who was seated opposite me on my first morning at the breakfast table.

"Those who have been here for a while trust that I would not risk the sanctity of our community. Please remember that fate brings opportunity and steely determination delivers the actions that lead to change. So, is Stig here because he couldn't get a flight home? Well, let's find out."

"Thank you, Baldur, for the opportunity to speak to you all today. I have always been intrigued by human stories. I guess my first foray into journalism came when I was eight. I was so impressed by my grandfather's tales of heroism, that I made my own newssheet. For Christmas I received a red t-shirt with the word Editor emblazoned across it. I was punch proud. I had cultivated an insatiable hunger for information, the differing viewpoints and, like amassing the pieces of a jigsaw, I worked hard on my conclusions."

I was in the middle of extolling the virtues of my journey from university to working for a local newspaper when the grizzly bear with the ginger hair, stood up, glared at me and proceeded to make as much noise as he could as he exited the room, slamming the door on his way out. It echoed like a beat from the hostile drums of war.

"Tell us something about when you first encountered editorial policy?" said Baldur.

"I was a young and naive reporter for the local newspaper in Kent, and I wrote a piece that was heavily critical of a local company. I thought they were guilty of exploiting a loophole that had the government heavily subsidising the wages of foreign workers, tipping some local folk out of their jobs. When I took my story to the editor, expecting a glowing approval, he introduced me to the boss of our parent company. He was the same man I relentlessly harangued for a comment on my exploitation report. At university it would have gained me top marks, but this was the real world and so, I had my first lesson in finding balance between news and commerce, and never biting the hand that feeds."

I had recounted this anecdote many times before, particularly when lecturing students of Journalism about the harsh realities of the profession. People mostly laughed or smiled at my embarrassment. Not at Heimdall falls.

"So, truth can be bought, right?" said Baldur.

"There's no real conspiracy. I mean, you can't just print what you want. We were able to give them the benefit of the doubt and I was able to keep my job," I said.

I delivered it word for word but yet it seemed to lose something in translation, sounding somehow different here among Baldur's clan.

"So, what is that if not a conspiracy to keep the truth from the public?"

"It was a little more complex than that, I should have been more diligent, and I have always made it my intention never to mislead anyone," I said, in the kind of heedless manner I denounced politicians for.

There was a murmur of disapproval in the audience and I started to regret accepting the offer to speak.

Everything here seemed to be viewed in stark terms of black and white. Perhaps you can do that when you are so divorced from the grid of human politics and commerce. Looked at from afar, I did struggle to justify some of the overcomplicated and illogical ways of modern journalism.

"It would be unfair of me not to mention the good things Stig has achieved in his line of work but is perhaps too humble to mention. He is known as *the Fearless Pen* and nearly lost his job exposing a large-scale child rape network operating in England."

As if someone had adjusted the thermostat, I felt the temperature in the room move from icy cold to a more comfortable climate.

"He also ran a newspaper campaign to get homeless veterans off the streets and into community accommodation in his native England, when others were full of ridicule for it. He raised awareness of the debilitating eating disorder Anorexia that is skyrocketing, in no small part by the promotion of waif-like models on the sleazy catwalks of the fashion industry. He has reported from warzones and on one occasion saved the life of an injured US soldier in Afghanistan," said Baldur.

His research on me was incredibly thorough and I could see the last item had bought me some much-welcome kudos among the group, even if the description was a little overcooked.

"As you all know, Stig came here to write an article on Heimdall Falls."

I had sent Baldur my finished piece to illustrate to him what I considered was a fair and interesting take on life in his community.

Baldur handed me a photocopy of the newspaper article taken directly from the Capital Post website. I froze on the spot, just staring wide-eyed at the reproduction. The headline across the eight-page spread 'With friends like these' was an onslaught focused on President Trump. Among the attacks on assorted oddballs, racists and anti-abortionists was a section on Heimdall Falls with a photo of Baldur under the subheading 'Trump's Fool on the Hill.' The inhabitants had been called bitter losers who were simply sad and lonely, described in print as *Hicks without chicks*. My text had been savaged, yet my name remained pinned to the top. Maxwell had done a number on me and I was now wondering if one of the people seated before me would be asked to fetch the rope.

I had described Baldur as a generous man of principle and while there was much to debate with him, he had not appeared as the caricature I read about prior to visiting Heimdall Falls.

"I have read the piece he wrote and have to say it was a pretty studious article which made the comparison of our harmonious life in the clear blue skies of this beautiful mountain with the cut and thrust of the metropolitan existence in the big cities. Of course, it differs wildly from the published version."

I had been handed the shovel. I would dig myself out of this hole or try and turn it into an escape route. I had nothing to lose. I wouldn't try to justify the things that were so badly wrong with my industry.

I stood up, took a deep breath and spoke from the heart. "You are right to be sceptical about what you read in the newspapers. Almost everything I have ever written that has verged on the controversial side has been tinkered with, butchered or redacted, sometimes to the point that my conclusions have been completely turned on their head. I'm not proud of the fact that I haven't always succeeded in protecting my work when faced with the editor's knife."

My lecture was turning into a rally cry and if they were surprised, I could assure them there were none as shocked as me. These sentiments had been simmering within me for years, suppressed for the sole reason that expressing them threatened my job.

"I have to tell you how I ended up here. I had the audacity to question the UK government's draconian policies implemented on the back of an international health scare. I never purported to have all the answers, but I'm in no doubt that they sent me here to silence my questions. I have rebelled, spoken out and clashed with my bosses but inevitably accepted the unacceptable because I have a mortgage and a comfortable lifestyle to upkeep. Baldur offered me an olive branch when I was stranded, and I have been shown a kindness that I will never forget. On reflection I think I was stranded in more ways than one. Sometimes you need to get a bird's eye view of life to really take stock. Standing atop of this mountain I have seen the path of my life more clearly than ever before. I accepted the status quo, even though I could see its negative reverberations. I promise you that I will not allow my words to be manipulated to serve any agenda other than the truth."

I amazed myself with the diatribe I had just delivered. When I finished, Baldur stood up, his impassioned applause spreading throughout the hall.

Baldur shook my hand enthusiastically before addressing the gathering.

"Thank you, Stig. For your dignified words. I'm aware of what those crooks in the media call me, but I will never kowtow to those lizards. I've seen good people tie themselves up in knots in the hope that the poisonous ink-dippers would say something positive about them. Me? I am the Eagle in the sky, I am the wily fox, I am the roaring Lion and the gentle Deer. I am all those things and more because I chose to be free. Freedom isn't just about unlocked doors, fighting dirty politics or campaigning against corrupt legislation, it's a state of mind. Today, my kinfolk, Stig Fisher chose Freedom."

These words received another burst of rapturous applause.

I waited until the hall emptied out before approaching Baldur.

"I had no idea what they had done to my piece about Heimdall falls," I said.

He took the published version of the article from my hand and crushed it in the palm of his hand.

"The hard road is mostly taken by necessity and rarely by choice," he said.

I shook his hand fervently.

"Thank you, Baldur."

Dylo was waiting for me and so I sidled off to talk with him and we slowly made our way outside.

"You all right?" he enquired.

"I survived." I said, as I exhaled a long stream of air.

"They loved it. I mean, the fella what walked out, that was Ernie Bartmann, he was a professor of History until a hack started digging around in his past and found some outta favour protest group that Bartmann had been loosely affiliated with. It cost him his job, his home and, after the relentless campaigning from various interest groups and media outlets, it destroyed his marriage. You ain't ever gonna win over folks like Bartmann."

Dylo took me over to a spot half-way down the mountain to a nook close to the waterfall. It was mesmerizingly beautiful, and the sound of the water made it feel so serene.

"It's strange really," I mused. "Baldur is a good orator, he has the poise, a trustful face, but all in all, he doesn't really tell you anything you don't already know."

"He tells you what you need to hear, not necessarily what you want to hear," said Dylo, just loud enough to overcome the cascading water.

"I bare a great debt to that man, although that's probably not how he would have it," he said.

His head darted upwards and I followed his gaze to see an eagle in the sky.

"Wisdom is a strange thing, there in plain sight if you could just recognise it for what it is," he said.

I assumed he was talking about his son.

"My life would have taken a different road had I known then what I know now. Baldur showed me that you have to learn to take strength from the pain. The best pain killers are those I get from helping other folks, particularly when I act against those who harm children," said Dylo.

Sometimes a pregnant silence is enough to prompt someone to go deeper and get something off their chest. If he needed to pour his heart out to me, I was willing to listen, but it would be on his terms.

In the end, Dylo failed to shed more light on the circumstances surrounding his son's death. We remained seated for some time just enjoying the view and letting the sound of the waterfall encapsulate us.

I didn't want to trouble Baldur, so in the evening I slinked away to the diner where I ordered a coffee and made use of their free wi-fi. The signal was pretty weak from where I had parked the car, but it was enough of a connection to reply to my emails.

I called Jasmine and we chatted. I hadn't seen her in over three weeks and, although that wasn't particularly unusual, our separation seemed to weigh heavy on me. I told Jasmine about my day and how mad I was at Maxwell for stitching me up with the article, but she didn't see the big deal, it was the nature of the beast. She was simply regurgitating the words I had parroted whenever there was ethical questions about the way the paper appropriated my work.

As I was telling her about the lecture, I caught myself saying 'the folk here are good people'. There was a gap of silence as we both considered what this meant.

"Are you ok? Sounds like you need to get yourself home," said Jasmine.

I knew it sounded a bit strange, but my time on the mountain made me see things a little differently. I can't ever remember having such clarity.

"I'm fine," I said. And I was.

Jasmine said she was anxious about catching the virus. She was perfectly healthy and knew no-one with it, but I could sense that the fear had gripped her. As the temperature in the car started to plummet, I drew the call to a close.

"I better get back," I said.

"Go on then," she said. "I don't want you to miss your place at the cross burning or whatever it is you're getting up to tonight."

8. The Ice Maiden cometh

Just when I thought I was getting the hang of being at Heimdall Falls, things started to get a little crazy. I was invited to join a small group who go for a weekly dip at the waterfall. Dylo said that I would feel wonderful afterwards. With the ice forming on the cabin windows, I could see that his secret stash of gin was doing what gin does best.

I woke early and poked my head out of the door and the icy breath of the mountain made me shiver. It was definitely the wrong side of zero outside.

Eight of us gathered at the auditorium. The strikingly beautiful woman with long pleats of blonde hair, who led the yoga, took charge. She introduced herself as Freya. "Some of you, I know, will be new to this. What we teach at Heimdall is balance and control. Baldur has shown you how to de-program your brain and take control of your life. I am here to show you that you can master the power of your body through the focus of your mind. You have faith in Baldur and now you can trust in your own mind, trust in what I am saying, and you will trust in the synchronicity of your body."

Freya put us through a short meditation ritual before focusing intensely on our breathing.

"This will be your method of control. It will prevent your body from succumbing to the cold. Everybody has the ability to neutralise the bite of chill," she said.

It was perilously cold, and I had been encouraged to shed my layers and join the others on the path down to the bottom of the falls in nothing more than a pair of shorts and a t-shirt. I began breathing in stallion-like proportions.

Once there, we repeated the breathing exercises and Runic Yoga movements. We were psyching ourselves up, both mentally and physically. In my heart I feared I would not be able to match the strength of their focus.

"The water is a gift from mother nature. Respect it. Do not fear it," shouted Freya, above the din of the falls' relentless cascade. "The water is inviting you to share its power."

A few minutes later we gently allowed ourselves to sink up to our necks in the freezing, gushing torrent. Each millimetre of water was another shock to my system that I was told to fend off with the concentration of my mind and the firm control of my breathing.

"You must temper the pain of the raw biting chill with the strength of your resolve, your focus is your destiny. Embrace the water. Be at one with it," bellowed our winsome motivator.

I did as I was instructed, my eyes never left the fast moving, frothing water. I had flashes of realisation that I was conquering the cold, but my mind told me not to celebrate but to focus on the method. If it all went wrong, I couldn't even think how long it would take an ambulance to reach the wilds of Heimdall and this was not how I fancied shuffling off this mortal coil.

The first two or three minutes were the toughest, but then the technique took hold, and I felt an enormous rush of adrenaline and positive energy. The power was overwhelming. I experienced a deep sense of relief turn into an invigorating feeling of invincibility.

After breakfast, I was back on the chain gang building the cabin. I found myself engulfed in a cloud of positivity that was enhanced by the physical labour. I toiled with them and I revelled in their common purpose. When we sang, I found the words enthusiastically bursting from my lips.

After my shift, I returned to my cabin. There, I was visited by Baldur, who enquired about my wellbeing. I told him I had never felt so good in my life. I was pacing the room excitedly as if I didn't expel this energy I would simply explode.

"I don't know what to do with all this energy. I feel so… so inspired," I said.

"Do what you were born to do… write," he said calmly.

"Write about what?"

The Heimdall piece that had been bastardised by Maxwell, I should redress that.

"Write about here?" I said.

"No," he said. He pointed to my heart. "Write about there."

I understood what he meant. I was no longer hesitant to embrace the knowledge he had shared with me. I will leave here tomorrow a bigger man than I was when I arrived. This all sounded so crazy, so bumper sticker. If I said this to anyone I knew in London, they would think me a victim of cultish cliché? But it felt so visceral.

"Many struggles and challenges lay ahead. Let your love guide you. You have what you need. Instinct, inner strength and purpose," said Baldur.

"I want to thank you, Baldur, for believing in a cynical old bark who had lost all faith in what it means to be human," I said, as he opened up his arms to hug me.

"You will be heading back to the bosom of your family tomorrow. Before you leave the mountain, come and join me at my house for dinner," he said.

After he left my cabin, I stared out into the unimpeded view of nature at its rawest and drifted into a state of reflection. Powerful emotions racing through my brain until they slowed and settled on one overwhelming feeling, that of happiness. All parts equal, I was happy. I missed Jasmine and the boys, but I had never been more content with who *I* was.

If I was going to be his guest, then I would need to find a gift for Baldur. I rustled through my luggage but there was nothing that would be of interest to him. Perhaps I could dash out and buy him some wine, but I wasn't sure whether he drank alcohol. I decided I would take his advice and write him a poem.

I arrived at his house with Dylo. Freya and her husband, Robert, were there. We conversed at the table while Baldur put the finishing touches to a dish of roast chicken. Freya and Robert worked as private tutors, him in Maths, her in Geography. They spoke about the challenges of an education system that ate away at the self-esteem and identity of the children. Their methods attempted to counter that, their own six children having been home schooled.

Baldur's house was furnished modestly, the glaring omission being the requisite television set of virtually every other home in my social circle in London. The bookcase in his living room was packed to the rafters. Freya said her ancestors were from Scotland, not too far from where my father had grown up and where my youthful imagination ran wild on summer holidays in the pine forests and coastal paths of a Highland idyl that was forever ingrained in the more colourful corners of my mind.

Mead wine, made from local honey, was served with the meal and we toasted the success of Dylo's latest mission. He was working with a group in Grand Rapids who laid traps on internet chat rooms to ensnare paedophiles. His work had led to the successful conviction of over fifty child abusers. He explained that community police welcomed the leg work he and his fellow hunters provided, but that there was pressure on a federal level to prevent any collaboration, particularly after the group unearthed three senators, a judge and a high-profile lawyer. He said that if the avenues of conventional justice were considered compromised, they would, on rare occasions, 'send their target away on a long holiday'. It was clear what he meant but that didn't seem to trouble anyone around the table, as it may have in the liberal circles I frequented in London. In fact, it was more like a cause of celebration.

"If you gotta choose who to protect, an innocent child or some creep who thinks he's untouchable because the court system is rigged, it don't take no time to come to a suitable conclusion," said Dylo, proudly.

With the mead providing that little bit of Dutch courage required for such occasions, I got to my feet and delivered my poem in tribute of our host.

Fresh water is falling at Heimdall Falls
A beacon is burning as the bald eagle calls
It heralds a passion so timeless and deep
And a strength to climb mountains no matter how steep
People are gathered, they work, and they sing
And worship the sunshine, new life that it brings
A taste for the old myths and legends anew
Food to replenish and his own secret brew
Thank you, Baldur, you came to my aid
Another lost wanderer you valiantly saved

Baldur sprung up and embraced me with a hug.

"This is for you," said Baldur.

He presented me with a pendant on a chain.

"An arrow," I said, looking at the engraved design.

"It is the Tyr rune. Runes have many meanings, it's part of their power," he said. "When you wear this, it re-establishes your oath to truth, honour and courage. Symbolism is important, our ancestors used the power of the runes, but the early Christians banished them and much of their power lays invisible to us these days, but it is there, connecting us to our subconscious the way it did so many moons ago."

I thanked him and we refilled and chinked glasses into the early hours. He was as drunk and rumbunctious as any of us, full of funny stories of daring do. Maybe it was the ample servings of mead, but if he had been on a recruitment drive for soldiers to fight in a war, I would have signed up without a moment's hesitation, such was the allure of his aura. He transmitted a sense of self-belief that released something in you.

From this day forward I promised myself that I would live my life by nobody's editorial policy but my own.

9. Empty

It was strange, after my time with Baldur, Dylo and company, to be confronted at the airport by neurotic creatures in masks, panicking about whether everyone else was adhering to the strict distancing rules that they were now self-declared denizens of. The airport was lacking its usual hustle and bustle of eager holiday makers, frazzled parents and bored businessmen. Many shops were shuttered, and vast areas were cordoned off. It resembled a retail mall on its last legs.

I checked in and settled down in the first-class lounge with a coffee and a newspaper. Before long a Boeing 747 would take me to Paris where after a two-hour gap I would board a plane for Blighty. The fact that I couldn't fly direct but could enter the UK via France was indicative of the nonsensical nature of the madness gripping the planet.

On arrival at Heathrow, I was delayed once more. I hadn't completed a pre-flight health questionnaire. They held me in a white cubicle awaiting my virus test results. I was offered tepid drinks of tea and my choice of junk food. I declined everything, exasperated at the lack of consideration and pitiful organisation. I was clearly not ill. The man in charge said there was a delay, but after four hours I think he'd forgotten what it was we were waiting for and let me go.

By the time I arrived home to Clapham I was shattered. It was teaming down with rain and I got soaked just walking from the taxi to my own doorstep while I rifled through my suitcase in search of keys.

It was eight o'clock in the evening and there was no sign of life in the house that would normally be alive to the sound of teenage tantrums, video games, loud music and kitchen clutter.

My mobile phone was dead, so I looked for the house telephone that usually gathered dust in the hall, but it was missing. I plugged my mobile in to charge and ten minutes later the binging started.

Rather than wade through the messages and voicemails, I called Jasmine.

"Where the hell is everyone?" I blurted out as she answered.

It sounded more aggressive than I meant it to be, but I was wrecked, and my fuse was getting shorter by the minute.

"Change your tone and get down here, we're at St. Thomas's hospital," she snapped.

"Hospital? What's happened?"

"It's your Mum, she's got the virus," she said.

"Oh shit. When? What's...?"

"I'll explain when you get here," she said.

"Okay, I'm on my way," I said.

I could hear Jasmine remonstrating with someone and then the line went dead. I arranged a cab to take me to the hospital. While I waited, I had a quick refresh in the bathroom and threw on a clean sweatshirt.

When the cab arrived, the driver made a fuss about my lack of a mask. I shuffled in my pocket but the paper one I pulled out was filthy.

"I'm exempt," I said.

"Yeah, they all say that," he said, in an accent derived from somewhere between London and Lahore.

"Can you just get me there quickly, please? it's an emergency," I said.

I could see his piqued face in the rear-view mirror. He drove like a maniac, shunting me around like he was scolding a petulant child. I didn't care as long as I got their fast. When we arrived, I rustled in my wallet and gave him a twenty pounds note for the twelve pounds ride.

"Keep the change," I said and went to leave but heard him click the internal locks.

"I can't take cash, man. New policy," he said.

"What the hell?" I stormed.

"It's the virus, innit, can't take the risk," he said.

I got out my credit card and swiped his gadget and he got his twelve pounds.

I rushed into St Thomas's hospital and was immediately barracked for not wearing a mask, I explained I had just got off a plane and the security officer told me to wait while he went and got me one. The place was unusually quiet. The guard, in a full-face welder-style mask, told me the building was on partial lockdown due to the virus. He ushered me over to a booth where I could speak to a similarly masked attendant behind a Perspex screen. She checked her computer and confirmed that my mother was in the intensive care unit.

"Intensive care? What the hell happened?"

"I'm sorry, I can't give you any further details," she said. She wore a weary expression that said she wanted to be anywhere but here. I asked her for directions to the ward and she looked at me as if I had just asked for her credit card and pin code.

"I don't think you understand, sir. All wards are out of bounds. You will not be able to go through. It's the new regulations," she said.

"But my wife is already there, I just spoke to her a few minutes ago," I said, my voice raised in aversion to such a cruel imposition.

"Sorry, sir, no-one is there, there are no visitors in the hospital, it's the new-"

"-regulations, yes, I get it," I said.

I hit the pause button on my recently revised opinion of the pandemic. The Michigan militia may have had all their statistics lined up correctly, but this was my dear old mum. Had I been suckered? listening to dangerous fools who were convincing in their argument that it was all one enormous scam?

I caught sight of my son, Iain, standing outside. I reasoned I would get a better idea of what was going on from him. As I approached him my heart sank as I realised he was wiping tears from his eyes.

"Dad, it's really bad, we can't…" he stammered.

His normal teenage nonchalant façade was usurped by sadness, as he buried his head in my shoulder.

"Is Mum with Nanny?" I said.

"No. She's gone to put more money in the parking meter," he said.

"So, who's with Nanny?"

"No-one is," he said. "We're not allowed in, Dad."

Jasmine appeared with little Harley and she burst into tears on seeing me. He ran and hugged my waist and we all embraced.

"I tried to see her, Stig. We can't let her think we don't care," she sobbed.

"What happened?"

Jasmine composed herself and I lessened my grip.

"The care home rang to say she had been taken ill-"

"-with the virus?" I prompted.

"Yes, with the virus. I spoke to her while you were away, and she was all anxious about some residents who were returned from hospital still suffering from the virus. I thought she was getting things out of proportion and told her it would be ok."

The floods of tears burst open once again.

"And now they won't even let us see her. She'll be frightened, she won't understand why we're not there for her."

I spotted a doctor on his way into the hospital, so I unhooked myself from Jasmine and raced to get to him before he entered the main doors.

"Excuse me, doctor," I called.

He looked around and flinched at the sight of me approaching.

"My mother is in the ICU, can you please allow me to go and see her? she will be extremely distressed, she suffers from dementia and this will be a really frightening ordeal for her," I begged.

"I'm sorry, they should have informed you that there are no visitors allowed." he said, in a matter-of-fact way.

I grabbed his shoulder to stop him going in.

"I'm not a visitor, I'm her son," I exclaimed.

"I'm sorry. I can't help you," he said, as he looked for help from the hospital's new bouncers.

He shrugged me off and I was instantly confronted by a security guard.

"I'll wear a mask, a gown, a bloody space suit. whatever, just help us please,"

"I'm sorry, I don't make the rules," said the doctor.

The security guard was now blocking my way.

"Sir, I understand your concern, but we are in the middle of a pandemic. You are not the only person denied access to-," he said, before a burst of my anger cut him off.

"Pandemic? What fucking pandemic? Where are all the emergencies? You've got a long line of ambulances outside here, sitting idle."

"Sir, it's the rules, there's nothing-"

"-This is madness," I shouted.

I could hear Harley's distressed voice beckoning his mother to intervene, followed by Jasmine trying to temper my rage.

"Leave it, Stig," said Jasmine.

"Sir," said the doctor.

"No…," I raged. "I'm not leaving until I have seen my mother. This is inhumane," I stormed.

Reinforcements arrived, and I was manhandled outside into the cold. I stood staring at the guards, my nostrils flaring like a Bull about to charge. They kept their eyes trained on me as they eagerly flanked the doors to deter any hasty attempt to get back in.

I returned to Jasmine, Harley and Iain. Jasmine gripped my hand.

"I thought she'd be safe in the care home," said Jasmine.

"She should have been," I said.

"She should have come to live with us," she said.

"With our busy lives? We talked about this. She needed proper care," I said.

"And *this* is proper care?"

"This is not our fault," I said.

At home, the despair of waiting was so chokingly mundane. We were caught in a void, clutching to the hope that she would pull through. Everywhere you looked, you were confronted with fear. Death and case numbers were reported on the news like an Olympics score board. Ominously, there was no data on the number of people who had recovered.

Mum was old but physically healthy, a long-distance runner in her prime, she rarely got so much as a cold.

Then dementia struck. She thought the world was out to poison her, she blamed the tap water, the food and the pollution. I remember when we first took her to a McDonalds, she was aghast that people ate 'that stuff' as she called it.

The children adored her. She often forgot their names but no matter what she was doing, it could always be put aside to make time for them.

Every time the phone rang, we jumped out of our skin, mentally preparing ourselves like Firemen awaiting the next shout. The punctuation was always a false alarm and although you instructed your nerves to stand down, they remained on heightened alert.

With my head still reeling I reluctantly returned to the office. On arrival, I was asked to grab my things and leave. Before the receptionist had finished her sentence, I exploded.

"Oh, it's like that is it?" I ranted, pacing around in a rage.

"No, Mr Fisher. Mr Fisher, you don't understand."

"Do you know how long I have worked-"

"-Mr Fisher, did you not receive the memo?" She said.

"What memo?" I cursed.

"Everyone has been asked to work from home," she said. The receptionist informed me that the building was crewed by skeleton staff and I was to take what I needed and work from home. I apologised for my embarrassing outburst and took my blushing face to my desk and scooped a few things in my rucksack before leaving.

On my journey home, I checked the messages I had been ignoring and right enough there was the information about the new office procedures.

I used my next column in the paper to rally at the inhumanity of family members being shut out of hospitals while distressed and bewildered loved ones lay suffering inside. As before, the editor's red pen removed most of the bite and it had instead been recommissioned as a rally call to support the government's message of keeping everyone safe. As safe as the caged animal that will never feel the warm breeze of the sun or drink freely from the stream.

Then it came. The news we dreaded. Jasmine clung to the phone desperate to hear of any progress first-hand. I saw the translation on her face even before she relayed it. They were sorry, but they couldn't save her. My mother was dead. The news travelled from the handset like an all-encompassing poisonous vine. Everything was covered. All we could do was try not to choke on the toxic fumes. I watched helplessly as, one by one, it slayed us all. They said she was peaceful at the end and that the hospital chaplain had been by to read a prayer from behind the Intensive Care unit window.

Jasmine relayed the news and promptly collapsed on the floor, weeping uncontrollably. Iain stood at the top of the stairs and shouted at the top of his lungs.

"Fuck off!"

He repeated it and repeated it until his throat grew sore before he retreated into his bedroom with a colossal slam of his door that shook the house.

Fuck off indeed to those cold in-human bastards who kept us apart. Fuck off to the government ministers who had imposed these fiendish orders. And fuck off to the person who decided that it was a good idea to send ill people into the heart of a nursing home full of vulnerable residents.

Seconds passed like hours on a tick-less clock. Everything was blur-like. I had never taken hard drugs but imagined that this would be the come down from some hazardous hit that left you tinkering on the edge of wishing it had stolen your last heartbeat, as this government had stolen my mother's.

I awoke in the night with a jolt. The sharp blade of reality preventing me from returning to sleep, I walked downstairs and hunched over a notebook on the kitchen table, I started scribbling. When I awoke it took a moment or two to work out where I was. Then it hit me like a sledgehammer. Mum was dead. I would never see her again. My poor gentle old Mum. I looked at my spidery handwriting on the pad. At the top of the page, I had written 'I am broken.' What followed was a poem.

I am the sails with no wind
I am the tree with no leaves
I am the heart with no beat
I am the love that now grieves

I am the game with no joy
I am the toy with no child
I am the lungs with no breath
I am defeat that runs wild

I am the noise with no sound
I am the hymn with no words
I am the dog with no bark
I am the sky with no birds

I am the room with no air
I am the touch that can't feel
I am the tear that won't fall
I am the wound that won't heal

10. Death lies heavy on my Gut

Unwanted obligations are an imposition often alleviated with cards and flowers. We received plenty of heartfelt messages of condolence and a few from family members who were clearly relieved that they could hide behind the virus restrictions as way of avoiding my mother's funeral.

Under any circumstances, this would have been a quiet family affair, but the constant reminder of the virus restrictions invaded its sanctity. At the crematorium the chairs were separated and fixed to the floor and government signage jarred amongst the religious paraphernalia. When Jasmine's friend, Gemma, rushed to comfort her, as my mother's coffin disappeared behind the curtain, I saw the usher move to intervene, but a sharp look from me had him swiftly reconsider and return to his base. It was a gesture so inappropriate in this setting, I half considered halting proceedings while the disrespectful wretch was marched out of the ornate building and thrown in the gutter.

I read my poem 'I am broken' and Jasmine eulogised about their special bond. Iain recounted a humorous tale about how they had played a game of *feed the donkey* when he was little. To keep him from crying, she had to munch through a bag of carrots every time she called around.

"We played it so often, by the time I was seven I was sure she had gained an orange glow," he said.

I received a box from UPS containing an unusually coloured solitary flower. Inside the card, the words 'in deepest sympathy' were accompanied by a strange three pronged whirly symbol. Iain spent some time later on researching it and told me it was an old Norse emblem that meant 'the gift of the sea, sky and land'. I assume it was Baldur, although I can't imagine how he found out.

My own newspaper, the Capital Post, joined some of the others in reporting that my mother's death was a good reason why children should stay away from their grandparents. A doctor at the hospital was quoted as saying 'Young people need to be separated from the old'. In the article, there was no mention at all of the cause of her untimely death and the insane procedure of sending contagious people back to care homes.

A few days later, as the numbness began to dissipate, I headed off to Trafalgar Square on a mission, grief and anguish cursing through me like a live wire on a wet road. On the underground I got stares from everyone because I hadn't bothered with a mask. I didn't care. No virus was ever going to scare me after what I had just experienced. Most of those staring were doing so out of envy because they didn't have the guts to go against the grain, to step off the conveyor belt of blind conformity and breathe the free air.

The in-house scheduling app indicated that Maxwell was in the office, so I bounded into the building and headed straight into the newsroom. I could see Maxwell sleazing around a smartly dressed young woman that I didn't recognise. Like a wolf in sheep's clothing, he was toying with his prey. No matter how much cologne he bathed in, the air around him always reeked of decay. Maxwell didn't see me approach and when I grabbed him by the scruff of his neck, his face turned white.

"You bastard," I stormed.

He was flustered, wincing and panicking like the coward I knew him to be.

"Stig, what are you-"

"-My mother died because they sent sick patients back into care homes, but you already know that don't you," I growled, inches from his face.

Maxwell put up no resistance, fumbling for a defence only to iterate a gooey line of 'but, but's.'

"Why didn't you call *me*? It's *my* mother for god's sake" I sneered.

"The doctor, we spoke to the doctor," he spluttered.

I relinquished my grip on his throat and he crumpled against the wall before quickly straightening up. He stood there caressing his collar while I seethed. As the fog cleared, I realised that an editorial meeting was in process, with no masks or distancing. It was deathly silent, all eyes on the commotion, no-one stepping in to help their boss or offering a kind word for their sorely bereaved colleague.

"You're all cowards," I roared at them.

I headed for my office and grabbed my possessions from my desk drawer and shoved them into a bag I had hanging behind the door. As I was about to leave, I stopped and pondered at the glass statuette I had been awarded for a Capital Post investigation into people smuggling. It dawned on me just how meticulously deceitful Maxwell had been to ensure certain names were kept out of that story. In this light the award suddenly took on the mantle of a badge of shame. I grabbed the statuette and hurled it at the wall, hoping it would smash into a thousand pieces, but unsatisfactorily, it lightly dented the partition before floundering feebly onto the carpet.

As I exited my office, Maxwell was in the corridor, flanked by two security guards. I knew them well and recalled how they spent most of their time bad mouthing the man they were now protecting.

"You're fired, Fisher," he spat, whilst positioning himself a safe distance from the *mild man gone wild*.

"I wouldn't work in this liars lair if you paid me all the hush money ever to dirty your pockets," I said.

On the journey home, I questioned the kamikaze nature of crashing my job in such a manner. As good as it felt at the time, I needed the stability of that job to keep our home life from nose diving and the somewhat risky mortgage we had taken out three years ago, in order to complete a quite unnecessary house extension.

When I arrived home and told her, Jasmine went berserk, smashing plates and lashing out at anything within a few feet of her. I instantly realised that this was not about my job, I had opened the pressure valve of grief that had been waiting to burst.

"You idiot. Are we not suffering enough? You want us turfed out on the street?" she said.

"Those snakes lied about my mum," I protested.

"What does it matter? She's gone and she's never coming back," she said, as rage tipped into despair.

"I just want the truth for her, that's all," I said.

"You want the truth?"

She was so close to me her spittle was flying all over my face as she blew up once more.

"The truth is, *we* shipped her off into the care of strangers. *We* did this to her. It was *us* who signed her death warrant."

Jasmine flew up the stairs and slammed the bedroom door shut.

I had never witnessed such incandescent rage in her. Jasmine loved my mum as I did, they were as thick as thieves. When it came to hospitals, she was well-aware that things don't always go to plan. Her own mother died when Jasmine was in her early thirties after a botched operation to remove gallstones.

Even though the mists of old age had encompassed her, my mother still retained a glint in her eye. She had been sharp witted and could be incredibly funny. One minute she would be recanting old stories that had been altered and inflated as they passed down the generations, the next she would have us all singing around the piano. For Iain, his grandmother had been the heroine in the story of his young life. She opened his heart to a knowledge and understanding that could never be reached via his parents or his schoolteachers.

Now, Iain had taken to bolting himself in his room and drowning out the world with heavy rock music. He didn't want to talk and any open discussions about his beloved grandmother, would see him run for cover. The Government had restricted him from seeing his girlfriend and his school day consisted of staring at his laptop for six hours, with a three-hour bonus of homework, also on the laptop. Even lab rats had more rest time than these young students.

My head was in a constant spin trying to reconcile my moment of enlightenment in Michigan with the new reality of my home life in the age of the virus. I took my pain and my thoughts out onto Clapham Common. As soon as I pulled the door closed behind me, I felt the chill cold wind fly up my back. It was an unusually cold day for spring. I needed a coat but had left my keys inside, so I decided to tough it out.

I walked over to the bandstand, shivering a little, in the winds that swept across the upper plain in London's south western district. Sitting on the edge of a well-worn wooden plank, almost without thinking, I started the breathing regime I had learned at Heimdall falls. With all that had happened recently, my time on the mountain seemed like the faded pages of someone else's memories. I could feel the heat come back into my body as I entered a meditative state.

I started to think about Baldur, and also Dylo, and the dark fog of London life lifted a little. They had a freedom that no-one I knew could even contemplate. I had mused over the idea of an idyllic existence in the countryside so many times with friends and colleagues, knowing full well that none of us were ever likely to expand the concept past extended weekend breaks and holiday homes. We were the mice in the wheel going around and around until we went pop. Affluent mice, but mice all the same.

My mobile rang, it was Pam Sowilo, a solicitor friend of ours. I prompted her to investigate if we had grounds to sue the care home. Money couldn't bring my mother back, but a successful case might prevent some other poor souls from going through the hell we were struggling with.

"It's not good, Stig," she said, with a hint of trepidation. My heart dropped. Small stones were causing enormous great ripples on the surface of my mood.

"All residents were asked to sign a contract with the care home that contained an indemnity clause. So basically, I have to advise you that a case of negligence is unlikely to be successful. They have sewn it up with the government," she said.

"Bastards," I said.

"There is one thing you can do," she said

"What's that?"

"Shine a light on it. You're a journalist, Stig. Write. Get the story out there."

11. Questions and Answers

Scanning my Twitter feed, I resumed full connection to the time thief they call the online world, losing myself in the cloaked manifestations of zeros and ones, as I had so many times before. I was lifted momentarily at the many messages of condolence, mostly from people I had never met.

I soon caught up with the jibber-jabber of the world of politics. The prime minister was implementing compulsory masks to be worn in shops, schools and busses in the name of saving the health service. The opposition were asking for the restrictions on the British people to be tougher. The Scottish parliament wanted to trump them all by banning people from visiting another person's property for any reason whatsoever, thus isolating the old and infirm even further.

Everything was going unchallenged and laws were being passed without so much as a moment's debate in parliament, or in the pages of the broadsheets where the government's message looked like it was being parroted verbatim.

To some extent, I had been guilty of this blind compliance too. It was always recognised that supplying the oxygen of publicity to people such as the global warming denier, Piers Corbyn, was dangerous. That argument had never been enforced so vigorously as it was now. Radical people make the best interviews because if their diatribe really is bizarre and outrageous you simply give them enough rope to hoop around their ideology or viewpoint and watch them swing into obscurity. Alternatively, different viewpoints bring fresh ideas and there is nothing healthier to do than test and challenge your own prejudices or status quo, let alone society's.

With clear eyes, it was easy to see that each edition of the paper was becoming more and more condescending to its readership. News stories were being replaced by instructions. The media would decide everything for the nation, there was no longer space for debate in the broadsheets, the so-called intellectual press. My recent employer, the Capital Post, had now become a governmental mouthpiece, the likes that had never been seen before, at least not in my lifetime. And if the truth was hiding in the small print, they would be only too aware that it would be a very niche readership.

However, online, the debate was raging. It was led, in some cases, by people who had previously muddied their names with outlandish conspiracy theories. The weight of their new revelations would always be off-set with the corrosive baggage of a tainted past that could so easily be exploded by the mainstream media at any given time. Strangely, there was no genuine organised opposition to the restrictions to our public freedoms. All established political parties were dancing to the same tune and so the resistance was a rudderless ship of disparate parts that couldn't politically challenge the might and financial reach of the state's machinery and its allies in the media. One personal message caught my eye, it had been sent to me both on Twitter and Facebook. It was a biblical quote.

'Are we not counted of him strangers? for he hath sold us, and hath quite devoured also our money'.
It was followed by a question. 'How does a medical adviser to the government spend his *pocket* money?'

The sender simply signed off with the initials WB. Curiosity got the better of me, so I got to work on unearthing the answer. Of the three health and scientific advisers with the ear of the prime minister, two, David Rissle and Ben Ducant, had shares totalling four hundred thousand pounds with various pharmaceutical companies, including those directly benefiting from government contracts. Will Cockburn, chief pandemic adviser, held shares worth over a million pounds with Rothbairn Pharmaceuticals, the vaccine developer awarded a four billion pounds contract by his own department.

I called around ex-colleagues and managed to speak to Jeremy Green, sub editor at The Guardian. I knew Jeremy pretty well from University. He said he was interested in my story and would float the idea of getting me a more permanent role with the paper.

The Guardian ran my story about the conflict of interest among government scientific advisers on their front page and it was the lead story on TV and social media for days. Two prominent politicians demanded Cockburn resign. I was back in the game and my mortgage payments would be secure for the moment. I hoped that this change in fortune might add some much-needed stability to my home life.

Cockburn would not have survived a storm like this a few years ago, but UK politics was so detached from the electorate, and so mired in the gutter of corruption that he simply brushed it off. In days gone by his colleagues would have ran for cover, avoiding the public stain of any association with him. Now, many were brazenly championing him, as if this blatant act of feathering one's nest was somehow virtuous and the real villains were those unearthing the fraud.

With a second full lockdown being imposed so soon after the first one had been temporarily reduced, it felt as if Harley's life was being frozen in ice. His school was closed, the swimming pool was shut until further notice and even his favourite playground on the common had 'Police - No entry' tape across the entrance, as if the virus had specifically chosen that place to set up HQ. Unlike on Baldur's mountain, pandemic rebels seemed few and far between. Fear was the real virus ripping through the community. There were hourly scare stories on TV and radio news, saturation advertising enforcing social distancing, masks and regular hand washing with Bio soap that, a homeopathic doctor warned me, destroyed any natural resistance to unhealthy germs. All of it started to feel like something out of some bleak sci-fi movie. This health emergency pumped fear into the air and I was picking up the scent of something resembling regime change and, just like in Russia and East Germany, the uniforms were replaced but the faces stayed the same.

We were sitting in our living room, like millions of others, transfixed as the prime minister addressed the nation from Downing Street. It was a reconstruction of those faded images of families sitting around the radio hoping to hear the end to hostilities announced, praying that their brave loved ones could return home in safety. The PM spoke in the language of war. 'It was a battle we would win', 'the enemy would be defeated', 'collectively we would conjure up the Dunkirk spirit of world war two'.

He was playing at being his hero Winston Churchill, but his reference to Dunkirk was ill chosen. The Battle of Dunkirk had been a moment of panic and poor judgement made by generals a very safe distance from the carnage of the conflict. Hundreds of thousands of troops were cornered by the German Army. Hitler, for whatever reason, had refused Himmler's Luftwaffe the go-ahead to wipe out the Allied troops and so opened an opportunity for them to flee back to England, on any vessel they could find willing to take them. It was an epic effort by everyone from fishermen to pleasure boat owners to save every poor soul they could reach. 80,000 died and thousands more were captured, it had been a major Churchillian catastrophe that was swiftly whitewashed for the history books.

Prior to a new allegiance with international bankers, Churchill had been against the war but, as his estate was miraculously saved from financial ruin, he became a tub thumper for conflict.

The Churchillian resolve was another media invention. He would pose in his RAF jump suit, visiting the smouldering bomb sites, in the safety of daylight, telling those who had family killed and homes destroyed that it was all worth it. Championing the bulldog spirit for the cameras, as night fell and the common people eked out meals from strict rations and braced themselves for fresh bombing raids, he would be chauffeured to the sanctuary of Oxfordshire to scoff caviar and puff away on expensive cigars while he got absolutely blotto on expensive bottles of Brandy.

Now, as he spoke to the British people, eighty years on from that day of humiliation, death and disaster, the prime minister was ratcheting up the fear.

"An estimated one million people will perish if we do nothing," he said in a sombre tone, his usually unkempt wavy blond hair appearing even more wild, as if done so deliberately.

He talked about how they were 'consulting the science,' as if science was indeed one almighty being of godly acumen. The science he was referring to was in fact, Derek Berkson, the computer programmer who had built a mathematical code of predictions. His previous attempts for Bird Flu and Foot and Mouth disease had been so vastly inflated they had been quietly airbrushed from the compendium of virology history.

The prime minister leaned in and directed his next message to the young. It was the bombshell that he knew would dominate the headlines and send a shiver through households.

"Don't kill Granny," he said.

"You already have, you bastard," I shouted at the telly. I could stand it no more. I grabbed my coat and made my way to the bandstand where I stomped around trying to douse an internal fire that was raging out of control. In my head the echoes of the newscaster were being invaded by Freya's voice, channelling the phrase she had used when training us for her cold-water therapy. 'Focus and focus some more. Life is a struggle and angry heads make poor judgements.' I launched into the breathing exercises I had learned at Heimdall falls.

As I concentrated on my heart rate and the rhythm of my deep breaths, I was interrupted by a loud hailer announcement coming from a police car.

"Stay Home. You are only permitted to leave your home for work or to buy food. Please comply. This is for your own safety and the safety of others."

It was like scene from the film V for Vendetta. Dystopia had come to our green and pleasant corner of the city and fear was suppressing even our most basic freedoms. I ignored the cop car and continued my breathing with renewed vigour.

My blood was pumping, and I felt an overwhelming urge to try and redress the balance. I needed to write. It was what I was on this planet to do. I needed to find the next story.

I needed another exposé.

I was astonished that, on returning home, my unopened email messages contained another golden nugget from this mysterious benefactor who signed off as 'WB'. The timing was incredible. It was too easy. I was being aided, but by who? Was this Dex? Or maybe Baldur from America? How would he get access to this kind of information half-way up a mountain in Michigan?

I read the message aloud.

"And I made the discovery that the law whose purpose was to give life
had become a cause of death."

It was another biblical reference, and it came with a link to a page containing photographs of classified Whitehall documents exposing the state's intention of actively encouraging the vociferous hounding of any dissenting voices on social media by inciting righteous fury in other, more malleable users. Just as Dex warned me, they had created a 'Nudge' unit to actively turn citizen against citizen, the way social media had successfully divided the nation over Britain's vote to exit the European Union. There was also proof of collusion with the tech giants who promised to give the government free reign and root out anything that conflicted with the state narrative.

My initial rush of excitement was suddenly tamed by the thought that I may be walking into a trap. Why was I receiving this anonymous help? Who was this mysterious WB? What was in it for WB? I would need to be meticulous with my investigation before I could hand anything over to anyone, not least The Guardian. In my world, if you want to remove a player from the game, give them the scent of victory whilst leading them to their own inglorious demise. Was this a poisoned chalice? I had earned the scalps of some high-profile politicians, businessmen and celebrities during my time as a reporter, many of whom would love to see my face drowning in the contemptuous ink of my own Rabelaisian well.

I explained the situation to Allen Charlton, an old colleague of mine from the London Standard. He was a fervent Tory basher and railed against everything they did. His stories were mainly picked up by fringe media companies. He also ran a successful podcast online where het let loose about everything from 80's punk bands to statues to Confederate generals.

Allen warned me about stoking up the anti-maskers, in what seemed like an attempt to put me off my stride. When I asked if he'd traded in his red rosette for a Tory blue one, he suggested we meet for a beer. It had to be clandestine because of the lockdown restrictions. It was all a bit 'nudge, nudge, wink, wink', but I think he got a thrill out of those cloak and dagger manoeuvres.

I assumed it would be more difficult to get confirmation on my revelations now that the democratic process was under the heal of an autocratic leadership.

"On the contrary," he said. "They have rushed through the digitisation of everything and, we have ways of accessing things we haven't always been able to see, shall we say. I found some explosive stuff on World War Two that, if I dared publish, I might find my abode for the rest of my days to be an eight-foot cell or a six-foot hole in the ground."

My tip off paid dividends and, although the newspaper couldn't get full access to the document, what they did receive was confirmation that it existed. Allen informed me that it had been placed in an online void created specifically to avoid the scrutiny of any bothersome freedom of information requests.

The story was green lit, so I got to work putting the meat on the bones. I was convinced that what I had stumbled upon was the blueprint of a new kind of authoritarian form of government that never existed before in the UK. Amongst the pages were new laws sanctioning the removal of people from their homes and placing them in secure quarantine centres. Bizarrely, one section permitted private dwellings to be destroyed if it was considered that they were contaminated. The new edicts would also allow for citizens to be forcibly vaccinated.

With that kind of information dynamite, it wasn't difficult to write what I thought was a striking piece of news copy and hurriedly sent it off to Jeremy, picturing the scandal as the cabinet ministers responsible for this outrage, read the frontpage story in the Guardian that would herald their imminent demise. Jeremy's response was strangely out of sync with my thought pattern.

"It's not quite the angle we're looking for," he said.

"This is massive. The government wants to forcibly jab citizens with an untested vaccine scooped out of Big Pharma's very expensive magic cauldron," I replied.

"I'm sorry, Stig. Just for the time being we need to put this on ice," he said, sheepishly.

"If you tell me the approach you are looking for, I can salvage it," I said, visualising another pay cheque drifting off down the Suwannee.

"Let's just wait and see, eh?" he replied.

"Jeremy. Is there something you're not telling me?"

"To be honest with you," he said. "And don't quote me on this. The management don't think it's the right time to break ranks on the whole virus thing," he said.

I appreciated his honesty but was completely baffled by the decision.

"Are you no longer an independent organisation, then?"

"Even *The Guardian* has to draw a line somewhere. Got to keep the investors happy," he said.

"Those investors, they wouldn't be major shareholders in the pharmaceutical industry by any chance?"

"I'll make sure you get paid, if we can just put it on hold for now, can't say fairer than that," he said.

My new online blog about the treatment of my mother received a wave of sympathy and a strong response from those who were aghast at the government's handling of the pandemic. I soon found that when it had been shared on Facebook and Twitter it was being adorned with a 'Fact Checkers' slogan declaring that the article contained false information. This kind of intrusion to our free speech had never before manifested itself in such an overarching and spurious manner. 'For Fact checker read thought police' read one meme on Twitter and I was inclined to agree. Who were the factcheckers? What gave them the authority to declare what was truth or lies? Where were the factcheckers before this crisis? On investigation I found that their biggest sponsors were branches of big tech and front companies for pharmaceutical conglomerates.

I recognised the pattern. I fired off a cutting email to Jeremy, receiving an almost embarrassed response stuffed to the brim with pathos.

One thing was for sure, I was never going to turn back from my pursuit of truth. It had become an obsession. I thought about the torture I went through giving up cigarettes. As a forty-a-day slave to nicotine I had been through the ringer, this new preoccupation was on a different plain and perhaps it would turn out to be considerably more dangerous.

12. Follow the Money

I was fishing in the undercurrent, hooking in a few hints and whispers from my Twitter feed. It wasn't the most substantial of leads, but to give them their due, some were backing up their conspiracy claims with some very credible source links. One name kept reoccurring. Gill Baits, one of the richest people in the world, was being singled out as puppet master, just as he had during my time in Michigan. The more I delved, the more transfixed I became.

I tried to talk about it at home, but Jasmine made it clear that this subject was out of bounds. They were just about coping with the ever-changing realities of day-to-day life, much of which had been transferred onto the internet.

Every morning I awoke with the same confusion. Is this real? Am I in a dream? The lack of control prompted me to assert that I had to do something, I couldn't just stick my head in the sand.

My investigations hoovered up all my time and often sent me on wild Goose chases, with some pretty far-out characters as company. Social media platforms were targeting and removing those who were successfully reporting the evidence from medical whistle-blowers. Joining the dots wasn't easy. The more convoluted it became, the more I wondered whether I was being duped. Yet, each time I doubted my endeavours, some new stonewall revelation would hit me between the eyes. To translate any of this I would need coherent and verifiable facts. It was unrealistic to expect the mysterious WB to keep feeding me lines, but that didn't stop me constantly checking my messages with the hope of catching another. Again, I didn't have long to wait. There it was blinking at me from the top of my inbox. It was the same format with biblical quote and brief instruction.

'Trust not in oppression and become not vain in robbery: if riches increase, set not your heart upon them.'
Follow the money. To control the message, how would you buy the messenger? W.B.

I took an A3 sketch book out of Harley's cupboard and started to place sheets upon the large pin board on my office wall, like I had suddenly been transformed into a *TV Super Sleuth*. I began to map out my thoughts. Clearly, you'd want to control the Press and TV's narrative from the top down, that's obvious. You would need the scientists on board, the experts that TV and newspapers use as sound bite generators. You're looking for the influencers. I remembered my training and how to invert the situation. The BBC seemed to be choirmaster-in-chief of what some people were now referring to as *the Plandemic*. Who was untouchable? Who could you not criticise?

Jasmine wandered in and took one look at my wall, shook her head and walked out. I caught Iain on one of his food runs between his room and the kitchen. I tried to talk with him, but he just stood there listening like one might listen to an extraneous announcement at a train station.

Once I had exhausted myself, he said "I don't care, Dad. I'm not interested," and he slid back into his room and closed the door.

Iain's girlfriend was out of bounds, her parents had flipped and became government torch bearers. They embraced the fearmongering and would not consider even the slightest bend in the rules, even if it would alleviate the mental distress of their own daughter.

We were paying the price of the bombardment of a health and safety doctrine, that had gone to such a length as to become self-restricting. All his life Iain was taught to stay safe, be careful, take care and do the right thing and never challenge authority. Now, the right thing was to rebel, but it seemed that it was such an alien concept to him and his generation. Sure, they had the fake rebellion of noxious rap music and soft drugs, but if you pulled the threads on that one it usually led to some faceless money-making corporation.

Back in my office room, I scoured the Baits Foundation website and there, in plain sight, was a list of the recipients of millions and billions of dollars in donations. In amongst them was the BBC and Jeremy Green's Guardian newspaper.

World Health Foundation $4bn
John Hopkins University $860m
University of Oxford $250m
Gavi vaccine alliance $3bn
The Guardian $9m
The BBC $53m

Royal College London $270m
National institute of allergy and infectious diseases NIH
(USA) $20m

No wonder my reports were hitting a brick wall at The
Guardian, they were never going to throw dirt at their
billionaire benefactor. Other newspapers were just as
protective of the man constantly being painted as our
vaccine saviour. This was the same person who stood to
make twenty dollars for every dollar he pumped into this
macabre circus.

Baits was buying the influence of every major player in
this whole sordid affair and in return was touted as a
modern-day saint. Unless this was exposed, he would get
away with it.

I contacted Dexter Harris, who was still working for the
Russian broadcaster, RT. I told him about my plight, and
he seemed delighted that I had found my way to his view
of things and that he might be able to engage in some
serious feather ruffling.

"You can't foist it on anyone. Best you can do is point
them in the right direction, the rest is up to them," he
said.

"It took a while for me to get my head around just how
big this thing is," I replied.

"Oh, it's a full-throttle, hold on to your hat, mind fuck,"
he said.

Dex agreed to float the story with his bosses and get back
to me. He told me that Baits' computer company had
been all but removed from Russia. There was only one
boss in the *land of the bear*, and it wasn't Baits.

RT agreed to run a slightly watered-down version of the
Baits funding story and asked me to focus on another
name that was frequenting the message boards of
Twitter, the Eastern European tycoon, Gorgi Natassi.

Natassi, who once boasted of breaking the Bank of England, was one of the richest people on the planet and was funding various anarchist and far-left groups. His companies and non-government organisations, a set of tax dodging pressure groups operating under the guise of charity, had also been asked to leave Russia.

There was an abundance of information on Natassi. I even found a link to the Man-Boy association of America that claimed its campaign to lower the age of sexual consent to ten years-old received money from my target, but without more evidence it was too much of a tenuous link to ratify.

A week or so into my research, I received a call from Michael Rose-Newman, offering me a three-month assignment to Italy, where he was making a documentary about Alberto Sconetti, one of the money men behind Formula One motor racing.

"He'll pay triple what you're currently on, put you up in a hotel and provide you with a private driver," he said, in the tone of a radio quizmaster.

"What about the regulations, I mean, they're saying everyone must stay home and not fly," I replied.

He laughed. "You don't think those rules apply to people like Alberto? You'll be one of his team. I guarantee you, restrictions will not be a problem."

The thought of escaping the rut I had got myself in was very tempting.

"There's only one condition," he said tentatively.

"Only one?" I said with a chuckle that attempted to hide my cynicism.

"You need to drop everything and come over to Italy immediately. This will demand your full concentration."

"I'm not sure I can do that," I said.

"Sure, you can. While everyone is locked up with their masks and mandates, you will be in wonderland, hobnobbing with racing drivers, gorgeous models and flamboyant millionaires. It's the assignment of a lifetime."

"Why me?" I said.

"I saw the thing you did on Baits, and I thought, here's our man," he said.

"Sorry, Michael, I'm a bit tied up I'll have to pass this time."

"Whoa, really? You're not interested?" He laughed. "Oh my god. I have to ask, what are you working on? I mean, it must be something pretty special," he said.

"A vulgar Billionaire," I said.

"Abramovich?"

"No."

"Baits?"

"No."

"Who?"

"… Everyone's favourite Hungarian," I said.

"Gorgi. Ah cam on. I love Gorgi. He's a great guy. Don't believe all that baloney about him on the internet, he's one of the good guys."

"Not from where I'm sitting, he's not," I said.

"Alberto wants you. You can literally name your price. Talk it over with Jasmine and give me a call," he said.

Rose-Newman hung around money like beggars hang around train stations. A pen for hire. All of Natassi's billions couldn't pay off the mortgage on that man's soul.

I mentioned the 'dream offer' to Jasmine and I was surprised when she told me I should take it. She wasn't happy with me being an outspoken opponent of the virus narrative that everyone she knew had accepted as genuine.

I went for a walk to the bandstand and paused in contemplation. Everyone within the media was hiding the biggest story in world affairs and if I dropped it now for an easy life, how long before it came back and bit me on the arse? On the other hand, kicking sand in the faces of some of the most powerful people on the planet would no doubt come at a heavy price and I wasn't exactly cut out to be Superman.

A few days passed and I received a string of text messages from an anonymous sender. The texts contained visual hints about the consequences of investigating my current research target. The tone was as blunt as a knock on the head with a billy club, which was one of the outcomes insinuated happening to me if I didn't cease my exploration forthwith. Being a hero in print is a fleeting moment of glory, tomorrow's chip paper and all that. Right now, I felt the cold claw of threat on my shoulder. Not a fear of bacteria, but billionaires and their bully boys.

13. False Gods

I knew the day was done for before I even had a chance to wipe the sleep out of my eyes, I stubbed my toe on the way to the kitchen, knocked my favourite cup onto the floor and found that Jasmine had used up the last of the coffee.

I threw my baggy tracksuit on and ventured over to Jolly's convenient store. In autopilot, I grabbed a few items and handed the requisite coins to the new guy, who was anything but jolly about my aversion to the mask rules.

On the way back across the road I almost lost more than my shopping when a motorbike, that seemed to come out of nowhere, forced me to dive out of its way. I cursed my absentmindedness in not spotting the bike.

While I attempted to retrieve my scattered groceries, the biker returned, flipped open his tinted visor and confronted me.

"You ought to be more careful, Mr Fisher," he said.

He revved the bike.

"You could get yourself killed," he said.

He flipped his lid back and took off up the high road towards Balham, leaving me shaken and dumbfounded. I scowled as I watched in earnest as my bread was flattened by a passing 12-wheeler juggernaut.

Scuffed and bruised, I dragged myself home. I was well aware there would be consequences for exposing such a powerful character as Natassi, but seeing that threat at close quarters was truly frightening.

I couldn't find anything substantial enough to put a dent in Natassi. Like Baits, he was funding virus treatments and vaccines, which seemed to be the game in vogue at the Billionaires casino. I wondered if I was getting too deep. I knew he was up to his neck in it, but I doubted I would ever get through the shifting layers of obfuscation he had built around himself. He probably had a team of people working around the clock to suppress anything he didn't want the public to know.

Perhaps a part of me wanted to stop pushing and maybe focus on another baddie.

I was starting to think I had championed a cause that would reward me with a bullet in the head and no-one would be any the wiser.

As rattled as I had been by the bike incident, I couldn't stop. My obsession was pushing out the one thing I most held dear: my family. I couldn't discuss this with anyone, and the pressure was splitting me in two. On the other hand, if good people didn't stand up to this then there was no chance of regaining our freedoms. Why did it have to be me?

As if to force my hand and banish any uncertainty, the journalistic angel on my shoulder delivered more heavenly tidings. The timing was incredible.

'The liar's punishment is that even when he speaks the truth, no one believes him'
Who is dancing quick step with the Devil? W.B.

The message was a little more obscure than before but there was no mistaking the revelatory dynamite in the accompanying links.

A Photograph of Gorgi Natassi, all robes and rapture, in what looked like a Satanic ceremony at a private party in Davos, during the January 2020 World Economic Forum. Also present were banking billionaire David Ropegyte and the eco-protester Gretel Greenberg.

The second link was a photo of a New York city police charge sheet in the name of Gorgi Natassi accusing him of soliciting underage boys.

The remaining links confirmed both allegations. This was massive. I had him bang to rights. My blood pumping, I wasted no time in writing up my story, leaving out absolutely none of the salacious details.

W.B. had come up trumps again. I made subtle hints to Dex about my digital benefactor, but he didn't offer up any clues, so I struck him off the list of suspects. It had to be Baldur, but how? I couldn't just get in touch and ask him, I would sound ridiculous and even if it was him, the fact that the messages I was receiving were anonymous meant that whoever was sending them didn't want their identity revealed, not even to me. It was the modern-day equivalent of *the Elves and the Shoemaker*. I phoned Stefan Wolf, a tech genius I knew at the Post and arranged a meet.

I greeted Stefan on the steps of the National Gallery, the other side of Trafalgar Square from the Post's HQ. He asked for my phone and, when I handed it over, he slipped it into a pouch.

"Faraway bag, you should get yourself one," he said. "Cuts all signal. Can't be tracked or recorded. Believe me this is common practice for anyone fishing in the waters you've stuck your rod in."

I showed him my laptop and the recent message from W.B.

Stefan was the newspaper's black ops director. He just about survived the phone tapping scandal of 2008. I helped cover his tracks back then. It was a moral dilemma that only years later I truly understood the gravity of. From then on, everything Stefan did was cloak and dagger. He wasn't employed directly by the newspaper and procedures were put in place to render him invisible to any possible investigations.

He produced a gadget and transferred all the emails from my secret benefactor. As I went to converse with him, he held up a warning hand and we waited for the files to copy before he returned my laptop into its bag and placed it by our feet. His paranoia trumped mine and some.

I offered Stefan a fee, but he said the intrigue was payment enough. He said he would keep it hush hush and would get back to me.

As I walked back across the square I bumped into Isaac Grossman, one of my sparring partners at the Post. We had a chat and after a couple of sly digs about his amazing scoops and rocketing promotion, into my old position at the Capital Post, I found myself drawn in.

"I don't need the Post, I'm taking down Natassi," I blurted out.

"Gorgi Natassi?"

"That slimy creep is gonna bite the dust," I said.

"All the nukes in Russia couldn't take that man down," he said, dismissing my claim.

"Hundred percent," I said, boastfully.

"You know who worked for Natassi, don't you?" He said.

"Who?"

"Maxwell. He was Natassi's PR man for a while," he said.

"Birds of a feather, eh?" I said.

A couple of hours after returning home I took a call from Isaac.

"The Natassi story, show it to Maxwell," he said.

I took this with a pinch of salt.

"The Post wouldn't have the balls to print what I've got," I trumpeted, with a touch too much arrogance.

"I floated it with Maxwell," he said.

"You did what?"

I had a sinking feeling about this and wished I had kept my big mouth shut.

"Maxwell hates Natassi with a passion. He will push it, it's personal between those two." He replied.

"I think you're forgetting about our last meeting," I said.

"There's not a journalist in London that hasn't crossed swords with Maxwell. He doesn't care. You should know that better than anyone, he's not in this business to collect Christmas cards."

He had called my bluff so now I would have to front up or look foolish. My pride would never allow that.

"I don't know," I said, trying to work out a strategy in my head.

"Unless you don't... y'know, really have a story?"

"Oh no. I've got him hook, line and sinker, don't worry about that.," I boasted.

We met the following day and made the deal. They checked out the validity of my piece and said they would run a teaser in the Saturday edition. I was just happy they were willing to run it at all and the fee blew RT out of the water. When I informed Dex, he said I would have been an idiot to turn it down. Just before he ended his call, he said something I wrestled with during a particularly restless night.

"Strange that a man so steeped in secrecy would let not one, but two masks slip. You got lucky there, matey," he said, in his usual chirpy tone.

I did get lucky. The Post had checked it out, they wouldn't print without checking it stood up. But why was I getting lucky? Who was WB?

Saturday came, and although the teaser did not actually mention Natassi by name, the full explosive revelations were promised in the following day's paper. 'Dark secrets of a Davos Devil,' declared the headline, this was accompanied by a silhouette of what could only be the hunched and bloated figure of the financier who had set himself up as one of the world's biggest philanthropists. The story was out. Like an old soldier proudly donning his uniform once more, I was back at the top of my game, my doubts a distant memory. This was who I was born to be.

By Saturday afternoon, my joy faded like a floundering firework. There was a problem. I was summonsed to an urgent meeting with David Nathan, head of the legal team at the Post.

I was the first to arrive and the receptionist, who I had never seen before, led me into the boardroom. David Nathan arrived twenty minutes late, bustled in, removed his mask and took a minute or two just silently staring directly at me as he retrieved paperwork from his briefcase.

"Mr Natassi is deeply hurt by your character assassination. His lawyers want your head on a platter, and I don't think they mean metaphorically," said Nathan.

It transpired that the photographs, the story and the highly convincing links were part of a sophisticated hoax. An orchestrated attack on Natassi. I thought I was treading the journalistic boards of Broadway, but the rush of excitement had distracted me from the rules of the game and I now found myself inadvertently walking the plank. My credibility would be shot to bits.

"I thought the legal team went over this with a fine-tooth comb?" I said.

"This is about you, Stig Fisher. The company put its faith in someone they thought they could trust. Now, I have no idea what your motivations were, but they contravene everything we stand for at the Capital Post. It will be your retraction appearing in tomorrow's paper."

The way he spoke, it was like his little speech was being performed for an invisible audience.

"Mr Natassi has influential friends in high places, so I think your apology will likely be the very last words you see of yours printed in a newspaper anywhere in the world."

I knew he was right. There was no paddling back from this. I was finished. Dex's legendary misdemeanours were misprints in a schoolboy's home-made fanzine compared to the journalistic crime I had just committed. Nathan produced my retraction, the only contribution from me being my signature.

As I left, I found Stefan lurking in reception. He handed me a ten pounds note.

"For the coffee the other day," he said solemnly, shielding his face from the receptionist.

"The coffee was on me, you don't need-," I protested.

"-Put it in your pocket, Stig. I can't afford to be dragged into whatever mess you're in," he said, loudly.

In the lift, I put the note into my wallet, then pulled it back out. On a small post-it note he had written a message. 'Travel section, Smiths, TCR 4.30'

The travel section of WH Smith's Newsagents and bookstore on Tottenham Court Road was empty, the government restrictions meant the general public wasn't out buying books about far-flung places they were prohibited from travelling to.

When Stefan arrived, without a word he opened a pouch, and I deposited my phone inside.

"Keep it. You'll need it," he said, passing the pouch to me.

He made it clear that this wasn't going to be a meeting of old pals as he avoided eye contact and talked directly to the bookshelves.

"I tracked your emails," he said. "The first three came from an office in Whitehall. Although the paper would be laying the blame with Russian misinformation, in fact it was Israeli in origin. The last email was sent from an IP address in Tel Aviv. Natassi has friends in dark places and enlisted the help of espionage firm *Blue wave* who faked the lot. The photographs were staged. You have been played."

I could somehow accept how I had been lured in, some sophisticated hackers had invaded my communications, singled out my modus operandi and invented the perfect honey trap. What I was most cursing myself for was my sloppy face value acceptance of it as genuine.

The quote *'The liar's punishment is that even when he speaks the truth, no one believes him'* was directed at me. Although not the liar, my truthful words will count for nothing as they will never be free of the liar's tag that had just been stamped across my reputation in indelible ink. To rub salt into the wound, Stefan asked me if I had spotted that the first three quotes were from the Bible and the final one was from the Talmud, suggesting a wry smile was currently spreading across the faces of Israeli intelligence or whoever was behind these black ops.

"You do realise that the people you named as being compliant in Devil worship; Gorgi Natassi, David Ropegyte and Greta Greenberg are all Jewish?" said Stefan.

"Shit, I never saw it in that context," I said

"They start calling you an anti-semite. Game over, it's the kiss of death," he said.

My whole body was on power down mode and I relied on autopilot to get me home. I slumped in the armchair and simply stared into oblivion. This time last year, I had a career, a happy marriage, a relatively happy family and a future. My sanity was now hanging by a thread.

When she arrived home, Jasmine brought with her a completely different attitude that caught me by surprise. Sitting on the edge of the chair opposite me, she leaned in towards me. The caustic cloud of contempt was slowly dissipating. Just for that one moment in time, this embrace made everything feel better. She touched my core with a caring that only comes with knowing someone intimately.

"You know, there's a lot of people who care about you Stig. Including me," she said.

I really didn't know how to reply to her, my suspicions of an ulterior motive had rendered her act of kindness null and void as I prepared myself for a sting in this sweet-smelling tale.

"I know that," I said unconvincingly.

"I heard what happened with the Natassi thing," she said.

"Blimey, bad news has got the march on the speed of light these days," I said.

"Isaac called me."

"What's that prick want?" I railed.

"He's worried about you. We all are. He thinks the stress of your mum's death has got the better of you and you have been chasing shadows ever since. And that's why you've ended up here."

I sat bolt up, tensed defensively, playing right into the description she had just painted of my fragile state.

"No. I tell you what led to my public humiliation. Isaac pushing that story forward."

Jasmine huffed and positioned herself more comfortably on the sofa, her head now in her hands.

"I think you need help. You know, talk to someone, professionally," she said, her caring tone lined with exhaustion.

"Oh yes, they'd love that. I uncover the biggest scandal in history, and I'm shunted off to the funny farm," I said.

"But it wasn't true, it was a-," she said.

"-A lie, I know. But I'm not talking about Natassi. That was a set-up. I'm talking about all this virus bullshit and the pharmaceutical criminals behind it."

"Stig, listen to yourself," she said calmly. "You're not being rational."

"You know what they did to Mum," I said.

"I know, it was wrong, but it was incompetence, not some world-wide conspiracy," she said.

I was incensed and, even though I was absolutely exhausted, I still found the energy to plunge headfirst into a rant.

"All the evidence is saying the opposite. The masks don't work, the lockdowns will kill more than they save, and Big Pharma is stifling all other plausible medicines in order to push vaccines that they have somehow been able to pull from their arses at the flip of a coin."

Jasmine sprang to her feet.

"Stig, Stig, I know, you keep saying, but you've got to stop. You're destroying-"

"-*They* are destroying, it's them," I railed.

"What about us? What about Iain and Harley? Are there any bridges you're not willing to burn?" she said firmly.

"Just leave me alone," I shouted.

"My fucking pleasure. And don't say I didn't try to help you, you pig-headed…urgh."

She left the room, and I felt the bite of loneliness savage my soul.

14. Game Over

Jasmine made a couple more attempts at changing my
path, but we were at a deadlock. I had all the sympathy
in the world for her, but my frustration with my life just
stank up the place. I struggled to converse with those
who were not prepared to see what this government were
doing to our lives. The fact that they couldn't see through
the emotional blackmail of 'Saving the NHS' – The NHS
was there to save us, not the other way around. These
highly educated people had switched off their ability for
critical thinking. So, when I wasn't arguing about it with
Jasmine, she could hear me rattle off to friends who
gradually stopped calling. I was in a state of perpetual
anxiety. When listening to Harley read, my mind was
elsewhere and soon he got the picture and something that
had given me unmeasurable joy was tossed onto the fire
of an obsession I couldn't escape from.

I began to hate what I had become, but as much as I seriously weighed it up, all the dominating messages emanating from the corridors of power amounted to treason. No matter what the media and all the preachy celebrities pushing the state narrative had to say, I couldn't turn my back on what I had uncovered. I didn't want to face up to it, but I knew I may be forced to sacrifice everything in pursuit of justice. The one thing I felt deep down that I could never sacrifice was the truth. I couldn't shift the certainty in my heart that what the state was doing was evil and I couldn't stand by and see it destroy all our lives, even if the price of that stance would cost the decimation of mine.

It came as no surprise when Jasmine told me she was taking Iain and Harley and moving out. Iain had avoided me at every turn and refused to entertain even a word of my anti-government diatribe. The hurt that was ripping apart my family devastated me. I pleaded with Jasmine to stay, even suggesting that I leave instead. It wasn't just me, she needed a break from the house and the bad atmosphere that was damaging our cherished little boy, Harley.

I hoped against hope that this would be temporary, and perhaps they would return after the summer holidays, but Jasmine told me before she left that she had already applied for schools in the area.

It cut me in half watching as he waved from the backseat as they left. In the blink of a blinkered eye, they were beyond the horizon of the film set of this inner-city rat race that was our life. She ditched London for our holiday home, a beautiful four-bedroom house in the New Forest. That part of Hampshire was a place dear to us all. Although we agreed it would be the place we would one day retire to, every holiday there culminated with Jasmine's pleas to move there permanently. Now, with the daily diet of fear and worry, she had plotted her escape route.

The house was only a short journey from Dorset's Jurassic coast where we spent our honeymoon. Images of those days danced across my mind, each bubble of carefree memories burst by the gnawing pain of her departure.

My phone bleeping pierced my state of numbness. I received a text from the same anonymous sender who dished out threats over my research into Gorgi Natassi. 'Game Over' it read, within an animated meme. I knew that these operators were so advanced on their surveillance that they could tell what you were eating for breakfast before you'd even served it up, but I had to believe that the timing of this text was opportunistic.

Everyone except W.B. felt it was 'game over' and I received another message from my secret source. This time it came disguised as an Amazon parcel. I wasn't expecting anything, so I asked the delivery fellow to check it out. He called out my address from what he said was a virus-safe distance and when I confirmed that it was correct, he got in his van and drove off.

Inside the parcel was a copy of the King James Bible, and there, highlighted by a bookmark, was a quote underlined in red ink with a post-it note underneath.

And the Apostles gathered themselves together unto him, and told him all things, both what they had done, and what they had taught.

Your emails have been compromised. If you want to be free, walk into the light. Go be with your tribe. Tell them Truth sent you.

There was no further information or link, barring a leaflet for an anti-lockdown demonstration in Central

London being staged this coming Saturday. At least I knew the quote was genuine and in line with the good intel I had previously received. As for the flyer for the demo, I doubted that was fake, but I checked it out online all the same.

For the next few days, I degenerated into a stupor of demotivation. I wrote nothing, read nothing, but drank everything I could get my hands on. I had maxed-out on the virus propaganda, my fight for justice and anything to do with the rotten system that used to pay my bills. My mind must have realised I was heading for a bad place so encouraged me to flood it with alcohol and drag my focus away from my obsession. This resulted in me floundering in a pool of my own mess. Even though this was hardly a positive development, it had become a much-needed circuit breaker that gave my brain a rest from the technocratic *coup d'état*.

I didn't need to be happy, sober or contented to write, and so, just as I was about to slip into a state of slumber, inspiration came knocking. The following words almost wrote themselves.

Written in the stars

Hate doesn't drive you on
It rips the chords right out of your song
Lies can never help you build
It's a dead-end street for the weak willed
A grudge won't ever sail your boat
It's a dead weight impeding your chance to float
A curse won't make things bright and clean
No currency gained when you demean
Revenge alone won't steer you home
Where love once was, hate will grow
Greed can't ever amount to much
It turns to dust all that you touch

Cruelty befits an empty soul
A life with nothing good to show
So, take the path that leads to love
It's written in the stars above

15. An Audience with Hope

For any journalist, it was suicide to publicly nail your
colours to a political mast, particularly one that was
being so roundly condemned from every corner, so I
attended the demonstration in London's Trafalgar Square
with a touch of trepidation. I had joined the ants I used to
observe from the sixth-floor window of my old office on
the south side of the Sqaure. Today, they were amassing
in their thousands.

Unsure of what I would find, I was relieved to discover
the broadest spectrum of people I had ever encountered
at a political rally. There were national flags of all the
home countries, but no sign of right-wing extremist
iconography that was bandied about in the press. There
were a few hippy types and a handful of people dressed
in black who wouldn't have looked out of place in a
'Stop the City' demo. The far-left were absent, having

strangely sided with the billionaires. There were notably more women than men.

As I made my way onto the traffic island behind Nelson's famous statue, I had a leaflet thrust into my palm by a dark-haired woman who introduced herself as Florinda. She was there with her two daughters, all three were sporting identical t-shirts with the inscription: My Freedom doesn't end where your fear begins.' As I explained about my mothers' untimely death, I could see that she had a total understanding of why I had turned up. She insisted we head to the stage where she would introduce me to Piers Corbyn who was running the show. As we bustled through the thousands of people, many with homemade banners and placards demanding the end to the restrictions, I could sense an electricity of purpose in the air. I walked up the steps towards the National Gallery, where I recently met Stefan Wolf. We were slowed by the crush of the crowds and our attention was brought to a flushed-faced man in his fifties reciting a poem through a loudhailer as if his life was dependant on it.

Vaccination without consent
It could never happen here
crush opposition - No dissent
It could never happen here

The veins in his neck were throbbing and his hands were shaking as he delivered the crescendo to his verse.

You think you're so clever
you say you'd see it coming
But evil is marching,
yet you can't hear the drumming
They tell us all lies,
you can't smell their words rotting

126

They're dismantling our lives -
but can't you see them plotting
Wake up! Wake up! - Your future is calling
We will all be enslaved if you don't heed the warning

The crowd erupted into applause followed by a chant of
'Unlock the world, give us back our freedom' that came
from a rebel song by the anti-lockdown band 'The
Apostles of Liberty.' Their music videos featured on
some of the anti-masker's social media pages I had seen.
We took our chances and burst through to the front.
Although the event had a swathe of security, it seemed
incredibly easy to move into the cordoned-off area for
speakers and organisers. As a yellow-jacketed steward
lifted the tape for us to enter I turned to see that Piers
Corbyn had moved centre stage and was now delivering
his speech.
"They want to crush us, because they are… they are
planning to destroy our lives. They are liars. They are
listening right now. Let's send them a message," he
inhaled fully and then attempted to work the crowd into a
vociferous chant.
"Stop telling lies, stop telling lies," he repeated.
It would have been all the more impressive if he had
given it a little more thought before encouraging them to
join in. At that precise moment I was witnessing the
mouthpiece of the anti-lockdown resistance stood on a
stage surrounded by about fifty thousand people
shouting, 'Stop telling lies.' If campaign groups made
gag reels this would surely be top of the hit parade.
"The PCR tests were not invented to diagnose people
suffering from anything," he continued. "These are not
my words, that is, that-".
A squeal on the sound system put him off his stride.
When I looked up at the ancient, cone shaped speakers I

wondered if they had been bought on the cheap from the fictional wide-boy TV character Del-boy Trotter.

Piers continued. "These are the words of Kary Mullis, the inventor of the PCR. His system is supposed to be used to multiply molecules. If you multiply a molecule enough times you will find almost anything you want to find. It's completely unreliable after twenty cycles, the World Health Foundation insist on more than twice that number of cycles."

Although not being the most compelling orator, he knew his stuff and the audience showed him a great deal of affection.

Florinda, my newly acquired chaperone, told me that Corbyn, a slight man in his seventies, had been arrested at demonstrations up and down the country. Every fine he challenged in court was thrown out for not being legally binding, but he still had the inconvenience of sitting in a cell each time.

Corbyn finished his speech and made way for a man dressed in a multi-coloured drape suit, the kind you might see on Children's TV.

I missed the new speakers name but did catch him announcing that he was a children's entertainer. Some people at the front seemed to know him. I thought it naïve to make such an announcement when everyone in the media were 'pens at the ready' to shoot down anyone brave enough to publicly speak out. Ridicule was always the most successful weapon in their armoury.

I was introduced to Mr Corbyn. Off-mic he came across with a warmth, sincerity and confidence that had been missing on stage. Before I had got a few sentences into my story, he gripped my forearm and interjected.

"Let me just say how sorry I am to hear of your loss and the terrible circumstances," he said.

I continued explaining the path that took me here, minus the scenario surrounding WB, for fear of sounding like a complete nut. I was charmed by the gravity of his focus. As I finished, he pointed out to the throng of people that started a few paces away and ended somewhere near Downing Street where, earlier in the year, the chaos and constriction had been set in motion.

"There's one thing you must understand, Stig," he said. "This is not about politics, left, right or centre. It's not about race, gender or religion. This is about every decent human being on this planet standing up to the dictatorship of corporations and money men and saying *'We won't be your slaves'.*

Piers was ushered towards a tall blonde-haired woman in her thirties, who was today's compere. In the meantime, I watched the children's entertainer, who, although having a voice that mirrored his clownish image, was incredibly astute in his assessment of those who clock-in further along the road at the palace of Westminster. His indignation for Will Cockburn, the current health minister, stirred the crowd like a late goal in a cup final. Piers Corbyn returned to where I was standing, his eyes betraying some urgency. He pointed to the assembled masses.

"Stig, I want you to tell them, what you just told me," he said, as he leaned in to make himself heard above the squeal of the sound system.

He must have noticed me gulp as I looked out at the sea of faces.

"Do it for your family," he said.

He didn't need to utter another word. That one phrase was like a starting pistol and I felt a surge of pride, anger and righteousness erupt and, before I could rationalise it any further, I was out on stage, microphone in hand conversing with the masses.

"My name is Stig Fisher, I am a journalist."

A murmur of boos rippled through the audience. I took a deep breath. I pointed at the building overlooking the square.

"I used to work over there, at the Capital Post. I earned a good wage, pension, first class travel etcetera. But that all ended the day I stopped writing for money and started writing for justice. For truth and *not* coercion, for freedom and *not* the status quo."

A brief chant of 'Freedom, Freedom,' rang out.

"My mother, God rest her soul, was a victim of the care home scandal," I choked. "They put infectious people into a facility full of vulnerable residents."

I fought an overwhelming twinge of grief and utter nervousness and carried on.

"At the hospital, we were prevented from seeing my mother. So, she died surrounded by masked strangers. There's no comfort to be found in a room full of faceless ghouls. Her last days on this planet would have been filled with terror and confusion. The government did that to her. They killed my mum."

Inside my head I could hear the stifled breaths of each and every one of those people as they looked on. When I caught sight of two women crying to the left of me, I froze.

"When I…" my voice broke. Suddenly I was stranded. From somewhere, a subconscious strength kicked in and I regained just enough composure to carry on.

"When I started investigating, I found that the government had given the care homes full indemnity. It didn't matter if people died, no-one would be held accountable. But, worse than that, much worse than that. The people I used to call colleagues, the ladies and gentlemen of the press, went to every length possible to misrepresent her story, to protect the guilty and vilify the innocent."

I could now sense an anger in the air.

"You're all here for a reason, and I know what each and every one of you feels inside right now. What we are witnessing is a fraud so great, it threatens to destroy everything that we understand as normal life."

A wave of noise erupted like a volcano and I knew I had made a genuine connection with the those before me. The applause continued and I felt inspiration surge through me. Every inch of me was alive.

"I stand for freedom," I shouted. "Will you stand with me?"

"Yes," they shouted back at me and a relentless chant of 'Freedom, Freedom,' enveloped the arena like a scene from gladiatorial Rome. It was repeated and repeated, louder and louder until every voice in the vicinity was shouting.

I looked to my side to see all the speakers and organisers standing with their fists in the air. In that moment, I felt a community grow in solidarity with my words. And there, with tears streaming down her face was Florinda, hand in air, her chest puffed out, her pride on parade.

My face was also wet with tears as I realised that this was the most important piece of journalism I had ever partaken in and it came straight from the heart, not the keyboard. The power of this blistering truth came, not from facts, data or slogans but from one human verbally imparting his story to another, or in this case another fifty thousand.

The euphoria was short lived as, like some twisted Hollywood horror movie, this vision of hope and inspiration turned crimson as, truncheons flailing, police stormed the stage smashing everyone in sight.

A stocky, balding man in his sixties came rushing past me, blood coursing from a wound in his head, a policeman in pursuit. Instinctively, I flicked the microphone stand, an old steel contraption, into the path of the oncoming policeman and he tripped and landed face first on the floor, his riot helmet protecting all but his chin.

I had reported on all kinds of social unrest over the years but never stood this close to the eye of the storm. What frightened me most was the ferocity of Westminster's Bully Boys in Blue as they charged the unsuspecting peaceful demonstrators. If anyone bought the media's crass labelling of this movement as hooligans and far-right thugs, now was a good time for a reappraisal. Instead of fighting back against the brutality of unprovoked state violence, the people nearest the stage squatted on the floor with the two-fingered peace salute as a gesture of their commitment to non-violent protest.

I received a blow from a thrashing truncheon that knocked me off my feet. In the pandemonium I lost sight of Florinda, my view impaired by the blood dripping from a head wound. I wriggled in panic to escape the crushing of my lungs by a pile of six-foot stormtroopers determined to make me, and anyone else caught up in the melee, really suffer.

"We've got the speaker, copy." I heard one of them call into his radio.

"Van waiting, over." Came the reply.

The weight suddenly lifted from my chest as, gasping for breath, I was heaved up. They cuffed me so tightly I squealed in agony. I felt a sharp pain in my arms as they were pushed far up my back before I was eventually projected head-first through the crowd and into a waiting police wagon.

I shuffled into a more secure position, readying myself for the bumpy ride to the station. We took off and, much to the delight of the two G4K policemen accompanying me, I flew from one side of the van to another, unable to stop my head from crashing into the metal panels due to my hands being cuffed and positioned behind my back. Another jolt and the door swung open and a grey-haired man dressed immaculately in an expensive suit was ushered in. He too was cuffed, his hands in front of him, affording him a little more comfort.

"Great speech," he said, in an unmistakeable German lilt.

"Thanks," I said.

"I was due to speak too," he said, wryly and I suddenly recognised him.

"My name is Heiko Schöning, like you, my crime is-"

He was cut off in mid-flow as we jolted to a stop and I left out a howl of pain as I smashed my shoulder into a panel of the van wall. The doors opened, and Herr Schöning was dragged out by the arm, struggling to keep upright, landing awkwardly on the pavement as he disembarked.

"Good luck," I called after him.

I was shunted inside Saville Row police station and taken to the desk.

"Can you loosen these cuffs, they're cutting off my circulation," I ranted, but the policeman, who had a fistful of my coat in his hand, said nothing.

The custody sergeant was dealing with a beanpole of a man who was shouting the odds.

"Black lives matter set fire to cars and knock down statues and where are you pricks?"

The sergeant was unmoved by his rhetoric, a facial expression that told you he'd heard it all before, but the man continued.

"You got down on your knees for *them*. We protest so you don't have to wear those stupid nappies on your fuckin' faces and you go wading in, truncheons up. You're the biggest slaves of them all," he ranted.

As my newest hero was dragged off to the cells, I got my call up.

"Uncuff him and leave him with me," said the sergeant.

The biting steel wristlets were removed, leaving a red raw imprint where they had gauged into my flesh.

"Name?" said the sergeant.

"Excuse me, but I haven't even been told the reason for my arrest," I said.

He rolled his eyes, then proceeded to read me my charge and my rights. I was arrested for contravening the Virus laws 2020. They took my details, made me empty my pockets but, in a more appeasing tone, offered to have someone clean up my wound.

"No way," I raged. "This is evidence of what *your* colleagues did to me."

"Not my colleagues, sir," replied the sergeant catching the eye of another Copper filling in some kind of rostrum on a white board.

"And since when have they privatised the police force? Do you all work for 4GK now, huh?"

"If you have a complaint, I suggest you take it up with your MP," he said.

I demanded to call my solicitor but was fobbed off to a cell and told they would have to process my arrest before I was allowed to communicate with the outside world. Alone in the cell, the adrenalin subsiding, my heart rate returned somewhere close to normal. The high-octane intensity receded into the sullen nothingness of existence in a six-feet by eight-feet concrete box, its aroma a mixture of disinfectant, vomit and body odour. The vile stench of human decay. As time slowly passed, it felt like the walls were moving in on me which added to the unnerving feeling that I had been abandoned in here to rot.

I understood why they took my belt and shoelaces. This wasn't one of the inhumane cesspits of south east Asia, or a rat hole of deepest Columbia, but for a fragile mind, a few minutes in a place like this would be enough to inspire the kind of desperation that could make death an attractive exit strategy.

16. Cell Mates

"Say nothing," said Pam Sowilo, my solicitor friend,
who told me she would do her best to get me out as soon
as possible. With the political nature of my incarceration,
Pam feared I would be ripe for a stitch up and told me to
prepare to sit it out. I said I would, but inside I knew that
each minute of imprisonment was gnawing at my already
frayed nerves.

When I returned to my cell, I found a welcome sight.
Heiko Schöning, who had been due to address the
demonstration, had joined me. We shook hands, and
suddenly the growing anxieties of my plight seemed that
much more bearable.

"What are you being charged with?" I asked.

"They caught me red-handed with the truth," he replied.

We shared a laugh and immediately I felt a bond with the tall, cool-headed German. He explained that he was from a group of over two thousand medical practitioners from all over Germany, called the Doctors of Enlightenment. They studied the science of the virus and concluded that it was no deadlier than seasonal flu. No-one had been able to separate its genetic identity, so any tests or subsequent vaccines would be based on a fraudulent and wholly unscientific foundation. The entire thing was a global scam. There were also groups of doctors working on similar research in Spain, Ireland and the USA.

We spent the following three hours deep in conversation. I was getting first-hand knowledge about the science, or lack of science behind this scandal. He told me that the PCR tests used to generate the thousands of reported cases was a completely flawed system.

Simultaneously, we turned at the sound of the spy hole opening, followed immediately by the clunking of the cell door. A glum faced policeman threw two blue paper medical masks at us and insisted we put them on before slamming the cell shut. We didn't need to discuss it, the masks stayed where they were on the dirty floor.

"Apparently, they were awaiting my arrival at Heathrow airport," he said. "But I chose to drive here. I think they planned to intercept me and either detain me until after the demonstration or return me directly to Germany."

"On what charges. It's not illegal for you to talk freely in the UK," I said.

He nodded in the direction of the face masks on the floor.

"It's not illegal to breathe fresh air but that hasn't stopped them imposing their will on the frightened population of every country on earth. They have not charged me with anything, because there isn't anything they can charge me with, but here I remain," he said, with his rational doctor's inflection.

I thought of the sacrifice Heiko made, risking his livelihood to highlight the criminality of the system and I felt guilty for taking up his time on the stage.

"I'm sorry if my speech, if you can call it that, took away your chance to speak."

"No, no, no. I wouldn't have missed that moment for anything," he said.

"But we should be more organised," I said. "You should have spoken first. We know the state can play these kinds of dirty tricks, so we need to be better prepared." It suddenly dawned on me that I was talking in terms of 'we' and not 'they'. I ventured along to the demonstration as a spectator and within a matter of a few hours I had crossed the line and gained a small part of communal responsibility for this rebellion.

Our evening meal arrived, delivered by an officer with a G4K tag. A non-meat burger for Heiko. KFC for me. Although the pangs of hunger were snapping at me, the food, cold and stodgy, remained untouched on the edge of the bench. Heiko, a vegetarian, said that in Germany they had invented a burger made from the mulch of mushroom waste, it wasn't much more than dirt in a bun. He was not willing to find out whether this EU-backed invention had made its way into the UK.

"If this really is a battle for our survival then we need a multi-pronged attack," I said, with a growing confidence. "Demonstrations aren't for everyone, we need an alternative press as well as a strong presence on social media. We need science, music, comedy, literature. We have to find a way to counter what they are doing."

He nodded throughout my diatribe and a glow on his face told me I was hitting all the right notes.

I suddenly caught myself. "I mean, perhaps they already exist, in which case the focus should be how we bring that to a bigger audience," I said.

"They are manipulating the people with fear and lies, specifically targeting them with the powerful emotions of guilt and shame," I continued. "We can use the same methods but with a difference. We have truth on our side. Facts are important, we need facts, but the truth alone won't win this war. I have seen first-hand the truth turned on its head and served up for mass consumption. The odds are impossible but what choice do we have? The technocratic future they have envisaged for our children is also impossible, impossible to accept. It is our duty to fight this, this evil."

He patted my shoulder.

"I think you have the makings of your next speech right there, my friend," he said in his booming German accent. "I have been a journalist all my working life, and sure, I know how media campaigns sway public opinion, but I still find it hard to accept that millions of educated people just follow this narrative without so much as a question or two. I guess things haven't changed much from the trenches of Belgium, where decent men were willing to venture over the top to almost certain death."

"It is indeed baffling how blindly compliant people have been," he said.

We both turned at the clank of the door springing open.

"Schöning," bellowed the policeman, ushering him to stand.

"Good luck," I said, as he was removed from the cell.

"If you want to know how all this is works, find Brian Halliday," he shouted as his voice disappeared along the corridor.

"You were supposed to put *the inebriate* into cell eight, not the bloody German," called a rattled cop.

I could hear someone being barracked for allowing us to share a cell and I could see why.

Heiko was a treasure of reliable information and a true inspiration. He was probably on a comfortable wage and social standing, yet he was willing to risk it all for the truth.

As the old Greek saying goes; The secret of happiness is freedom, and the secret of freedom is courage, in this dingy dungeon Heiko had helped me find mine.

17. A Truther like You

At the time of my arrest and detainment, adrenaline equipped me to fight my corner, but on release, my courage began to deflate. I wasn't cut out to be a troublemaker and deep down it rattled me. I had been in hairy situations before but always as an observer. Thankfully, I wasn't charged with anything and the damage to my head was superficial.

I looked at the baggy, weather-worn reflection of myself in the hallway mirror and almost chuckled at the thought of myself as a rebel. With my thinning hair and conspicuous paunch, I was the archetypal middle-aged professional. I submitted some controversial and challenging articles over the years, regularly stuck my oar in where it wasn't welcomed, but any personal crusades I pursued were hidden behind others I had championed.

In my private life, compliance could well have been my middle name. Like every good citizen, I paid my parking fines, TV licence and council tax on time. At work I was never tempted to take liberties with my expense sheets. Jasmine called and freaked out about my arrest. As the conversation eventually settled down, we made arrangements for me to come down and celebrate Harley's birthday.

Everything in my life was out of sync. Our house in Clapham seemed to have folded in on itself. Our little family unit packed so much into this house over the years, but with only me rattling around inside, it simply became four brick walls and a roof. Jasmine, Iain and Harley, they were my home.

I spent days searching online for Brian Holliday, the name Heiko Schöning called out while being led away into the depths of the Cop shop, but all I could find was a country and western singer, a piano tuner and a professor of Celtic studies, none of whom sparked a link to the Government's lockdowns or vaccine programme.

I joined online freedom forums that appeared and disappeared on an almost weekly basis. The social media companies ramped up their war on 'misinformation,' removing, blocking and suppressing any alternative view on the World Health Foundation's virus narrative. It's funny that people aren't questioning why these vast resources of control and suppression had never been used to hamper people smugglers, drug pushers and child molesters.

After the futility of discussing current affairs in the family home, I promised myself the trip to Hampshire for Harley's eighth birthday would be politics free. The separation was very painful, and I needed to tread lightly. Iain lost his girlfriend in the move and I hadn't exchanged much more than a 'hi' or 'bye' with him since he was last here. I spoke regularly with Harley. Somehow, he found a strange resilience from the lack of control he had over the situation. He survived in the framework provided for him and being a sociable little fellow, he found a new group of school friends without too much bother.

From the day we bought it, our holiday house quickly became a home from home, but now it took on a whole different vibe. It felt odd, like slipping your feet into your favourite slippers and finding they were two sizes too small. This was now Jasmine territory I was invading. On entering, I clocked that she had made some distinctive alterations to the décor.

As Jasmine cooked up Spaghetti Bolognese, as only she could, I ventured into the kitchen where the aroma that caught my breath was not that of the mince simmering in garlic and fresh tomato, but the place of comfort and solace that I so badly yearned for. Just being in her presence could warm my heart. There would never be a good reason for us to part. It would always be the breaking of something that was fated to be eternal.

"Did you wash your hands when you came in?" said Jasmine.

I moved towards the kitchen sink.

"I'll do it now," I said.

"No. Use the bio soap at the front door. How can I get the children to do it if we don't," said Jasmine.

Back in the kitchen, I slowly but purposefully inched myself closer to her.

"How did we get here, eh?" I ventured tentatively.

"You tell me, Stig?"

The tone of her voice brutally countered the escapism I was searching for in her natural fragrance.

"It's like we've ended up in parallel worlds," I said.

"Well, while you're flying around in circles in your superman cape with your pants on the outside of your trousers, in my world, I feed the kids, send them to school and then get to work."

"Don't be like that, eh?" I pleaded.

"You're the one that's doing this to us. I just want a bit of normality, that's all."

"Well unless we fight this madness, we will never get anything like normal back," I said, in a raised tone.

Harley appeared, his face beaming from experiencing a light-bulb moment.

"Daddy, it's alright, my teacher says they are making vaccines that will make everything go back to like how it used to be," said Harley.

"What do you know? You're only eight-years-old," said Iain interjecting.

"She did. Muuuuum. Iain's being nasty," responded Harley.

"Alright boys, that's enough," said Jasmine.

I crouched down and spoke directly to Harley.

"The thing is, son, it takes a long time to make a vaccine," I said. "I wouldn't trust anything that wasn't tested properly."

"Yeah. That's what John says," said Iain.

"Who's John?" I said.

"My friend Fynn's dad? He knows someone who works at that big hospital they built in London," he said.

"The Nightingale?"

"Yeah, he said it's been sitting empty for six months, but he's not allowed to tell anyone."

"You don't know that. That's all just rumours," said Jasmine, issuing a stern frown at Iain.

"You see, Dad?" said Iain.

I was surprised and a little buoyed by Iain's stance, but it was threatening the fragile peace in the house.

"Well, let's allow Mum to do the cooking eh?" I said, as I tried to shuffle them back into the living room.

"It's a massive con. They only care about how much money they make. They're gonna jab everyone, little kids, pregnant women, anyone they can," said Iain.

I was thankful that Jasmine only had one ear for the conversation and was dashing between pots, pans and dishes.

"It's only for grown-ups, Daddy," said Harley.

Jasmine stopped what she was doing and faced us.

"Get this straight. They're not going to vaccinate the kids or pregnant women and it will never be compulsory, that's just scaremongering."

She had activated her warning siren and I was desperate to tread lightly.

"Well, as long as none of you get jabbed," I said.

"I thought you believed in freedom, what about our freedom to choose?" said Jasmine.

She had a point of course but without all the information on the table, and the impossibility of assessing the long-term side effects, it would not be a genuinely informed choice.

"These jabs are so different from normal vaccines they shouldn't even be classified as such. They halted animal testing because they all died. Anyway, you never rushed to take a flu jab."

"This is not the flu, Stig," said Jasmine, becoming more and more rattled by the conversation.

I couldn't stop, I was triggered and, even though I was reaching out to them with meticulously researched information, it was obvious to everyone where the thread of this talk would lead.

"It's a similar death rate. You have a 99.97% chance of surviving-"

"-So, the doctors, the scientists, they're all wrong, huh?" blurted Jasmine sarcastically.

"It would be funny if it wasn't so twisted, the way they talk about consulting the science, as if it is one boffin on some throne of irrefutable knowledge."

"What's irrefu…irrefootball?" asked Harley.

"It means truthful," said Iain.

"Science is a never-ending sea of questions, debate, theories and predictions." I continued. "Except for this situation, we have no debate because anyone who questions the narrative is silenced or damned. Look what they have done to me."

"Look what you have done to yourself," said Jasmine. You could have built a modern city in the space that suddenly developed between us. I edged myself out of the kitchen and sloped off out the front door and into the front garden feeling utterly defeated.

I had scared Harley, and now I could hear Jasmine telling him that I was not very well and not to take any notice of what I said. I was livid, but I knew an explosion of anger would make it so much worse, so I tried to keep myself in check.

Iain appeared behind me.

"Dad, d'you want to come and see the den me and Fynn made?"

"Okay."

"Cool," he said.

"Better check it's okay with Mum," I said.

Iain dashed back inside and reappeared moments later with a camouflage rucksack over his shoulder and we headed out into the country lane.

"Go easy on your mum, eh?" I said.

"Dad, you don't see it. She's mental. She sprays everything, she has days when she sprays me with disinfectant when I come home. She has the shopping delivered to the garage because she is scared the delivery driver has put the virus on the bags. Last week she told

Harley to wear two masks in the shops, until she realised he couldn't breathe properly."

"Oh, Jesus. I didn't know she was that bad."

"Why d'you think I'm always out with Fynn."

Fear was the real contaminate.

We continued walking while my mind searched for a way in which I might be able to bring some sanity back to the household.

"Dad,"

"Yeah," I said, recognising that puzzled look that used to appear before he had bombarded me with questions when he was little.

"Why do you think they're doing all this? Y'know the lockdowns and all that," he said.

"I don't know. The pharmaceutical companies are incredibly powerful and normally what rich and powerful people want is more wealth and power. But it seems like it's a bit more than that."

"How?" he said, studying me.

Part of me wanted to move the conversation onto the latest Marvel superhero film or what seemed to pass as Doctor Who these days. Walking him down the road I have taken was going to lead him into a world of pain, ignoring it would probably end in double, but that would come later. I wondered if it might be better for him to just stay in his bubble.

"Dad," he prompted again.

"People think it's impossible that the whole of society could be pulled in one direction to serve such a tiny group of billionaires," I said. "But what they don't realise is that the main shareholders of all those companies are the same people who own the pharmaceuticals. They also own the media groups, big tech companies and they fund the universities, public broadcasters and political parties. Their money ties everyone to their mission."

"But why don't more people stand up to them?"

"Most people believe what they're told. Others succumb to fear and enticements. Fear of losing their jobs, fear of being attacked online, fear of losing their reputations. And for some people it's financial incentives to keep quiet, to not rock the boat," I said.

"Is that what you did after Nanny died?" he asked.

"I had no choice. Once you see the truth, you can't just unsee it."

I was trying a bit too hard to convince him and he must have picked up on the desperation in my words.

"It's alright Dad, I believe you."

I looked at him to see if he was simply pacifying me, but he was deep in thought.

A short walk from the house, Iain cleared some detritus from the ground, and we arrived at a homemade shelter. You would have never known it was there. It looked fit for the SAS.

"Wow, you built this?" I asked.

"Yeah, Dad. Me and Fynn made it. He knows everything about surviving in the woods."

"I'm impressed."

His face beamed with pride.

"D'you want a cup of pine needle tea?"

I didn't, but I knew there was only one correct answer, so I nodded the affirmative and he set to work creating a stove, lighting it with a spark from flashing two flint pieces together. As I nursed my cup of pine tea in my hands, I was instantly brought back to Heimdall falls where I first encountered pine tea and so much more.

"Fynn is really cool. Next weekend we're camping out with no food."

"What will you eat?"

"What we catch," he said.

"Be careful eh, the only thing you've ever caught to eat is a packet of crisps thrown from the other side of the living room."

"Fynn has shown me. We caught a rabbit and cooked it. We gathered mushrooms-"

"-but you hate mushrooms," I said.

"No, I don't. Anyway, it's different when you cook them yourself,"

"So how does Fynn know all this stuff?"

"His Dad showed him."

"Who's his Dad, Robin Hood?"

"Very funny," he said.

"I'm only messing," I said.

"You'd like him. He's a Truther like you."

A Truther. My son was referring to me as a Truther. I had found the holy grail. Fatherly respect from a teenager. I tried hard to suppress my elation for want of not spoiling the moment.

"He showed us these videos of doctors talking against the lockdowns and one about a man who used to do a hypnotic show on TV, it was amazing. You probably know him, Billy, something, erm, no. Brian Holliday or something like that."

"Brian *Halliday?*"

"Yeah, I think that's his name, anyway he showed how they do this stage act and the government have used the same trick on the British public. I can get you the video if you want?"

"Yes, do that. Thanks," I said.

My mobile phone rang.

"Hi there, Mr Fisher, It's Ali Redplum, Benjamin Dunderbach's assistant."

She sounded exacerbated.

"Benjamin would like to…"

She was cut off mid-sentence and the actor and A list celebrity, Dunderbach, crashed in.

"Stig, Stig Fisher. It's Ben Dunderbach."

He announced his surname as if introducing himself on to the stage at the London Palladium. Dunderbach was clearly off his face.

I interviewed Dunderbach a few years back, the session was so controlled, with limitations on what questions I could ask, and more importantly which subjects were off-limits, but because of his stature, the paper agreed to his demands. I was also told not to look directly into his eyes. On the day, the four walls of the palatial hotel suite struggled to contain the arrogance of the man.

"Look, Stiggg, we, err, we discussed doing a 'Day in the life' thing or something," he slurred.

"That was five years ago," I said.

"I'm here rrrraring to go. What say we action it, huh? Hundred percent access. No cock and bull."

"Thing is I'm not really-"

"Ok, 'Day in the life' is old hat, what about…"

The line went silent.

"Hello…Benjamin" I said.

"What about a piece on,,, my art collection. I've got the finest Bacon this side of the Hard Rock Cafe."

He paused and I thought he was probably imagining himself receiving a rapture of laughter and applause in his head. This was the best evidence yet that he didn't write his own material.

"I've got a Tracey Emin too," he continued. "Err, second thoughts, scrub that, that thing's falling to fucking bits. Conceptual art, Stig, don't waste a nickel or a fucking dime…where was I? Oh yeah, exclusive piece, what d'ya say, huh, Stiggy Wiggy Stardust?"

"Ben, I'm not at The Capital Post any longer," I said.

"What? But you're, what about the magic pen or whatever that fucking thing Mel Gibson called you? You saved *his* arse. Come on, man."

Ben Dunderbach, actor and darling of the celebrity circuit, like a performing monkey desperate for the oxygen of fame, was demanding I feed his narcissism. How very sad.

"I'm between jobs," I was trying, but failing, to get a word in edge ways.

"No work, Tell me about it, darling. I'm climbing the fucking walls here."

"I can't help-" I said.

"-You can pull something out of the fire for me. I know you can. This is fucking ridiculous, I'm begging, you got me begging here, you enormous cock."

Suddenly I remembered that he had joined a bunch of celebrities in a condescending obnoxious advert guilt-tripping people to stay home and wear their masks.

"I tell you what, Benjamin, why don't you take your own advice and stay home," I said, and I cut the call. Every editor and sub-editor across the country must have shuddered at that moment and would never know why. It was like turning down an invitation to Buckingham Palace because your favourite sitcom was being repeated on the TV, but it felt good.

"Who was that?' asked Iain.

"Oh, nobody… an absolute nobody," I said, with relish.

18. An unexpected Visit

I was driving on empty all the way back to London. The wrench of leaving my family was unbearable. Jasmine made one more half-hearted plea for me to get help for the nervous breakdown she was convinced I was suffering from.

When I was in Hampshire, I caught glimpses of the woman I had fallen head over heels with and I yearned for us to be together. Brief moments where the softness in her face, that had comforted me so many times in my life, broke through the harshness of a conflict borne out of our contrasting visions of the future. When it came to communication, we were on different continents, talking very different languages.

When Jasmine stopped listening to my warnings, I became like the spurned dog who's every waking moment was spent attempting to win her over. I needed her to understand what we were up against. I didn't have all the answers, but I had identified the problem and if I couldn't open her eyes to it then my family was in great jeopardy.

I tried to make excuses for Jasmine. We trusted each other impeccably, our love was deep and strong and, while many of the marriages of our friends crashed and burned due to some frivolous indiscretion that infested their relationships like sewage slowly contaminating the water supply, we had always remained true to our wedding vows. Our united front was obliterated now that my colours were so publicly nailed to the Truther's mast and she had sided with the mob who ran like headless chickens jumping through whichever hoops the prime minister recommended on his daily TV brainwash briefings.

Iain was an unexpected spark of light. He had spent much of his time on our previous holidays in Hampshire complaining about being bored, constantly bemoaning the lack of a games console to while away his time, yet now he was a fully-fledged explorer of the great outdoors. Sometimes you just have to cross paths with the right people at the right time. He had done that with Fynn.

I couldn't rely on Iain to find the key to banish the spell of fear and propaganda that hung over his mother and his little brother, it would be like using a hand grenade to clear the autumn leaves from your door.

A couple miles from home, I stopped off in a supermarket and was navigating the aisles on autopilot, my head enmeshed in my family woes, when I was accosted by a security guard who came running to alert me that I wasn't wearing a mask. The red-faced

151

overweight man in his forties had the kind of zeal one would expect from someone urgently clearing the store due to a recently discovered terrorist bomb or gas leak.

"Sir, Sir, you have forgotten to put your mask on," he stammered.

I was ready for him.

"It's okay," I reassured him.

His face was a picture to behold as I delved into my pocket and fished out a small stone that Iain had found on the forest floor and threw it up in the air and caught it.

"I've got my lucky pebble."

The security guard looked at me, his eyes dropping towards the stone and then back at me again. This wasn't in the script. Jaw agape, his face was such a delightful huff and puff mess of confusion. I felt the urge to burst out laughing, but instead I left him in my wake and continued shopping.

At home, a strange sensation hijacked me during the mundane task of putting my shopping away. Something about my house wasn't right. Nothing appeared to be broken or missing and there was no sign of a break-in, but I had the unnerving feeling that an uninvited visitor had been here. I stared for a moment at the portrait of Harley and it somehow jarred. I suddenly realised that it had always hung opposite the clock in the dining room, but his smiling cherubic face was now beaming at me from the wall by the front door where the oil painting of a cove, on the east coast of Scotland, normally resided. I urgently searched around the remainder of the house but nothing else had been disturbed. In my office, I recognised that someone had rifled through the paperwork on my desk. The notes were rearranged, and a writing pad of mine was open on the page that contained a list of names under the heading – People of interest. Gorgi Natassi's name was crossed through and my own name had been added in a red pen.

I picked up the phone, and then hesitated. Was there any point in phoning the police? If I hadn't inadvertently become an enemy of the state, I was certainly off their Christmas card list. Calling up your very powerful adversary to express concern that you were being targeted unfairly was like standing on the gallows pleading your innocence with the hang man as he secured the noose around your neck.

I poured myself a drink and collapsed onto the sofa in the front room. My mobile phone bleeped, and a message flashed up from Iain. He was bemoaning the lack of consideration he was receiving at home for airing his views about the government restrictions. I had departed Hampshire but left an echo. This would undoubtedly resonate badly with Jasmine.

It was strange, up until all of this madness exploded into our lives, Iain had been something of a loveable, but fairly docile, individual. He acquired the requisite teenage cynicism, but it was mostly gnat bites at dawn. No angry youth rebellion, not the spikes of the punk rockers of my youth or the bovver boots of the skinheads, no snarling psychobilly razor-quiffs or football graffiti. No headbanging metalheads or perfectionist mod fashion snobbery.

V*irus mania* hits and he finds his voice. As much as I admired his new-found pluckiness, what Jasmine needed least right now was a teenage rampage under her roof, particularly one that flew the same contentious colours as her estranged husband.

How have so many educated people bought into the government narrative? It was the question that tormented me, and I'm sure everyone else who spent time researching the facts behind the propaganda. With all the people I loved and respected unconditionally complying, I kept chiding myself for reading the whole thing wrong. After seeing so much evidence, the scientific papers declaring face masks useless, the manipulation of virus data, the empty hospitals and the renowned doctors speaking out at great risk and being removed from YouTube, any doubts about my own conclusions were blown out of the water.

My eldest son was backing up his rhetoric with self-education and we began exchanging information. Upon activating one link Iain sent me, the Bryan Halliday video filled my screen with an important part of the jigsaw. The state's use of deliberately unsettling and repetitive propaganda mimicked the preparation Halliday undertook for his hypnosis stage show. The use of particular colours that represented fear and authority, coupled with the ritualistic sloganeering, was all part of their assault on our brains.

The charismatic Scotsman explained in great detail the process of creating a sense of vulnerability and anxiety in his subjects so they became suggestable to the point that he could get them to do anything without question, even if it contravened all their social instincts and taboos.

The government was doing this on a grand scale and the trick was being repeated in virtually every other country in the world. People were guilt tripped into never questioning anything and this was coupled by the contrived peer pressure that reinforced the message of compliance. They were robbing your courage while they picked the pockets of your conscience.

Halliday included a clip of a man who was convinced people around him were deriding him and he flew into a rage anytime one of them spoke to him. Such was the control Halliday had over him, the man was prevented from ever leaving his seat simply by the power of suggestion.

With a better understanding of the problem of communicating such an urgent message with my fellow citizens, it allowed me to think about ways of beating the hypnosis instead of having the frustration of constantly banging my head against the wall. The information was sailing over the heads of people who had been so completely uncoupled from their intuition. One thing became clear, the facts were not enough. Statistics were important to back-up every claim you made, but mostly they just bounced off the uninitiated. Emotional intelligence seemed to be the only thing that had any chance of really hitting home. Tales of personal strife and suffering could snap people in or out of this media induced trance.

People like Bryan Halliday would pay a price for speaking out. He lost bookings and found himself de-platformed. This often had a reverse effect, boosting their following and strengthening the target's resolve. His video had been taken down on numerous occasions, but someone always re-posted, and it became viral in spite of the tech giant's attempts to censor it. People power was still alive and thriving on the internet.

I was invited by two separate Freedom groups to speak at what seemed to be the same event being planned in three weeks' time in central London. I had become aware that there was some jostling for position behind the scenes, but it was confusing.

My last speech was off the cuff, but this time would be different, so I got to work preparing what I would say.

Ladies and gentlemen, my mother is dead. My mother has been used as a Government statistic, there to prop up a lie and join thousands of similar lies. My mother died frightened and alone. Like many care homes up and down the country, and many more around the globe, the agents of death were visited upon the facility where she was a resident. Ill patients were returned from hospital on the authority of the Minister of Health. It was no surprise to those who called out the plandemic a lot earlier than me. What was a surprise, to those, like my family, who assumed there was still a modicum of moral integrity in the system, was the assumption that once the alarm was raised, the practice of mixing the ill with the seriously frail and vulnerable would immediately cease. Rather than halting, the process was ramped up and repeated three months later on a far greater scale.

At the same time that decisions were made to continue this practice, a decree was also made for all care homes and elderly patients of local doctors' surgeries to adopt a 'Do Not Resuscitate' policy, coercing old people to quite literally sign their lives away.

And all this for an illness that has over 99.5% survival rate.

A recent study has shown that Lockdowns do more harm than good, and like the flimsy masks being touted as requisite protection for halting contamination, they do nothing to stop transmission in the community. The comparison of the American states of California, which did lockdown, with Florida, which didn't, indicated an almost identical rate of infection. Another study focusing on the UK versus Sweden showed the Scandinavian nation, that refused to impose a lockdown on its citizens, fared better than our country.

In all probability they will have doubled world poverty within twelve months. Millions of people will starve to death as a result of putting the planet in the invisible chains of tyrannical hysteria. Some countries rely on tourism for eighty percent of their income. Even the World Health Foundation, a major player in this corruption, are publicly stating they do not agree with the policy of Lockdowns.

Can you spot the emerging patterns of a deliberate cascade into chaos? Policies turned on a sixpence. Within twenty-four hours a government announcement can completely contradict itself without explanation. You will remember our lofty prime minister insisting 'Masks don't work' only to change the narrative to 'We must all wear masks' in a matter of days.

George Orwell has gone from author to prophet in the space of a few months.

This whole charade deliberately pivots on an emotional vicious circle of boom to bust that has been contrived to generate fear, anxiety and uncertainty.

A UK study completed in August found that 86% of 'patients' experienced no viral symptoms at all. It is literally impossible to tell the difference between an 'asymptomatic case' and a false-positive test result. The likelihood of being asymptomatic and actually having enough viral load to contaminate another person is not just low but extremely low. This was confirmed in June by Dr Maria Hoe, head of the WHF's diseases unit.

When it comes to the validity of imposing mask mandates, some studies have been done claiming to show masks give protection against the virus, but they are all seriously flawed. One study relied on self-reported surveys as data. Another was so badly designed, a panel of experts demanded it be withdrawn. A third was withdrawn after its predictions proved entirely incorrect. The WHF commissioned their own meta-analysis in the Lancet, but that study looked only at N95 masks and only in hospitals. Aside from scientific proof, there's plenty of real-world evidence that masks do nothing to halt the spread of disease. For example, In the United States, North Dakota and South Dakota had near-identical case figures, despite only one having a mask-mandate.

In the past, no-one was able create a vaccine for this virus, a strain of influenza, yet scientists have been able to come up with six in the space of five months

Scientists have been trying to develop a SARS and MERS vaccine for years with little success. Some of the failed SARS vaccines actually caused hypersensitivity to the

157

SARS virus. Vaccinated mice could get the disease more severely than mice that were vaccine free. Another attempt caused liver damage in ferrets.

Traditional vaccines work by exposing the body to a weakened strain of the microorganism responsible for causing the disease, these new shots are mRNA vaccines. mRNA (messenger ribonucleic acid) vaccines theoretically work by injecting viral mRNA into the body, where it replicates inside your cells and encourages your body to recognise, and make antigens for the 'spike proteins' of the virus. They have been the subject of research since the 1990s, but before 2020 no mRNA vaccine was ever approved for use.

And get this, this really is the cherry on the cake. If the vaccine kills or damages you, the manufacturer has complete indemnity – awarded by our government – the people paid to work for our best interests.

The only conclusion that makes any sense is to reject their vaccine programme, avoid their demonic propaganda, refuse to mask up and do not engage in their flawed testing system. Our future freedom depends on it.

I sent my speech to the *Freedom4U* group and it wasn't long before a message came back from a man using the epithet 'Mugzie'.

'Respect!!!! You are the man!!! You smashed it!!!! That is massive!!!!! We are gunna put you mid-show. About 3pm. Make yourself known in the roped area. I'll have people looking for you. 4Freedom – Mugzie.'

He typed more exclamation marks in that one paragraph than I had in my entire journalistic career. A wise old owl once told me that the use of exclamation marks generally meant one of two things. Either the writing was flat, and you were relying on the punctuation marks to give it some oomph, or alternatively, you had written the sentence correctly and were garnishing it with a self-congratulatory pat on the head, or in Mugzie's case sixteen pats on the head. The exclamation should reside in your words, not your punctuation.

I was pleased it hit the right notes with them, but something was niggling me. I poured myself another coffee, my eighth of the day, and stared out onto the common and streets beyond. I watched as people hurried along in their useless paper masks, a fancy dress parade of worriers. Some of them stopped to wipe the condensation off their glasses, others hung the paper strips around their chins. I saw children being barracked by their parents for being too close to other humans, as if brushing past one would instantly turn them to ash. The plastic police tape flapping in the wind caught my eye as it transmitted its alarm, warning children not to play in the happiness of their adventure park. I saw people metrically delineated along the pavement like a modern-day chain gang queueing for their chance to buy groceries. Others stepped into the road, choosing to risk a collision with a car or truck over making their way through the perceived danger of oncoming pedestrians. Every bus that passed was emblazoned with the ritualistic slogans insisting everyone clean their hands, hide their faces and stay away from each other.

I had written my speech for those folks who were living in the darkness of their own ignorance, victims of a cruel spell that finely weaved one lie after another until the victim had been suffocated by disinformation and paralysed by its fearmongering. As I continued to sip the black stuff, surveying the emotional hotch-potch of human misbehaviour, it dawned on me that none of those individuals would be at the demonstration. It was the right message, but the wrong audience. What I had forwarded to Mugzie and the Freedom4U organisation was a piece of journalism. It's powerful and extensively researched, but it's been written in the wrong key for such an event. So, I returned to the drawing board.

Last night, the man that some within our ranks appointed as a saviour, US president Donald J Trump, failed in his attempts to be re-elected. Just as Dex had predicted, it was apparent that some jiggery-pokery was going on behind the scenes, with glaring anomalies appearing in the counting process.

Trump was brash and outspoken and seemed to really shake it up on that side of the pond. He couldn't catch a break in the media. If it rained in America that would prompt a widescale editorial policy blaming the Orangeman in the Oval office.

And now the good folks of America elected the bewildered little old man I had encountered in Chicago, whether they liked it or not. The president, even some Democrat commentators were christening 'Sleepy Joe,' was at the helm. Something didn't add up, and not just the digital vote counting process.

Trump had been the wind in the sails of some Truthers across the globe, but when it was time to really stand up and be counted, he began vigorously championing the vaccine. On live TV, he declared that he would get it delivered into the arms of every US citizen in warp speed.

Maybe he wasn't part of the criminal cabal that ran the world, but he certainly wasn't the great messiah many had hoped he would be. Surrounded by the usual bankers and moneymen, he left me wondering if it was just another puppet posturing and playing to the crowd.

19. A Smashing Time

On the morning of the demonstration, I was glued to social media. Swiping through my feed I found striking pictures of the resistance in all its international colours and flavouring. In cities all around the world, the masses were gathering. It emboldened me in preparation for my official appearance at the afternoon's rally.

Last night, the prime minister used his 6pm Orwellian address to the nation to announce that the vaccinations had been approved and jabbing had already commenced. What he failed to mention was the authorisation was for emergency use only, the trials were not due to end until 2023. It was yet another example of the government's obfuscation. The real catastrophe in this country was not taking place in our hospitals, it was in our parliament where there was a crisis of honesty. The politicians were spewing out more toxic pollutants than the chimneys of Chernobyl ever did.

The PM's words were a worm-like ear infection that crawled into the brains of the unprotected, initiating a propaganda tumour of self-destruction. There was no vaccine for that kind of prognosis. The remedy was simple, turn off your TV, cancel your morning paper and step away from the caustic cauldron that was social media. If everyone did that, the pandemic would be over.

Mid-morning, I headed off to a clearing next to a clump of trees in the middle of Clapham Common and began my breathing and meditation ritual. I was still battling acute anxiety, but this act of self-care settled my mind and brought me some much-needed focus. Even though I could hear the 137 bus chunder along, battling with the juggernauts on the city's clogged arteries, when I closed my eyes, I was right back there with Baldur and Dylo at Heimdall falls. Maybe I would never see that place again, but it had grown in my mind ever since I departed its earthy rugged magnificence.

When I arrived in central London there was no sign of a demonstration. Eventually, I spotted a flurry of protestors and I followed them down Regent Street towards Piccadilly Circus where again things seemed rather quiet. We cut through the back of the National Gallery and were first met by the menacing presence of an army of Robo-cops, dressed for war.

We hurried on into the welcome of a carnival of colours, as people from all walks of life congregated with their striking banners and aptly marked placards. 'My Body My Choice,' 'The Media Is The Virus' and my favourite 'You want to vaccinate the entire planet, but you can't feed the starving.'

I spotted the enormous bulk of a man with wavy blonde hair cutting his way through the crowd in my direction.

"Mr Fisher," he shouted, as the masses melted from his path like a fireball through snow. He was wearing a black sweatshirt with the slogan 'My freedom is non-negotiable.' The last few obstacles gave way for this man-mountain and my sense of anxiety from being part of this very public rebellion hitched up a notch or two.

"Mr Fisher," he said.

His face had warmed a little and before I knew it, his giant frame engulfed me in an all-encompassing hug.

"I wanted to thank you in person. My name is Joe Thornton," he said.

"Nice to meet you, Joe," I said.

"Most people call me Thor," he said.

There was no confusion as to how he acquired that nick name.

"How they treated your mother was a disgrace. My mum was in a similar place, so I busted her out. They are supposed to be gentle places, but have the kind of harsh restrictions you wouldn't expect at a prison for dangerous criminals. They tried to stop me, but I pushed my way in. I found her, gathered her stuff up and took her home. The staff were going crazy and, because she is mostly away with the fairies these days, she found it all a bit of a wheeze, laughing inappropriately and waving to them as we disappeared into the night just as the police were arriving in the opposite direction."

"Wow, that's... amazing" I stammered.

"In the following three weeks, eighteen residents died," he said.

"Thank you for sharing that with me," I said.

"No, Mr Fisher. Thank you for saving my mother's life," he said. "If I can ever be of any service to you, you will only need to ask once."

I put out a hand to shake his but was once more wrapped in the bulk of his Viking-like embrace.

As I looked at the swelling crowd before me and the stage, on the other side of the Square, under Nelson's column, it struck me that my new friend could be just the guide I would need to propel me through such populated terrain.

As we arrived at the roped off area, I sensed a less than amicable atmosphere. I told the man in a yellow vest and skinny jeans, who was guarding the plastic rope encircling the area, that I was due to speak at 3pm and, although he acknowledged my name, the barrier remained between us, with me on the wrong side of the tape.

"There's been a change of plan," he said.

A young woman, I didn't recognise, started her speech and we were drowned out by the initial roar of the crowd's approval now that proceedings were under way.

"We've been around the country with our battle bus. It was just like being back at Uni," she scoffed, hardly able to contain her self-satisfaction that so many people were listening to her.

"And if I learned one thing over our time together it was this," she said, pacing the floor.

I expected her to relate a gem of knowledge about how they had taken the temperature of the nation and the fight was on.

"If Sebastian asks you to do something. Run away," she chuckled. "Run far away."

What was this drivel? Why was she wasting such a vital opportunity? How many more chances would we have to get our message across to such a vast collection of people, both here in the square and watching online?

I turned back to confront the steward.

"Listen," I said. "I was invited by Freedom4U to give a speech today. And I was told-"

"-It's not up to Freedom 4U, they're not official associates of this event."

"But their logo appears on the leaflet." I protested, as I pulled it from my pocket.

"That's not the official leaflet," he replied.

"Sorry, are we not all here for the same reason?"

"I'm just going by the sheet," he said, flapping a piece of paper at me.

"Find Mugzie, he'll tell you," I said.

"Mugzie was arrested on the way here," he said.

"I was also invited by Time-4-Change," I said.

"Wait here," he said, and he disappeared into a heated conversation with five people whom I assumed were the main organisers.

In the meantime, the millennial's speech had gone from bad to worse, but the grin on her face indicated that she didn't think so. I looked at Thor and shook my head. He squeezed my shoulder and reassured me everything would be ok.

Our gatekeeper returned.

"Harvey said he never received anything from you," he said.

"I don't know who Harvey is, I sent my piece to Mugzie. I thought you all worked together."

At that he rolled his eyes.

"I'm sorry, it's all set out now. There will probably be another demo in a about a month, you could send something in for that if you like," he said, a little too nonchalantly for my liking.

Thor, who had been quietly monitoring proceedings suddenly tore the rope in half and headed for the organisers. He drew them in to a huddle, but I couldn't hear what he was saying. The prima donna on stage was taking her final bow.

Thor returned and said they had reconsidered and that I would be speaking as originally planned. It was like the starting gun for the Butterfly Olympics in my guts. I would need to deliver. Perhaps I had been a little tough on the first speaker, maybe she prepared an inspirational mantra of truth but bottled it and reverted to chit-chat and banter. Would I also buckle in the spotlight?

Piers Corbyn followed and, although he garnered a lot of affection amongst the thousands present, his rallying skills were something of an anti-climax. I could see some folks drop their heads. Judging by the recent message boards, many Truthers hadn't forgiven him after he was caught in a messy bribery sting. Approached by two men purporting to be representatives of a pharmaceutical company, Corbyn was offered twenty thousand pounds if he dropped their company's name from his list of targets. Incredibly, he agreed to take the money and within hours was exposed in all the major newspapers and TV news programmes. It was a low trick, but he had fallen for it. There were mounting whispers from people concerned that, perhaps due to his family's deep ties to the Labour party, he was controlled opposition. His presentation skills, tramp-like demeanour and his failure to capitalise on his appearances on mainstream TV programmes all added to the rumours. Without any real evidence it was a harsh appraisal for someone who was relentless in his attempts to spread the message.

While watching proceedings I was approached by a tall, weather-worn individual who introduced himself as Darren Nesbitt. He had launched The Light paper, an alternative to the mainstream news with an intellectual pitch somewhere between the Telegraph and the Guardian, minus the political bias. He had financial backing and distribution hubs all across the British Isles that would ensure a large and varied readership. He couldn't offer me much in return for my writing services but said he had hoped to meet me here and make me an offer. I was so pumped up by the afternoon's events I would have agreed to almost anything.

"Count me in," I said.

It was clear by the animated faces and constant clock watching within the stage area that the next speaker, a medical whistle blower, was over-cooking his goose. Listening to his talk reinforced my instinctual sense that the first speech I wrote had been the wrong approach. He was full of scientific facts and was trying hard to sell people a ticket they had long-since bought. I surmised that most of the speakers were fairly new to the game, or still clutching age-old methods of address. When I thought of all the speeches I had seen over the years, there was a clear evolution to make them much shorter, sharper and designed to punch. This wasn't the 1970's where hard facts were harder to acquire. Thanks to the internet, humans were overburdened with information and it was almost a full-time job disseminating the useful stuff from the rubbish.

My moment arrived. Thor, possibly recognising my apprehension, gave me a hug.

"Good luck, Stig. Make it memorable," he said.

I stripped off my jacket and handed it to him and took the mic.

"You are not the majority," I said, and I could instantly see puzzled faces appear in the crowd. "The majority are distracted, lazy, ill-informed and quite content to continue on the treadmill as long as they receive the soothing, sleep inducing creature comforts of modern convenience. You are the minority. You are the resilient, well-researched and principled minority. You are fiercely protective of your rights and the rights of your children, your community and your country." I ramped it up.

"You… Do not…have to be…the majority. It is always the minority that makes the difference. Throughout history it is true to say that it always has been the minority that drives change, and it always will be."

I took a deep breath and continued ramping it up.

"You… are… the… power," I shouted

I looked to the side of the stage and received a subtle but meaningful clenched fist from Thor.

"They try to silence your voice with their censorship. Will you ever be silenced?"

"No," they replied in unison.

"They try to coerce you to submit to their corruption. Will you ever submit?"

"No," came the shout, louder than before.

"They try to drown you in their lies, blackening your name and testing your resolve. Will you buckle?"

"No," was the steadfast response.

"The unions have betrayed us. The schools and universities have betrayed us. Religious leaders, politicians, the police and the law courts have betrayed us. So many people blinded, bullied and blackmailed. But the stronger they push... the stronger we push back."

There was a communal roar of approval that ran from the back of the crowd, reverberating around the arena shooting right up my spine like a bolt of lightning.

"We will never surrender to this tyranny," I said.

The moment was nothing less than spiritual.

"Nothing they do can ever break the freedom that resides in the hearts of each and every one of you, because you have the power. We will accept Freedom and nothing less."

I left a pause and then delivered a shout of 'Freedom' that was repeated ferociously like the ripple of an earthquake that spread out four ways from the stage, to the people standing in Whitehall, those positioned on the Mall, the Truthers blocking Charing Cross Road and the swell of folk at the mouth of the Strand. The sound was deafening. Inside I was aflame with purpose.

"We will never accept the killing fields of Big Pharma," I continued.

"Fuck Gill Baits," shouted a man at the front, his face flushed red from chanting.

"I don't have a crystal ball. I can't tell you what the coming years will bring, but I can tell you now, looking out at all of you, good, honest faces, we will make a difference and if we fight hard, we will make a better world and a future for our children."

Again, I paused, and the ripple of 'Freedom' returned, projected with even more vigour.

"Let me tell you this, the crimes being committed will be met by the full force of our humanity. We will show no mercy to these devils. The BBC…"

The boos were deafening.

"Defund the BBC, Defund the BBC," shouted a section of the crowd.

"Gill Baits, Gorgi Natassi and all those gangsters masquerading as philanthropists."

"Boo. Hang Gill Baits. Hang Gill Baits," shouted the crowd.

The air was electric with revolution. It was at that moment I knew that these people weren't here for fact checking or a summary of the latest figures and statistics. They had already done their homework. They were here as a collective of power, feeding off each other. An energy was directed at all those who dared to block their path to liberty.

"Celebrities, fake pop idols and sleazy vulgar film stars," the boos reached fever pitch. "They are the empty relics of a world we will replace with justice, honour, loyalty and FREEDOM."

"Freedom, Freedom, Freedom," they shouted.

Behind me I saw an animated black man in dreads remonstrating with the organisers. Something urgent was developing and Thor ushered me over to come and join the heated debate going on at the side of the stage.

"Riot cops are moving in. They're going to attack, we need to warn the people," said the black man.

One thing was for sure, I had no intention of waiting for the rain of a truncheon on my head and the thought of needlessly languishing in a cell again added to the urgency to find a solution.

"We must ensure no-one retaliates," said Harvey.

"When the order is given, we will get battered. They will smash us if we are peaceful or not. They are under instruction," said the black man.

"No violence. We cannot afford to be labelled violent," said Harvey.

"They will brand us violent regardless. The days in which we concern ourselves about what the mainstream media call us are long gone," I said.

"We need a diversion. We need to control the situation," said Thor.

"Go out there and appeal for calm," said Harvey.

"We need to do something they're not expecting," I said.

"What can we do to stop them?" said Harvey.

The crowd was growing restless, an anxiety had quietened their fervour as news of an imminent police attack filtered through. Thor rushed on stage and grabbed the microphone.

"Thank you everyone for coming. Those of you who really want to make yourselves heard join us now as we march on the BBC," he announced. "Let's take it to their door."

A roar went up and "Fuck the BBC," was chanted in response.

Instantly, I saw the crowd re-engage and disperse north in the direction of Charing Cross Road. The police looked dumbfounded.

At the side of the stage, the organisers were fretting about what just happened.

"We must we keep things peaceful. If there's trouble at the BBC, the entire movement will be tarnished," said Harvey, his minions nodding in unison.

"Politely airing our concerns is getting us nowhere. We need action," I said.

"Sorry, but if you're not for peace then you shouldn't be here," said Harvey.

"The people who have lost jobs, been falsely arrested, had family die unnecessarily, what peace do you think they get? This is war," said Thor.

"We don't want your war," said Harvey.

"War is upon us whether you like it or not," I replied.

"Who do you think you are?" said one steward. "This is our day."

"Yeah. We've got music lined up, we've got a DJ. You've ruined everything," said another.

"This is not a fucking jamboree," said Thor. "We're fighting tyranny, nothing more and nothing less."

Harvey addressed the crowd, many of whom were already leaving.

"Remember, we are a peaceful movement. Please do not be provoked. Let's everyone keep calm," said Harvey, before trying to whip up the crowd with a chant of 'We want peace.'

We left them grumbling and made our way through the crowd and I could sense Thor monitoring the situation on the ground as we went, avoiding clusters of Robo Cops. The late afternoon sun slipping behind clouds brought a drop in temperature, I dashed into the doorway of a closed restaurant and pulled my coat on.

"I think this could get heavy," said Thor, extracting some foam character masks from his rucksack and insisting I put one on as way of disguise. I chose the Prince Charles mask, Thor donned a Prince Philip mask. A Truther in a red sweatshirt emblazoned with the slogan 'Freedom patrol' clocked what we were doing, and Thor handed him a Prince Harry disguise, handing a mask of Queen Elizabeth to the woman next to him.

All around me I could sense a different atmosphere. It was charged with righteous anger. The chants of 'Defund the BBC' became louder and fiercer.

The police, who had been monitoring everything were now scrambling to follow the crowd which was way too big and mobile for them to physically confront. Thor's intervention on stage had foiled their tactics.

As we rounded the corner into Regent street, the BBC offices a few hundred metres ahead of us, we were met with a line of Robocops blocking the way. Our convoy of Truthers was tightly packed which served as a good way to avoid police infiltration and to illustrate what a sham social distancing was.

I did a double take when I spotted what looked like Iain's camouflage cap bobbing along through the mass of bodies that surrounded us.

"I think… I think my son is here," I said, simultaneously pleased and concerned.

As we got closer, and the crowd became denser, I got near enough to confirm it. I lifted my mask so he could see it was me.

"Dad," he called out.

Thor manoeuvred people to allow him and his friend through.

"What are you doing here?"

"Fighting for freedom," said Iain.

"Cool speech, Mister Fisher," said Iain's friend, Fynn.

"Thanks," I said before swiftly turning back to Iain.

"Does Mum know you're here?"

"Don't know, don't care," Iain said, flashing a cocky smile at his friend.

I grimaced. "Oh shit. You'll get me strung up, you will," I said.

"I thought you'd be pleased," said Iain.

"I am. Just promise me, if there's any trouble whatsoever, you get out pronto."

"Chill Dad," he said.

"I mean it."

I could see he didn't like being chided in front of his friend. I didn't want to burst his bubble, but if he got in any bother today, it would be curtains for me and Jasmine.

"I'll keep an eye on them," said Thor.

I thanked Thor and introduced him to the boys. Part of my brain was saying march them to Oxford Circus tube station and send them on their way, but had they been Thor's boys, or anyone else's children, I would have complimented them on their courage. This fight was for them and the generations after them.

This was the dilemma facing all parents these days. There was a tendency to wrap the children up in cotton wool. They were always available on their mobile phones, just in case. Just in case of what? In case they actually chose to explore their own personal freedom? We all embraced this self-induced claustrophobia. This clawing confinement culture led to the instinct of a generation being supplanted by a blind adherence to a risk averse dogma of 'staying safe'. It was rife in school, popular culture and on social media. The children were being wired for control. Not-so-Great Britain had become the signpost nation. Incessant and unnecessary written instruction everywhere you look: STAY SAFE, CLEAN HANDS, SAFE SPACE, MIND THE GAP, WALK ON THE LEFT, QUEUE ON RIGHT, PATHWAY CLOSED, DON'T EAT MEAT, USE OTHER DOOR, NO BALL GAMES. It was producing a generation of people utterly unsure of themselves and completely lacking in self-confidence and self-esteem. A life contained is a life not lived. I also had to throw off those chains.

After a short lull, we carried on moving towards Broadcasting House and I could hear Fynn quietly quizzing Iain.

"Did he say his name was Thor?"

Affixed to the facade of the BBC building was a sculpture of a child sitting on the knee of a man that became the target of the crowd's anger. Red paint bombs were hurled and as one hit the middle of the stone structure the crowd cheered then began chanting 'Paedophiles, paedophiles.' The sculpture was created by Eric Gill, a heinous sex offender who raped his own children and his pet dogs. Petitions to remove the 'Paedo stone carving' were instantly rebuffed by the BBC.

As a journalist I had walked under that monstrosity over the years, until recently I had been oblivious to its history and real meaning. Now it seemed, the veil was being torn apart and we were witnessing the naked truth, not just about the nature of our national broadcaster but of all the pillars of our society.

The policeman in charge of fighting child sexual abuse in England recently bemoaned the reduction in resources during the first Lockdown. How interesting that in contrast the resources to silence any voices questioning the government's narrative were unending.

A clash between the police and a protester suddenly heightened the tension. As the protester was dragged away, some of the crowd started hurling objects at the line of Police and when they swarmed in to snatch the perpetrators, violent clashes broke out near where we were positioned. In the melee, some Truthers managed to break through the lines and swarm towards the BBC building. A trickle turned to a flood and soon we were all carried towards the doors in the melee. I felt my arm being tugged and turned to see a woman yelling at me.

"Stop them, stop them. We must remain peaceful," she pleaded.

She continued badgering me as we were swept along closer to the building.

"We don't need to fight, we've already won because we have truth on our side," she said.

Whether it was the added responsibility of Iain and his friend arriving, or the snarling riot police facing us, I had had enough of this woman tugging at my sleeve.

"Look, I'm sorry," I said forcefully. "We've got the facts, evidence, whatever you want to call it, but they're not listening."

"But they can't defeat the truth," she repeated.

"The truth is not enough," I hollered above the noise and I watched as the crestfallen face of the woman was swallowed up in the surging crowd.

We were crossing a line both physically and metaphorically, and although it made me nervous, something inside told me it was the right thing to do. They contained our street protests, and the media was, on the whole, wilfully ignoring us. There was a co-ordinated effort to silence our message. One thing was for sure, they would not be able to ignore this. The authorities will be spitting blood at our audacity, and even though we will be painted as devils, people would know we had the numbers and the commitment and courage to take our message to the people in whichever way we thought necessary.

Some BBC employees and security had been goading the crowd, safe in the knowledge that the cops would prevent the protesters from ever reaching them. Now they scrambled into the building looking for shelter. As they did, they enabled the mob to breach the broadcaster's security system and within seconds the premises was under our control.

We surged forwards and I looked back in horror to see riot police closing in on the boys and it looked like one had gripped Fynn's shoulder.

"Thor," I shouted and just as a truncheon was heading for Fynn's head, my giant friend yanked him forward and the blow skidded down the youngster's back and the policeman's grip was lost to the surge of freedom fighters now storming the BBC.

We scrambled on into the building and I was relieved to see that all four of us got through.

"Right, everyone turn off your phones. And you two pull your hats low and hide your faces from the cameras," Thor instructed Iain and Fynn.

Thankfully, the boys in blue decided not to follow us into the building. As I clattered through the doors, I pocketed some key-cards from the hastily abandoned security post.

"We need to get a message across," I shouted to Thor.

"Listen up," hollered Thor, and his voice rose above the excited cacophony of pumped-up protest that was bouncing off the walls of the vast palatial reception area, where portraits of the upper echelons of the world famous organisation were already being desecrated by the mob.

I held up a handful of passes.

"Take a pass and head for the studios. Be quick before they cut transmission." I shouted.

The key cards were swiftly snatched up, mostly by those who led the demonstrators into Broadcasting House.

Thor and I took off towards Studio 6 where I knew the 24-hour news was broadcast from. I had been a guest there during the North West England grooming scandal. I broke the story and was the first to interview Sara Rowbotham, the Rochdale Crisis Intervention Team co-ordinator, who was sacked after bravely blowing the whistle on what was going on.

The radio programme centred on my motivation for the story and barely touched on the plight of the girls.

We took the marble steps to the basement, where we found a small group of Truthers banging on the glass

walls of a locked office containing the Cardinal, David
Dullweed, and the Rabbi, Simon Simms. They were
presenters of the multi-faith morning show. They backed
the lockdowns and the closing of all religious buildings.
This country had never known a time when the religious
authorities barred the doors of their churches at such a
perilous time of need. They had always managed to
remain open, even during wars and plagues. It was
cowardly and another sign of the state's attempt to be the
only source of information and influence.

Luckily for Simms and Dullweed, none of the protesters
had passes. One swipe of a key card and they would be
in on them like foxes in the henhouse. We hadn't come
to spill blood and I was sure the so-called men of God
would be shaken enough by their ordeal to get the
message that there were consequences for their
cowardice.

There were six of us now heading for Studio 6, four in
masks and the two boys. It took us three or four attempts
to access the studio.

"These studios are soundproof. Whoever is inside may
be shocked by our sudden appearance," I said. "We must
use that element of surprise. Overpower the crew and
ensure broadcast continues as long as possible. We need
two in the control room and two on the floor."

The surprise on the faces of the crew was a joy to behold,
as the Royal Family burst in. Once inside Thor, in his
Prince Philip mask, took control. We had struck gold,
interrupting an interview with health minister, Will
Cockburn. Fortunately for Cockburn, the interview was
being conducted via the internet. If he had been in the
building, there would have been slim chance of him
escaping in one piece.

The presenter, Adrian Winkleman, who was paid more
than the prime minister, was a millennial so wet you
needed an umbrella just to be in his company. When he

saw us, he froze in puzzlement, perhaps wondering if it was a prank. I could hear Cockburn's whiny voice continue to drone on. One of our crew, a stocky woman in her forties who was wearing the Queen Elizabeth mask, grabbed the shaking Winkleman by the throat and forced him towards the door Thor was holding open. I could see that the 'Voice of Reason' or as Truthers had dubbed him 'the Voice of Treason', had urinated in his own trousers as he was thrown into a cupboard full of cables and old recording machines. The other staff followed shortly, putting up no resistance at all.

The boys got to work destroying the studio webcams that had been trained on Winkleman.

"Hello Adrian? Are you there?" Cockburn fumbled, perhaps sensing a change in the air.

"Perhaps you would like to inform the public about the hundreds of thousands of pounds you have invested in Rothbairn Pharmaceuticals?" I said, in as calm a voice as I could muster.

Ever since this attack on our liberty began, the media, my old colleagues included, hadn't asked one challenging question between them. It was a pantomime but now he was facing the music and found himself at odds with the new script.

"What?" said Cockburn, clearly enraged and not a little puzzled that the interview had gone off script.

"Perhaps you could tell us why you insisted on a Lockdown three days after your department downgraded the severity of the virus to that of the common flu?" I pressed.

"Well, that is true of course, but… We had to, errm. I don't know what is going on there, but this interview is over," Stammered Cockburn, and as expected, his line went dead.

"I'll tell you what's going on," I said, speaking into Winkleman's mic. "You and your government's wall of lies is being dismantled by the ordinary hard-working people of this country. The game is up. I plead to everyone listening, do your own research, ignore the mainstream narrative, they mean to enslave you. Search for Hugo Talks, Lockdown Sceptics and the Light Paper, also the online-"

The room went black before security lights flickered back on. They had cut the power.

"Right, let's get out of here," shouted Thor.

Fynn ripped the phones and intercom system from the wall as Iain poured a jug of water across the mixing desk and it sizzled like bacon on a barbeque.

"Come on boys," I shouted, and Thor hustled them out. Outside the door I had seconds to react. I could hear a great commotion from above and I realised that we would likely be captured if we retuned the way we came. I was aware that this building was something of a labyrinth. The Jimmy Savile debacle had exposed areas of Broadcasting House that were known in some circles as the petting zoo. It made my stomach turn at the thought of those who placated such a demonic individual. With all those victims and years of depravity, it was inconceivable that he had acted alone.

I took the decision to search for an alternative exit. I remembered that musicians like the Rolling Stones, Oasis, Madonna and Kanye West used a secret entrance to avoid the throng of fans that massed outside the main doors each time a big name appeared live on one of the stations.

We searched around the basement floor trying doors until we found one that only led downwards. Following it to what must have been the lower basement, we found a pipe-lined tunnel that was thin, winding and a little bit creepy. Little rooms with heavy metal doors sprang off the sides like a submarine. Eventually we found some stairs and followed them up to a fire door that none of our passes could open. We stood back as Thor charged and almost took the door of its hinges as he burst through into a small indistinct courtyard, a piercing alarm trumpeting our arrival.

"Wait," said the man in the Prince Harry mask and, without explanation, he took off back into the tunnel.

"We haven't got time for this," I said.

"What's he up to?" said our Queen.

"He must know what he's doing," said Thor, the only one of us with a modicum of composure.

The beat of my heart was suddenly competing with the shrill of the alarm. We ripped off our masks. The boys weaved off towards the busy street beyond, but I called them back. It was important we stick together, at least for the moment.

Prince Harry appeared at the door clutching a pile of workmen's boiler suits. We each pulled them on and after fastening mine I looked up to see Thor laughing. He couldn't even get his past his knees. The boys were in hysterics.

"Listen up," said Thor. "We must never talk about what we just did. Everything is either bugged or buggable these days and they will want their pound of flesh for striking at the heart of the beast. No text messages, no forums and no casual boasting." He pointed to his lips. "Keeping these zipped is your best form of defence."

"Come on, let's go," said the Truther who had worn the Queen Elizabeth mask, now dressed like a BBC stagehand.

"Heads down, stay smart," said Thor.

We exited the tiny courtyard and found ourselves in the hustle and bustle of Carnaby Street with its fancy boutiques and pricey shoe shops. Thor drew looks and I wasn't sure whether it was due to his mammoth size or his conspicuous 'My Freedom is non-negotiable' sweatshirt. Either way, it would be a problem if the police spotted him. He was obviously thinking the same thing.

"I should have turned my sweatshirt inside out. Can't do it now," he said.

"Once we're on the Tube we'll be ok," I said.

"If I get spotted just pretend you don't know me," he said.

As we shuffled away, Iain snaffled a t-shirt from a board in front of a shop selling tourist tat. As we rounded the corner, I scolded him.

"What do you think you're doing? Do you want us to get caught?"

With that he retrieved the t-shirt from his overalls and handed it to Thor. As the big man unfurled it, the design became apparent. It was a unicorn with a giant rainbow.

"Perfect," said Thor ironically, as we tried, but failed, to stifle our sniggering.

20. Truth Flowers in Winter

Every time the doorbell chimed, I felt my heart jump into my mouth. When a man arrived with flowers, I was so suspicious, I kept the door closed and told him to leave them in the porch. I felt justified in being overly cautious, but the mounting paranoia, constantly gnawing at me, was becoming a problem.

The social media pages of the major Truther groups were ablaze with debate about the nature of the events that followed the rally. The media tried to camouflage the incident, claiming the intentions of the 'criminals' who broke into the Broadcasting HQ were currently unknown. The movement was split, pro-violent versus non-violent. For me, it wasn't ever as clear-cut as that.

A ripple of rebellion sent tremors through the broadcast media, as copy-cat Truthers smashed their way into TV outlets up and down the country.

I closely inspected the flowers. Was this some kind of listening device? I put that out of my mind as I considered the various devices in my home, no less the mobile phone that rarely left my side, whose cameras and microphones could be activated at any moment without my knowing. It wasn't a conspiracy theory, it was common knowledge, but we all accepted the infringement on our privacy because so much of our daily routines were wrapped up in it.

I read the card that came with the flowers, 'Dear Stig, many congratulations, WB.' As I placed the flowers into a vase and crunched up the wrapping paper, ready to chuck it in the bin, something caught my eye. Printed faintly, on the inside, was a load of blurb about how to look after the flowers and the care that had gone into choosing them, but towards the bottom there was a message.

'The robbery of the wicked shall destroy them; because they refuse to do judgment.' YAHOO! Take the right path to discover the BUSINESS of who is running the world. The share is unfair, is it not?'

If this was my newest clue, it was a little more abstract than before. There were no accompanying links, which, on the plus side, meant whatever I found was my own research and although that made the task more difficult, it gave me confidence that the message was genuine. My inquisitive brain wouldn't even wait for me to pour a coffee, I set to work dissecting the riddle. 'Who owns the world?' I kept repeating.

I searched on the Yahoo internet browser and after wading through speculation about the Illuminati,

Freemasonry and the much-maligned Protocols of the Elders of Zion, I came upon information about the world's primary feudal landowner who it stated, was Queen Elizabeth II. She is Queen of 32 countries and head of a Commonwealth of 54 nations in which a quarter of the world's population live. The image sold to us that Lizzie Windsor was just a nominal figurehead, and kindly old lady who shook hands and smiled a lot, was absolute bunkum. Something told me that she wasn't WB's intended target, but all the same I thought it something of a sick joke that the British public constantly stumped up taxes for the richest woman on the planet.

Yahoo has a business section that lists the shareholders of all the companies in the world. I started with the big ones and found that the same two investment companies, IllorStone and FleeceGard, were shareholders in every company I looked into. Companies pitted in public as bitter rivals were owned by these same two behemoths. They had a controlling stake in every major tech company, every mainstream media company, Gas, Oil and Steel. Their grip included Airlines, Food and Beverage companies and all the Central Banks. It came as no surprise that all the big Pharmaceutical corporations had their inky black fingerprints all over them. It was an enormous scandal. They were not even household names, yet they owned everything. It took a while to sink in. The implications were obvious, those two institutions could dictate virtually every major commercial decision made in the modern world. Finding out who the lords of finance behind IllorStone and FleeceGard was not so easy. The identities of the major shareholders of these two investment companies were hidden. I spent the night and the best part of the following day digging. I couldn't find concrete proof, but it was obvious that they were some of the villains in the

Conspiracists' top 10 baddies. If there was a new world order, as had always been surmised by those who knew where the bodies were buried, then this was where you'd find its masterminds. I swallowed hard as I came across stories of the mysterious deaths of those who had been on the path to exposing these uber-gangsters.

I typed up my first draft and went to bed. I slept for what seemed like days but was really just over six hours. I wished so much to remain in slumber, but the home phone was ringing off the wall. I would have ignored it but the only person who ever called me on the land line was little Harley. I missed him so much.

I launched myself out of bed and down into the hall. "Hiya little man," I said, as I swept the handset up and placed it to my ear, still trying to flip the heel of a slipper in place.

"It's me," said Jasmine, in a stern manner that told me I was in trouble.

"I thought it was Harley. I haven't heard from him lately," I said.

"So, you poison Iain's mind and Harley is next in line, is that it?"

She was over a hundred miles away, but I could feel my face burning from the hot lava she was spitting at me. Age hadn't dented her beauty, but rage transformed her in an instance.

"What are you talking about?" I stammered.

"I know what you did. I know about the BBC," she said.

"What?" I murmured.

My unconvincing act wouldn't have secured a minor role in a toddler's Christmas show.

"To throw your career away is one thing, and attach yourself to those, those bloody nutcases is another, but to drag your son into that shit… That's low, Stig. Really low."

"I didn't drag anyone anywhere," I retorted.

"Oh, just to let you know. I have received my offer of a vaccination," she said.

"You would be utterly mad if you got jabbed," I interjected, as I felt my anxiety reach fever pitch.

"I want you to know that it will be my choice. Nothing you say is going to change that."

I knew the data on the vaccine – it wasn't pretty. They had never used a gene manipulation medicine on humans before and here they were rolling it out, without any proper trials, across the entire planet. How could I preach to others about the real reasons behind the lockdowns, our evaporating freedoms and the use of vaccines to control us, when I couldn't even successfully convey that message to my own wife? Albeit a wife currently living far away under a different roof.

"Please don't take it, Jasmine," I pleaded.

There was silence and then I heard her holler sternly at our young son.

"Harley. Your father is on the phone."

I kept *Virus mania* out of the conversation and tried to enjoy a little oasis of normal in this sea of chaos. I couldn't get it out of my mind how reckless Iain was to allow his mother to find out where he had been that Saturday. More importantly, I hoped that spite wouldn't lead her to play Russian roulette with her health and take the jab.

I could hear Jasmine barking at Harley to say goodbye, but he was reluctant to. She snatched the phone from him, and I heard him call out. "Miss you, Daddy."

Those words filled and then ripped at my heart, echoing in my head long after the telephone line went dead. What a world we had found ourselves in.

Over the next few days, I sent a string of 'call me' texts to Iain. I needed to put him straight about his loose tongue. There was no response and I wondered if he was blanking me for fear of a rollicking waiting for him at the

185

other end of the line, or whether Jasmine had confiscated his phone.

In the meantime, I lost myself online unearthing evidence of vaccine damage. People dying hours after being jabbed, some dying minutes after the procedure. A media blackout on the long list of ailments and life-threatening conditions induced by whatever was in that shot. There were videos of people who couldn't walk without shaking, some whose faces had collapsed in response to the injections. The messages were dark and a daily diet of searching through these news boards and websites was blackening my mood quicker than an *EastEnders* boxset.

I needed a distraction and plumped for a movie. The Death of Stalin was superb, the politics of fear, coupled with the ultra-violent absurdity of Kremlin power games, was carried off with aplomb. However, watching it on my own, I found my laughs were soon usurped by the echoes of my loneliness. Dinner for one became a clarion call for my demons. I was becoming sick of my own company.

Breathing and meditation sessions, in the fresh air, went some way to cleanse the digital junk that had passed across my eyes and fogged my brain. I regained a bit of clarity, even though I knew it wouldn't be long before I was chained to my computer chasing ghosts once more.

By the time Iain finally returned my call, I had lost much of my ire.

"It's best not to discuss anything about our little adventure," I said.

"The BBC?" he said.

"What did I just say?"

There was silence and I wondered if Iain had returned to type.

"I'm not angry with you, it's just you need to remember what Thor said," I said.

"Dad, is he really called Thor?"

"It's a nick name," I said.

"Cool," he said.

"You really need to go easy on Mum," I said.

"Mum's a sheep," he said.

"She's your mother, you only get one. Just promise me you'll try not to piss her off."

"But Dad, she needs to wake up before it's too late. She'll take Harley down with her. He's such a little idiot, he believes anything," he said.

"No, no, no," I said, firmly.

"Do you know what he said? 'People who don't wear masks in the shops are murderers,' he's so stupid," he said.

"Just stop, okay. He's your brother. He's only a little boy, he shouldn't have to deal with this madness. None of us should, including your mum."

"But Dad."

"You'll only make things worse if you rub them up the wrong way, promise me you'll go easy," I said.

"Okay, Okay, don't go on… it drives me mad, that's all," he said.

"I know, son. I know," I said.

"I hate it," he said.

"It won't always be this way," I said.

21. Wrecked

Even though I could see through the intense propaganda and manipulation, I was still suffering at the hands of the government's psychological warfare. Just nipping to the shops could become a trigger-fest. This morning I set off to pick up some eggs and bread. My paranoia would not allow me to go anywhere without first scouring the immediate vicinity outside my front door. The worry that I was being monitored was ever-present, yet I had absolutely no idea how I would recognise those who might be engaged in such an operation.

As I exited onto the street, I could hear the latest warnings of doom from the BBC radio news booming out from a workman's van parked on the corner. The Bus shelter featured a giant poster that stated, *'Even if you don't feel ill you must pretend that you are ill.'* Outside the shop, the circular stickers placed to manipulate the masked masses into the distancing charade had been updated with even brighter ones. The newspaper rack was full of Tabloid front pages screaming with faux outrage, 'Christmas is over,' 'The man who killed Christmas' and 'Christmas cancelled'.

I paid for my eggs and bread. The muffled voice behind a blue paper mask, that looked like it hadn't been changed in days, thanked me for my custom and I exited the shop past a frowning customer who clearly took umbrage at my open face. Crossing the road, my heartbeat was ratcheted up further as I clocked the advert that screamed out in terror from the passing bus 'DON'T KILL GRANNY – WEAR A MASK.'

On returning home, I ignored my own warning bells and switched on the news to hear from the horse's mouth just what devilry the Scrooge of Westminster had in store for us over the festive period.

"We already know enough," the PM said, his hair over-ruffled, in a deliberate manner. "More than enough to be sure that we must act now. I met with members of the Virus Operations Committee last night and after much deliberation we agreed on the following actions."

He flipped the pages of his speech and was momentarily befuddled. Was this all part of the clownish persona he seemed to be inhabiting of late? Acting like an imbecile certainly had the effect of making people falsely assume that the never-ending nightmare they were enduring was not by design but the result of government incompetence.

"First," he continued. "We will introduce new restrictions in the most affected areas, specifically those parts of London, Birmingham, and the Southeast of England. People should not leave their local areas, and residents must not stay the night away from home. Individuals can only meet one person from another household in an outdoor public space for a maximum of one hour."

So, yet another government promise, a Christmas lockdown amnesty, would join the long list of U-turns performed over the last year.

The PM was being cruelly dishonest, this was not legally binding, it was advice, but he knew that if it played over the media as such, people would think it was law and most would adhere.

Everyone who had challenged the fixed penalties in court had their cases thrown out. Although very welcome, they were mostly hollow victories because news of these cases was being suppressed.

"It is with a very heavy heart, I must tell you, we cannot continue with Christmas as planned," said the PM. "All places of worship will remain closed. There will be no relaxation on the 31st of December, so people must not break the rules at New Year. They must… NOT… break the rules at New Year. It is very, very important to emphasize that."

"There we go, wrap it up and stick a bow on it. Happy Christmas citizens of Great Britain," I ranted at the Television.

They destroyed Easter, much of the Summer holidays, Halloween and now with Christmas and New Year, the keen collectors of other people's misery will have the full set.

Even though I half expected this oppressive manoeuvre, it still affected me when it was announced. Whether you were wide awake to their scheming or blissfully ignorant to the manipulation at hand, it was impossible to dodge the psychological malice at play. I was hoping that Christmas might be a time of reconciliation for me and

Jasmine, but now it was looking like I may have to enact a covert military operation just to join the family around the table for Christmas dinner.

For the remainder of the week, I was lost in a cycle of nausea and numbness. To the detriment of my wellbeing, my meditative trips to the wooded area of Clapham Common became less frequent.

The occasional burst of ringtone from my mobile phone was a sound that got added to the tinnitus of my mood. I knew the fog of darkness that engulfed me would only seep down the line and contaminate any conversation I had, so I avoided the green button.

I awoke with a start and for a moment I couldn't think where I was. I soon realised I had fallen asleep in Harley's room. Noises emanating from downstairs startled me. The TV was blaring but I could hear muffled voices. What if it was burglars? Or a hired thug sent to silence me? My mind raced. I urgently scanned the room for something I could use as a weapon. Whoever it was, they were now inside the house. My tentative breathing sounded like the percussion section of an orchestra in my ears. If I hid, they would surely find me. There was nothing for it, I steeled myself, took a deep breath and I ran to meet them at the top of the stairs, a child's tennis racquet my only defence.

"Who's there?" I growled.

"Daddy," shouted Harley and he ran up the stairs and threw his arms out wide. I dropped the racquet and embraced him. His little hands clutched around me, thawing me out like an open fire in winter.

"We were worried about you," said Jasmine. "What's going on?

"We've been phoning you up, Daddy," said Harley

"Sorry, I've been a bit out of sorts," I said meekly.

"I should say so, you look dreadful," said Jasmine.

"No, he doesn't Mummy, I love my Daddy," said Harley, squeezing me tighter.

I picked up the little man and walked down the stairs, catching my reflection in the hall mirror. She was right. I made Persey the Tramp look like the man about town. Harley delved into his coat pocket and pulled out a bag of sweets and offered me one. I helped myself to a chewy cola bottle and he scrambled on to a chair swinging his feet happily.

Jasmine gave me a big hug and I thought my heart would jump out of my chest and start dancing a jig on the living room floor.

"I do love you, Stig," she whispered in my ear and I could feel her words fly around the house like a mystical sword slashing at the cloud of doom I had been trapped in of late.

"I hope the Stasi didn't see you coming here?" I joked.

"A child has a right to see his father. They haven't outlawed that,"

"Not yet," I said, then instantly reminded myself to tread carefully. This was not the time to make sentient points, it was a rare time to bathe in the love of my family. Jasmine unhooked herself from my embrace, but I clasped her hand in mine for which I received a sweet smile in return.

"Iain's got an essay he needs to finish, so he couldn't come. With the house empty, I'm sure the call of the X-box will be louder than that of the teacher's threats, but what can you do?" she said

"Must be terrible to get your schooling through a computer screen every day," I said.

"It's an important year for him," she said.

"Yep, it is an important year." I said, careful not to load my reply with any overtones.

"You'll come down for Christmas?" said Jasmine.

"Say yes, Daddy, say yes," said Harley.

"I wouldn't miss it for the world. No rotten politician is going to tell me when I can visit my own family," I said. Jasmine helped me tidy up the house while Harley reacquainted himself with his old bedroom, periodically appearing at the top of the stairs to alert me and Jasmine of a toy or teddy bear he hadn't seen in a while.

Jasmine took charge of the entire evening and kept it light throughout. There is nothing so wonderful as spending time with someone who knows you better than yourself. The elephant in the room, my opposition to the lockdowns and vaccines and our teenage son's role in the fracas in London, was tied up in the back yard and starved of attention.

With Harley tucked up in bed, we relaxed in the front room with some episodes of the latest Scandi-noir dramas that had been the mainstay of our television consumption before the explosion of virus mania.

In the morning, I awoke on the sofa. Jasmine had thrown a blanket over me. I found her in the kitchen preparing breakfast, the utensils and other kitchen paraphernalia having been regimentally placed back where they were prior to her departure to our house in the New Forest.

I showered, shaved and suited up. I needed to halt the rot that had set in. This war that I had initially stumbled into was being fought on so many levels. Without a little more self-care I would have plummeted down into a state that was both useless to me, my family and my sworn commitment to fighting for freedom. I would not let them do that to me.

I was tempted to move the conversation on to us and the stalemate we had recently been enduring, but I could see that Jasmine was protecting us from the risks that such an exchange could bring to this very welcome oasis of harmony.

After they both left, I threw on an overcoat and walked the three or four miles to Chelsea Bridge. The icy wind whipping up along the River Thames bit into my hands and face, but my mind was fogged with a much more powerful sensation. Melancholy was in the air. What started as a yearning for my old family life drifted down the years to my early days growing up in this area. I remember watching the drag races across the bridge, jogging around the nearby Battersea Park and fishing with my friends on the banks of this sludge-ridden river. If we had caught and cooked anything back then I might not be standing here now, but fishing was an excuse to stay out late, sneak a glug or two of cheap booze and lark about. Life wasn't perfect but I felt free back then.

This was also the route I used to take on my morning walk to school across the river in Pimlico, less than a mile away from Parliament, where a succession of traitors had driven this great country into the ground. The iconic Battersea Power Station loomed over the skyline, but I felt the twinges of a heavy heart at the dissipating character of the community here.

Battersea was once a working-class hub of quick wit and fast hands. My parents arrived here as strangers in the nineteen-sixties. You had to be on your mettle, or they'd steal the steam off your coffee. This was balanced by the warmth of the constant banter and laughter that wafted up into the air like the aroma of fried breakfasts emanating from the working man's cafés that had mostly been replaced by Estate Agents.

You paid for your street wisdom with an eternal suspicion of outsiders. You constantly evaluated your circumstance and those you encountered in terms of friend or foe. Your essence of humanity would never be the same after growing up in an area and era as the one that raised me. It taught me that life was a negotiation of compromise and sacrifice. It was the measure of those two virtues that made you who you were and paved the road to your future.

Nowadays, depending on which side of the street you were on, the Cockney accent had been usurped by the Yuppie drawl of nearby Chelsea or replaced by the modern street slang that mostly belonged to the streets of New York and the ghettos of Jamaica. We were living in very different times. I was one of only three students from my school year that went to university. I soon realised that I would need to dial down my own Cockney inflection. It was a betrayal of sorts, but a necessary survival mechanism. This was long before the 'Mockney' vibe gained a novel coolness in some media circles. Back then, in most employers' eyes, Cockney equalled trouble. The TV was full of dim-witted characters who had been anointed with the rough London brogue for extra effect. Eras come and go but no matter how old I become, I will always be a Battersea boy of the nineteen-eighties.

My thoughts carried me homewards via Battersea Park and on up to Clapham Junction. There were very few people out and about. Abandoned pale-blue face masks fluttered around me like rudderless little kites caught in the breeze and struggling to get off the ground.

I stopped at the duck pond on Clapham Common and performed my breathing exercises. The weather was overcast and dull, but I hadn't felt so calm in months. Love will do that to you. Deep down it was what this was all about. The collective love of humanity standing against a conglomerate of cynicism, greed and corruption.

My new-found aura of serenity came to a crashing halt as I opened my front door to find my home had been trashed. This wasn't a mere opportunistic smash and grab undertaking, whoever had been here had really gone to town.

I collapsed onto the sofa with my head in my hands. Jasmine and little Harley had pulled me out of the doldrums and helped me climb the ladders to a higher plain and now the snakes had dragged me down once more.

Before the rot could really set in, I purposefully righted myself. Whoever had done this was not going to defeat me. I leapt to my feet and began clearing up the mess. It didn't seem like much had been taken.

I called 999 and reported the crime. I was well aware that the chances of the police catching who did it was slim, and it was just as unlikely that cops would even bother to investigate. Most victims of burglary are simply given a crime number for insurance purposes and that is the end of police involvement. Up until now, we had been very lucky, only having a couple of very minor break-ins, but our neighbours were targeted almost every year and I had yet to hear of any police investigations, let alone arrests or prosecutions.

I put the kettle on and made myself a cup of tea. I was drinking the last drops when the doorbell chimed. Not even twenty minutes after I had reported the crime, three policemen, one in uniform, two in plain clothes, all in pointless paper medical masks, were standing on my doorstep.

The one in uniform explained the procedure, like he was reading the small print from the back of a retirement policy, whilst the others entered my home and immediately began surveying the carnage.

"You left the house at 12.30, what was the purpose of your journey?" asked the uniformed copper.

"I went for a walk," I said.

"What time did you return to your property?"

"It was just before three," I said.

"You are aware that the limit to recreational activity in public is one hour?" he said.

I just stared at him.

"There is a pandemic, Mr Fisher, and we are advising people to stay home unless for essential reasons," he said, smugly.

If looks could kill, my eyes were currently picking flowers for his grave.

"Perhaps you could remind the arseholes who trashed my house that, if you ever find them," I snapped.

In the corner of my eye, I could see one detective make his way upstairs and push open the door to my study, while another kept me busy with banal questions that were going nowhere.

"Not in there," I shouted up at him. "They never went into that room."

"It's okay, sir," said the cop in front of me.

"I'm just looking for possible routes of entry," shouted the officer upstairs as he casually nudged the door behind him, giving him unabated free access to my work files. I suddenly felt like the Turkey relieved at being brought in from the cold who has just spotted the cooking pot. I cursed myself for inviting it on.

Almost every room, bar my study, had been trashed. Strangely, my computer, which I bought a year or so ago for a pretty penny, had not been stolen.

"Are you sure you didn't maybe leave the door on the latch as you went for your walk?"

I glared at the policeman in front of me as he continued with his inane questioning, before changing tack and advising me on ways of enhancing the security on my home. There was nothing I could do other than follow on, the sense in my gut warning me that this thing had been a rouse to search the premises.

Once satisfied that he had done his bit, the uniformed bobby handed me his crime safety appraisal form and a crime stoppers leaflet, before he was joined at the front door by the detectives.

"We have all we need for now, Mr Fisher," said the taller of the two detectives, his voice muffled due to the mask he was wearing. "The fact that some of your valuables weren't taken suggests that whoever raided your house may have been disturbed."

"Are they likely to return?" I said.

"The best advice I can give you is to stay home and follow the rules," he said.

Was he talking in code? Words were my livelihood, and I am sensitive to how they can be utilised both overtly and subliminally. I clocked the use of the word raid. Burglars don't *raid* houses, they *rob*. The police, however, do *raid* houses.

I gave a meek acknowledgement of gratitude and saw them out.

As they went on their way, the whole ordeal left me completely engulfed by my own rampant paranoia. All the positive energy from Jasmine and Harley's visit had drained out of me. Images of them installing listening devices flashed across my mind, although something told me these ideas of state surveillance were about two or three decades out of date.

I messaged Thor via the Signal app as advised. He agreed to come over. His place was about 25 minutes away in Thornton Heath, near Croydon. A couple of weeks ago, he introduced me to a network of Truthers who gather at Kim's Tea Rooms, a quaint little patisserie in a beautiful village outside Croydon. The group was made up of a wide spectrum of people with a definite leaning towards holistic medicines and spirituality. Their intelligence, honesty and focus was matched by their warm welcome and healthy sense of humour. If you could replace the government ministers with those twenty or thirty individuals, our country would undoubtedly grow and prosper like never before. I was lifted intellectually, emotionally and spiritually, all while sipping pine needle tea and munching freshly baked buttered scones.

Thor arrived swiftly and I felt the power of his aura fill the place. He brought some equipment with him and, before we sat down to talk, he scanned the house for bugs. By the end of the search, he lay 6 tiny button-hole sized devices on the parquet flooring and crushed them under his boot.

"That's a relief," I said.

"Your mobile," he said.

I tentatively handed him my phone, my heart in my mouth, concerned that it would meet the same fate as the listening devices. Instead, he took out a pouch and slipped it in and handed it back to me.

"It's a faraway bag, it blocks out all signals," he said. "Slip it on when you talk to anyone about *anything,* if you know what I mean," he said.

It was identical to the one my old colleague Stefan had given me when we met in Trafalgar square. I didn't mention to Thor that I already had one for fear of looking stupid for not using it.

"It's relentless. I can't help feeling fatigued," I said.

"They're ratcheting up the pressure," he said. "You need to build yourself routines and take time out of the struggle, watch sports, listen to music, anything that breaks the chain. Doesn't matter how awake you are, it will still get to you."

"I used to watch a bit of football," I said. "But now they play in empty stadiums and pipe in a fake crowd noise. That really grates with me, It's fakery pure and simple."

"Yeah, you need to find spaces where you're not going to be triggered," he said.

"Walking on the Common helps," I said.

"Thing is, there's not a day goes by when I don't wish that I was wrong, that somehow I had read it all incorrectly," said Thor. "The relentless propaganda can have you doubting yourself, but that's not a bad thing. Always question everything. It was really getting to me, y'know, the constant barrage of stories that the NHS was on its knees. Croydon Hospital is just up the road. I know it gets mega-busy there. So, I took a stroll up there last week, walked in and around the place. I had pictured a pandemic where ambulances are rushing the critically sick in every few minutes. In reality, it was like a ghost town. A and E wasn't even a quarter full. They are fucking lying to us, but seeing the truth first-hand helped my piece of mind," he said.

Thor assisted me straightening up the place and went online and ordered some surveillance cameras.

"There is a downside to these things," he said.

"Whatever you see through the camera, it's possible that they will hack the system and be able to see too, but I don't think you have any choice. You need to know that it's safe to come and go."

We spent the day chatting and ventured out for a stroll around the common. Thor was more candid there, regardless of the actions he had taken in the house, he warned me that it was still not 100% safe for everything and not to discuss anything that could be twisted to represent an unlawful act of aggression against the state.

"Never talk about the BBC thing," he said, in a hushed but firm tone.

His paranoia seemed to be trumping mine, but I trusted him, so took it all on board. It dawned on me that he had been here all day and in coming to my aid, he may have neglected his mum.

"She's being looked after by Jayne, one of the Truthers from the Tea Rooms," he reassured me.

"That's nice of her," I said.

"This is the power of our community. We are building an alternative society full of wise and caring folk. If we overthrow these devils, the Truthers will be the bedrock of a new and fairer society."

He spotted that I was wearing the pendant I had been given by Baldur.

"I wear the Runes too," he said.

He pulled up a sleeve to reveal a tattoo of various runes.

"They are symbols of power that you hold in your blood," he said.

"I don't really know that much about them, which is a bit embarrassing really as I am part Swedish on my mother's side." I fingered the medallion. "I like that this represents truth," I said.

"And fight," he said.

Thor promised me he'd get me some good books on the subject. He was a fascinating character, and one of those rare individuals that you instantly bond with. He had an aura that conjured up a sense of empowerment and brotherhood.

22. Christmas is Cancelled.

Will you? or won't you? Seemed to be the question on everybody's lips as Christmas Day approached. The government stated you could have four people at your family Christmas celebrations, excluding permanent residents in the same house. The fact that anyone considered complying with this nonsense was ridiculous. This draconian declaration was made on the same day the Daily Mail ran an article about a raucous City of London banquet that the PM, along with four hundred bankers, had attended. The published photographs showed that the only people adhering to the mask mandate were the staff serving the food and drinks. It was just another illustration of what many people were predicting; a society of the vulgar rich served by a slave class who were restricted from even breathing the same air as their masters.

My neighbour, Ray, told me he was having sleepless nights because, if he was joined by his son and daughter-in-law for Christmas, their granddaughter would push the numbers into forbidden territory. So, fogged by the propaganda and rattled by the fear of condemnation, he surrendered his ability to think for himself. He decided to play it safe and he, and his wife Cherry, would spend Christmas alone. The sheer cowardice sickened me to the pit of my stomach.

I arrived at our New Forest house in the early afternoon on Christmas Eve. On the way, I marvelled at the cottages and immaculately dressed country houses that wouldn't have looked out of place on a Christmas card. It was a majestic part of the world in any season.

When I arrived, I found Harley bouncing around like a jumping bean. Our estrangement had heightened his excitement for this family celebration.

At our Clapham Christmases, Jasmine had insisted on a fake tree, bemoaning the mess from falling needles, yet now she had bought a real tree that filled the front room with the aroma of natural pine.

I reminded myself of Jasmine's visit to Clapham with Harley, earlier in the month. That act of kindness and consideration was not lost on me. I decided that viruses, lockdowns, burglaries, vaccines and the prime minister's words of foreboding would be left at the door with the muddy boots and umbrellas.

When Iain arrived back from his latest den-building escapades, I had a word with him about keeping things light for the sake of all concerned. I got the sense that he had bulked out and, even in the short time that had elapsed since our adventures in London, he had lost some of his boyish looks.

"I've left a little something by the door for carol singers," I said.

"Carol singers, are you kidding me?" said Jasmine, laughing. "They'd walk two miles just to knock at four or five houses. You've got more chance of Snow White and the seven dwarves popping by."

"It's the magic of Christmas, anything could happen," I said.

We ate a fabulous meal of salmon and sauteed potatoes followed by a delicate peach desert that Jasmine made especially. She had taken to cooking everything fresh and, as Iain was turning his nose up at microwave meals, her cooking went into overdrive. It seemed like the country move had been good for her. If only I had been part of the package.

I helped Iain with the dishes while Jasmine set up a board game and we all gathered around the dining table and, before long, the air was full of laughter and good-natured chatter. I insisted we switch off our mobile phones which turned out to be easier than I had imagined. Jasmine wasn't drinking so I took care of her share of the wine. It was the first time I'd drunk alcohol for a while and it went straight to my head, and so the dad jokes were let loose much to the faux groans of the children. I didn't care if they laughed at me and not my jokes, just so long as they were laughing. I love being a father.

When I looked outside of the window, in the dimming light across the fields, I could just make out a light flutter of snow settling on the trees. I was living in the moment and I relaxed into a real sense of peace.

We all jumped at a loud rapping knock on the door.

"Ah hah," I said. "Carol singers."

"I can't hear any singing," said Jasmine.

"You have to open the door first," I said.

"Can I get it?" said Harley.

"Course you can," I said, and shared a smile with Jasmine.

He opened the door and immediately took two steps backwards.

"Iain Fisher, is he here?" came the curt but muffled voice of a policeman, in medical mask.

Behind him, I could see two other coppers flanking a police van. They all looked ridiculous their authoritative navy uniforms, with stab vests and padded coats, topped off with pale blue paper nappies stuck to their faces.

I spotted Iain scout the windows and doors before glancing at his wide-eyed little brother. There was no escape. With the front door opening into the living room, we couldn't exactly pretend he wasn't in.

"What's this about?" said Jasmine.

Iain began slowly getting up from the table.

"We need to speak with him, madam," said the officer.

"This is bullshit," I railed.

Uninvited, the policeman stepped into the house. As he did, his glasses steamed up so much, he was forced to take them off. He lowered his mask so he could breathe unimpeded through his nose, much like every supermarket cashier I had encountered during the year.

"Iain Fisher, I am arresting you for criminal damage committed at the BBC offices in London on Saturday 28th November 2020."

"Whoa, whoa, whoa. Arrest him? You can't do this," I hollered.

"You do not have to say anything," He continued. "But it may harm your defence if you do not mention when questioned, something that you later rely on in Court. Anything you do say may be given in evidence".

Iain looked to me and I could feel my blood rise.

"I can't believe this, it's Christmas eve, for God's sake," pleaded a distraught Jasmine. Her sobs adding to the cries of Harley, his wide eyes filled with fear.

"He's going nowhere," I said as I stood to confront them.

"Let's not make things worse, sir," said the cop.

Jasmine barged me out of the way.

"You can keep it buttoned," said Jasmine, her upset at their arrival turning to an anger suddenly directed at me. They cuffed Iain and lead him out.

"Where are you taking him?" demanded Jasmine.

"Charring Cross station, just off the Strand in London," said the policeman.

He instructed her how to get to there and, wiping her tears away, she grabbed the car keys from the side. In the meantime, the other cops had wasted no time in forcibly placing Iain in the back of the van.

"I'll come too," I said.

Jasmine, who was still tactically positioned between the copper and myself, turned and stepped towards me and I lost my balance before quickly steadying myself.

"No. You stay here." she said, her eyes burning at mine.

"This is your bloody fault," she cursed under her breath.

"I think it's best if you do as your wife said, sir," said the policeman, in a patronising tone.

"You can fuck off, and don't tell me what to do. That's my son you've got in there," I raged.

"Sir," he responded. "Let's not make the situation any more difficult than it has to be."

"Difficult? This is Christmas Eve, for fuck's sake," I raged.

Jasmine reached out and physically pulled my attention from the cop's face to hers.

"Who's going to look after Harley, eh?" said Jasmine.

"I'm not dragging him along to a London Police Station, and you've had way too much to drive," she said, poking me in the chest and tipping me backwards. She rushed out of the door.

"I'll call Pam Sowilo," I said, thinking of something practical I could do in my state of helplessness.

"Tell her to call me," she said, over her shoulder, as she jumped into the car.

"Don't worry Iain, you've done nothing wrong. We'll get you home," I shouted, but the van had taken off before I had finished my sentence, Jasmine's car following closely behind.

I stood for a moment, my head now spinning from the drink and the sickening feeling that my son was heading for a stinking cell and there was nothing I could do. I felt utterly useless.

As I closed the door, I caught a glimpse of a framed portrait of my mother that Jasmine must have affixed to the wall next to the coat rack.

"Oh, what do I do now, eh Mum? This world is so crazy, I think you might have had a lucky escape… we miss you so much."

Behind me, Harley had taken off, running up the stairs crying. He threw himself on his bed, his sobs becoming ever more animated, his little body jerking uncontrollably.

"It'll be okay, little man," I said. "It's just a mix up. Iain is a good boy, you know he is."

Still the tears came. I dashed back downstairs, my tipsy state, so recently a relaxed humorous joviality, had become an inappropriate embarrassment in a matter of minutes. I made Harley a glass of milk and grabbed some biscuits, picking up my phone on the way back up to his bedroom.

He sipped at the milk while I called my solicitor friend, Pam, knowing that the last thing anyone would want to hear at eight o'clock on Christmas Eve was a desperate plea for assistance. After apologising profusely, I explained, as best I could, the fate that had befallen Iain. She kindly agreed to represent him and correspond with Jasmine.

Harley's room was a pastel-coloured sanctuary of childhood paintings, family photographs, books and teddies. Jasmine had the magic touch when it came to décor. I chose a book from the shelf in his room and began to read, while he took sips, deep breaths and battled the hiccups. The book, The Potion Maiden by Ozzy Clop, was an old favourite and as much as I couldn't really focus on anything other than Iain's predicament, I could acknowledge what I missed so badly about living under a different roof from my little boy, as we snuggled in together.

I received a text from Jasmine informing me that Iain's friend, Fynn, had also been arrested.

The text was brief, but she did confirm that she was liaising with Pam.

After the third book, I suggested he try and get some sleep, but his eyes bulged at the thought of being alone in his bedroom.

"Will the police come back and get us, Daddy?" he said.

"No, don't worry, your completely safe. It was just a mix up," I said.

I told him we would grab his duvet and make him comfortable on the sofa, so he could join me in front of the TV. I put one of his favourite films on and he was out like a light before it had even got ten minutes in. I gently stroked his sleeping head in a way that calmed me too. The coffee I made was at last lifting my alcoholic haze. I called Jasmine, but she didn't answer. About an hour later, I received a text informing me that Iain had been interviewed and returned to the cells.

'Why don't they let him go?' I typed.

"Don't know,' she replied.

Two hours later, I heard the sound of a car followed by a firm knock on the door and I jumped to my feet. I peered through the spyhole to see a tall well-built man in an overcoat. I flung the door open.

"What the fuck do *you* want?" I ranted.

The man took two paces backwards and lifted his hands in a gesture of peace.

"Sorry, I know it's late," he said.

"It's two in the bloody morning," I raged.

"I'm John, Fynn's dad," he said.

My rage turned to deep embarrassment and I could hear Harley whimpering behind me.

"Who is it Daddy?"

"It's okay, it's okay son, you settle back down. It's Fynn's daddy," I said.

I apologised and ushered John into the kitchen, settled Harley down and returned to the kitchen and closed the door.

"What's going on?" I asked.

"They're keeping them both in for the night," he said.

My heart dropped.

"Bastards," I said.

"Perhaps your wife has told you, the police had photographs of them at the freedom rally and a couple of hazy shots of two lads with similar hats entering Broadcasting house. There is no evidence they have done anything other than perhaps trespass, but even that is unlikely to go to court. So, they will attempt to extract what they need for a prosecution by giving them the third degree at the station and hope they implicate themselves."

I was impressed at his understanding of the situation but horrified at the thought of my precious boy being treated that way by the police.

"We have to hope they're not made an example of, Y'know. But when I heard what happened in London, I did have a fear in the back of my mind that they would come for everyone they could find. So, I briefed them both on what to do if they ever got a tug from the law," he said.

He gave me a look that questioned whether we were on the same page.

"Y'know, say nothing, sign nothing and generally act dumb. I told them that the police would try and turn them against each other by pretending that one had ratted on the other, until one of them spilled the beans. I hope they understand the situation, very different in practice than theory," he said.

"Thanks," I said. "I had no idea."

"They're both pretty sussed lads. It's why they went to London in the first place," he said.

"Yes, I suppose so. Although I doubt Jasmine will see it that way," I said.

"I think your wife said she's staying there overnight just in case they are freed. I tried to explain that nothing would happen now until at least lunchtime but, you know, she's a mother. A mother's pain… it's in their blood," he said.

He had a good way of putting it. I offered him a coffee but he said he had to get home so he could be 'on it' in the morning.

"I just wanted to say, and I know that you don't really know me, but whatever you do, don't allow anyone to encourage Iain to make a statement. When you are innocent you have to be just as careful as if you are guilty," he said.

"Fair point. We have a solicitor friend who is advising and I'm sure she will agree with that. She gave me similar advice when I was wrongfully arrested at a demo earlier in the year," I said.

"Oh yes, I heard about that," he said.

At the front door he shook my hand.

"I love what you do. If we don't fight this, the legacy we leave for our children won't be worth a bean."

As he went on his way, I tucked Harley in on the sofa and ventured into Iain's bedroom. There hanging on the bedpost was the thing I was looking for. It was his favourite hat, and I wasn't sure that he would ever forgive me, but I took it downstairs and thrust it onto the fire.

As I watched over the sleeping Harley, albeit a little restless, the TV announced that it was now officially Christmas Day 2020.

23. Cold Turkey

Jasmine called early on Christmas Day. Her voice was muffled but, even through the face mask she was wearing, I could sense how utterly exhausted she was, so much so that she made no effort to argue. I hadn't dodged a bullet, she just didn't have the energy to pull the trigger.

With no indication of when Iain would be released, with Jasmine in London and me in the New Forest, there was no way we could contemplate Christmas celebration plans of any kind. It stung badly that our boy was languishing in a stinking police cell. I told her that I had negotiated with Harley about moving Christmas to

Boxing Day and he said he would do anything that would help his big brother.

I told her that John called around, relaying what he had said. The atmosphere changed instantly, and I felt the embers of her fury glow.

"He's no better than you. Another crackpot from the foil hat brigade," she spat.

There was no sign of any release for the boys, but Pam told her that she would make a strong representation to the sergeant when his shift began in the afternoon. I suggested me and Harley make our way to join her in London, but she flatly refused. She would wait in our Clapham house until Iain was freed. This ratcheted up the anxiety running riot in my gut.

When John arrived, I didn't want Harley to be party to the nitty gritty of what was going on, so we took a brief stroll in the fresh air.

"I have faith in the boys," said John.

"They do seem to have a very strong bond," I said.

"As soon as Iain arrived on the scene, it was like Fynn came to life," he said. "I mean, he's always been a good lad, but I think he was sick of walking in his father's shadow. Hiking in the countryside had become a chore, y'know, but now he can't wait to get out there, with or without his ole dad," said John.

"I can tell you, Iain's transformation was almost 180 degrees. Our relationship had gone downhill a bit. He's always been a bit of a mummy's boy up 'til recently. Moving here has also broken the hold of the games console. I reckon he must be the only teenager who leaves his phone at home when he goes out. I really appreciate all the help you've given him. He really respects you," I said.

"Iain's great," he said. "They are lucky. When you recognise what shit this society has in store for young folks, the bland, empty culture of, y'know, like self-"

"-Self-hatred," I hastily interjected.

"Yeah, that," he said.

I was reminded of the bad habit of finishing people's sentences. It was part of the overall anxiety that had become my constant companion of late.

"They put an airhead on Instagram and all the girls blindly follow," he continued. "And boys, well, they are so feminised, some to the point that they can't even recognise what gender they are."

I chuckled in agreement.

"The more you look at it, the more you see that almost everything is being bastardised in this world. It's why I spend so much time in nature. No matter what those crazy scientists and technocrats think, you can't beat the great outdoors," he said.

We wandered down to the small lake that reflected the all-encompassing grey clouds above. It was bleak but full of atmosphere. Behind me I could still see the house. My thoughts darted back to Iain.

"What do you think will happen with the boys?"

"Gotta have faith that they keep it schtum and hope there's no funny business," he said. "They didn't damage anything, so you'd think they would be more interested in the people who defaced portraits, smashed windows and graffitied walls. Probably fortunate that, apart from a bit of pushing and shoving, there seems to have been very little physical violence."

His appraisal of what happened in Broadcasting House wasn't exactly accurate and had definitely benefited from a fine coating of sugar. Punches were thrown and the damage must have been substantial, even the boys were guilty of wrecking some pretty expensive equipment, but I wasn't going to add to his worries by correcting him. I wondered if the boys may have been targeted because of my outspokenness. I'm sure the thought would have crossed his mind too. I was grateful that he didn't mention it.

He held up his mobile phone.

"This is our biggest danger, Y'know. It's a listening device, personal history database, photo album and tracking tool all rolled into one. I got the lads to remove apps like Facebook and WhatsApp… they are the absolute worst. But it's the unit itself, y'know. I haven't given up on it yet, but that time is fast approaching. I've seen what they can do, listening in on you, switching on the camera without you even knowing, even in airplane mode or if it's switched off, it says everything that our government allowed this," he said.

I pulled out the faraway bag that Thor had given me, and he smiled.

"Sorry, preaching to the converted, it's become something of a hobby this year," he said.

"Not at all. It's been the biggest struggle of my life, trying to convince the people I care about. The strangest thing is, the people whose lives were built on the mistrust of the Conservative Party suddenly fall in line and blindly obey the Tory PM, it's so surreal and trying to figure it out can be quite a strain on your mental faculties," I said.

"I know, they say, but it's about health," he said. "It's as if they think it can't be about control or political tyranny because they'd tell you. Educated people reduced to obedient clones."

We spent the next half hour validating each other's opinions until John received a phone call from the Metropolitan Police. The boys would be released later that day, pending further enquiries. What a relief.

We darted back to the house where John hopped in his Toyota truck and took off for London. I phoned Pam.

"Iain is a little shaken, but he's just happy to be heading home," she said.

My heart was lifted. 'Heading home', what a beautiful combination of words. I could have sworn that the smile on my mother's portrait had just widened a little.

"The case is flimsy," she continued. "But he will have to reappear at the police station in six weeks' time. They put the fear of God up him, but he did the right thing and followed my instructions. You've got a canny boy, there, he coped and that's all you can hope for in that scenario."

"Thanks so much for helping us."

"The Police know that two youths, of similar description, were part of a gang who trashed a studio, but although Adrian Winkleman was a witness to the vandalism, his description of the people who stormed the studio would not be detailed enough to build a case around. Even with police, erm, encouragement, shall we say, he said it happened so fast, it would be impossible to identify anyone with any real certainty. The rest of the evidence they have is not much more than conjecture."

After I thanked her for the umpteenth time, for sacrificing her Christmas Day for us, we said goodbye and a tear escaped from my eye and rolled gently down my right cheek and I took a moment to breathe it all in.

"Harley," I shouted with joy. "Iain's coming home."

His face lit up like our generously decorated Christmas tree and I hoisted him up and swirled him around.

I tried calling Jasmine, but her phone just rang on. Pam had told me that Jasmine was picking Iain up, so I was forced to content myself with the knowledge that he was free and would arrive home this evening.

I told Harley that Santa had saved our Christmas and we got to work preparing Christmas dinner. He was keen to lay the table and position the crackers above each plate. I put the Turkey in the oven and busied myself with the vegetables. I figured that all being well, they would be back about 8pm.

By 9.30 I started to worry. Jasmine's mobile diverted on to the answer machine and Iain's phone was still here on the table. I checked the security cameras on the Clapham house but there was no sign of life. When they finally arrived, it had just gone 10pm. I pulled the Turkey out of the oven to sit on the sideboard before dashing to open the door, an excited Harley by my side.

A subdued looking Iain was first in and Harley wrapped his little arms around him.

"Am I pleased to see you," I said, and I gave him a massive hug.

"Thanks Dad," he said, quietly.

"He's not some returning hero," said Jasmine.

"No-one's saying he is, I just…" my words cut down by my wife's icy stare.

"Get to your room," she barked at Iain and he slinked off upstairs.

"Oh, come on, it's Christmas," I pleaded. "Let's at least have dinner, eh?"

"I'm not hungry," said Jasmine.

"But Mummy, me and Daddy made the Turkey and I put the crackers out and everything,"

"Sorry, Harley. We'll do the crackers and the presents tomorrow, okay Sweetie," she said.

Harley plonked himself down on the sofa, utter dejection across his little face. Jasmine made a cup of tea and passing me as she headed towards the stairs, she whispered.

"You did this. No-one else, just you. I want you gone in the morning, understand?"

I didn't reply but her message landed square between my eyes, like a knockout punch. I couldn't pretend to myself that there wasn't an element of truth in what she said. It should have been me in that cell, not Iain.

In the morning I looked out of the guest bedroom window onto a blanket of frost that lay across the fields.

However cold it was out there, it would be a heat wave compared to the atmosphere inside the house.

We managed to exchange gifts, with Jasmine insisting she would open hers later. Harley was over the moon about the Scooterboard I got him. As Iain ripped the paper off one of my gifts to him, revealing a hunting dagger, I don't know who winced more, me or him. Jasmine got up and left the room, her face set like a sculpture moulded in an immutable disgust.

With his mother upstairs, Iain quietly complained that his mobile phone had been confiscated and he had been permanently grounded. He was desperate to see Fynn and discuss their ordeal. They had been kept in separate cells and couldn't really communicate through the walls for fear of implicating themselves within earshot of the cops. It had shaken him up, but I was proud of the way he handled it. That said, I felt further abasement at my inability to even attempt to negotiate a better situation for him with his mother. I promised him I would speak with John and let him know the situation regarding his latest incarceration.

Before long I was making my way back to London, my newly acquired baggage of marital ire, political retribution and family recriminations hanging heavy on my conscience. You would have to go some to chalk up a worse Christmas than this, I pondered, as I entered the near-empty streets of the Metropolis. Begrudgingly, I had to concede that whoever planned this whole debacle had got their homework right. I felt utterly demoralised. Just when you desperately need to stick to good routines of health and meditation, to help dig you out of a hole, why do you always seem to choose the things that plummet you deeper into the abyss? I neglected my breathing, healthy walks and fresh fruit in exchange for booze, junk food and the BBC 24 news channel.

Once more, I awoke fully clothed on the sofa, despair my waking bed fellow, my mouth as fresh as a chain smoker's ashtray. Sitting there in a numbness of a grief, the pain felt eternal. The silence was broken by my own words, spoken before I had really had a chance to contemplate them.

"What the hell am I doing?" My murmur turning into a gust of rage. "What the bloody hell… am I… doing?"

I had destroyed our Christmas, put my teenage son in a jail cell, caused untold stress for my little Harley and sacrificed the love of my life. For what? Did I really think I could change the world? Was I so enslaved to my ridiculous ego? So what if people were suffering from vaccines and lockdowns, my job as man of the house was to protect my family, yet I fed them to the lions to save people I didn't even know, people who didn't even want to be saved. People I had no business attempting to save.

I got up, grabbed my keys and exited the house into the biting cold. I had no jacket and the icy wind soon attacked me from all corners. I embraced the pain of that chill, desperate to feel the rawness of winter's razor-sharp punishment. I walked on, hands stuffed deep in my pockets, my arms so cold they were becoming numb, mirroring my emotional state. Eventually it forced me into deep breaths and my walking attained such urgency that I was almost marching. As I approached a row of park benches, I tore at the police tape placed there to prevent people from resting. By the end of my burst of fury, I was covered in the blue and white plastic strips, the ridiculousness of my appearance matching the conflicting nature of my mind and the grim predicament I had woken up to. Life sucks.

24. A Friend in need

The craziness of our world showed no sign of abating. At the big supermarkets in Wales, they were roping off some of the aisles to stop people buying what the state considered was 'non-essential' products. These included Tampons, children's shoes and alcohol. There was sporadic outbreaks of resistance. One man walked into a Tesco's store and smashed thousands of pounds worth of booze while screaming 'Fuck the new prohibition' at the top of his lungs. New and ever more ridiculous rules were being invented by the week, and not just in Wales. Perhaps tempting trouble, I decided I would sit on a park bench every day, even though the signs placed on them forbade you to do so. On the first day, a policeman confronted me, regurgitating some cobbled version of the virus rules. I refused to engage, knowing that there was absolutely nothing unlawful about what I was doing. The more I ignored him the more power drained from his authority and he told me he would give me twenty minutes and then sauntered off. An hour later there was still no sign of him.

By the third day I found that walkers were drawn to me for no other reason than to share a few minutes company with another person. Perhaps lonely at home, it may have been the only face to face conversation they had all day, a human need being wilfully blighted by the government and the media.

"I didn't think you were supposed to sit there," said an old woman who was ambling by.

"Thing is," I said, half sighing at the prospect of a pointless argument with a vocal member of the mask mafia. "You can either accept everything they tell you without question or you can recognise the absurdity of sealing off a bench in the middle of a park and refuse to comply.

"That what you're doing then?" she said.

"I guess so," I said, avoiding eye contact in the hope that she would just shuffle by.

"Would you mind if I join you?" she said.

"Be my guest," I said, and she parked herself a person space away from me.

We were sitting in silence for a short while.

"It's not right all this, is it?" she said, and I felt a little guilty for misjudging her.

"No, they're doing some pretty awful stuff and getting away with it," I said.

She took her mask off and placed it in her pocket.

"I'm seventy-nine, I am. I can say I've seen a thing or two in my time, I have. They say they're doing this to protect people like me. I don't know how many years I have left but I don't want to spend them locked up in my home. If the virus gets me, it gets me, I've had a good run," she said, her voice tired.

"They should have given people the choice," I said.

"I'm Doreen, by the way," she said.

"Stig," I said extending a hand to shake hers before hesitating should she be wanting to avoid physical contact.

"It's ok, Sid. I'm not scared to shake your hand," she said, extending hers.

I thought better of correcting her. We shook and she gave me a warm smile.

"It's the young 'uns I worry about," she said.

"Me too."

"My granddaughter, sweet little thing she is, 14, well, let me tell you, they found 'er looking up suicide internet windows on her phone screen," she said.

"That's horrifying," I said.

"She sees a counsellor now."

"That's good," I said.

"Is it? We didn't have counsellors back in my day. Life was tough and you just had to deal with it. But you had your family, your neighbours and your friends. They were your counsellors."

"World's changed," I said, wanting to remain a little neutral on the topic.

"Ain't that the truth, she replied. "And it ain't for the better, neither."

As we were chatting a young man, probably late twenties, came jogging past wearing a mask, got a hundred yards and then suddenly collapsed clutching his chest.

I raced over to check on him and I was surprised to see that Doreen was already by my side, opening his mouth to check he hadn't swallowed his tongue. She took his pulse.

"Right, lean him on that tree, back against the trunk," she said, suddenly taking charge.

I did as she said and took my coat off and threw it around him to make him more comfortable.

I pulled out my phone and called the emergency services. While I was talking with them, Doreen began conversing with the jogger who was having trouble breathing.

"They want his name," I said.

"Steve… Wooley," he murmured, and we managed to get his age, 28, and the information that he had no previous health issues and pass it on to the emergency services who said the waiting time for an ambulance was 45 minutes. I remonstrated but I knew it was unlikely to change anything. The advice was to keep him awake by talking to him, even if he didn't always muster a reply. Steve was stick thin and only wearing a pair of shorts and t-shirt. There was no way he could sit there for 45 minutes, he'd die of hyperthermia. I spotted a neighbour getting into his car and I called out to him. He agreed to help me gently carry Steve over to my house.

An hour later, there was still no sign of the ambulance. Fortunately, Steve seemed to be picking up a bit. He listed all the physically adventurous activities he did, including five London Marathons, a Triathlon and a couple of years ago he cycled from Land's End to John O'Groats.

"I started having a few issues last week when I got my first dose of the vaccine, but everyone kept telling me that it was normal and to be expected," he said, breathlessly.

Instantly, images and videos I'd seen of some terrifying vaccine adverse reactions popped into my head.

"What you go and do that for?" said Moreen, as if castigating her own child.

"I work with disabled people and the bosses wanted me to have it," he said.

It would be interesting to know just how many people were getting the jab for medical reasons and how many, like Steve, were being coerced or bribed with the promise of exclusive access to pop concerts and foreign holidays.

When the ambulance finally arrived, we explained what happened to the medics. They wrote down everything except the fact that he was convinced this was due to the vaccination. When I quizzed them about that they got all arsey.

"We'll let the doctors decide, eh?" was one reply.

"I think the fellow knows his own body," I replied.

Steve was packed up and we wished him well as he was driven off lights and sirens blazing.

Ray who had watched from his window was now loitering awkwardly on his front step.

"Heart attack," I said, knowing that was what he wanted to know.

"Same thing happened to my brother," he said.

"Sorry to hear that," I said.

"We've been lucky, Stig. I've had six people in my family get ill this month," he said.

"Lucky?"

"Well, if they hadn't got the vaccine, gawd knows what would have happened. Saved 'em it did."

At that point I thought it best to end the conversation, so I went back inside and made another cup of tea and chatted some more to Doreen, an act that broke another of the government's moronic rules of no non-family visitors allowed in our homes.

As the days passed, it seemed like the utility costs of the entire street were being chalked up and added to my bills. Things were getting desperate on the money front. I really needed to get things ironed out with Jasmine. I thought we should sell the house while the prices were high and make the move to the New Forest permanent. There was only one pretty big snag, I wasn't currently welcome there.

I cashed in the last of my shares and thought it wise to withdraw a few grand in cash, should I need the flexibility of anonymity if I had to suddenly escape. I bought myself a little rucksack and stuffed it with things I might need in an emergency. Every day, when I saw it at the door it prompted me to question my mental faculties and whether my paranoia was getting the better of me. Thor had suggested it and so I took it everywhere I went, hoping that I didn't give some mugger a late but welcome Christmas bonus.

I never heard from Jasmine. My attempts to contact her hit a brick wall. Iain's phone was dead, still confiscated I imagined. I relied on John for scraps of information. Harley's calls were the light that broke the darkness that haunted me. He was allowed to phone a couple of times a week, always random times which meant I missed some and, with no way of returning the calls, those moments were a complete downer when their number appeared on my phone's missed calls list.

I had been ignoring a frequent caller whose number I didn't recognise until one night, in the middle of cooking, I pressed the answer button by accident.

"Hello Stig? It's Jayne," said the voice.

It was the lady looking after Thor's mother.

"Hi Jayne, everything ok?"

"Do you think you could pop over?" she asked tentatively.

"Sure, when were you thinking?"

"Now," she said. "well, just whenever you can."

"Err, okay. What's up?"

"I'd rather not discuss it on the phone," she said.

I switched the cooker off, grabbed my coat and dashed off to Croydon.

When I arrived, an exhausted looking Jayne let me in. There was no sign of Thor. His mother, however, mistook me for an actor from the nineteen fifties. She spent the next few minutes telling me how wonderful my films were, until she got stuck trying to remember the title of one of her favourite movies that she'd seen me in.

"Don't worry, Maggie thinks I'm Jayne Mansfield most of the time. You know, the famous dead actress turned carer," she said, with a smile.

As Maggie fell silent, Jayne informed me that the police had raided the place and arrested Thor.

"They nicked over 50 Truthers," she said.

"Bastards," I said.

"He knew they would come for him. You've seen him. No matter how many masks he puts on, you can't hide a six-foot-four man with wavy blonde hair that's built like a tank," she said.

We were temporarily interrupted by Maggie who had nodded off and was snoring like a rattling door caught in a draft.

"What's the current situation?" I said.

"He's on remand in Wormwood scrubs," she said.

"Shit… Does he need a solicitor? I know a good one."

"He's got a solicitor. The evidence is kind of minimal, but he thinks they might make an example of him. Y'know to stop others willing to physically attack the elite."

"I hope not," I said.

"I don't know if you heard, but protesters stormed the studios of Sky, Channel 4 News, and ITV's morning show. Dr Shillary was saved by security, but I think he had to administer a new pair of underpants to himself after the ordeal."

"Is there a way of contacting Thor? Does he need anything sending in?" I asked.

"He doesn't want any contact from Truthers while he's in there as he knows he'll be monitored. He suggested you lie low and avoid public demonstrations," she said.

"I don't think I'll be invited back to speak at any more demo's after the last one," I said.

"Might be just as well," she said. "They're really turning the screw."

"How about yourself? How are you getting on?"

"Well, Maggie can be bit of a handful and needs round the clock care. They've frozen Thor's bank account so we're a bit screwed, I mean it's not cheap. If I charged Thor proper rates, he wouldn't even be able to afford me. But I've known him for years and he really helped me out when I was stuck in an abusive relationship, so I was only too happy to help him out. Problem is, it won't be long before we run out of money."

"What about the Tea rooms? Maybe we could raise some from the Truthers, they're a good bunch, I mean, we could all chip in, I'm going up there, I could mention it if you like?"

"Yeah, maybe," she said, fatigue playing across her face. Maggie suddenly awakened and exploded into a string of expletives.

"This is normal. She doesn't know where she is. I'm going to have to get her sorted."

I took that as a signal to leave and made my way back out into the street.

Getting into my car, I started the engine, paused and turned it back off.

I rummaged in my bag. I pulled out a book and ran back up to Thor's and knocked on the door.

When Jayne opened the door, she was all rubber gloves and exasperation.

"I've got something for you," I said, opening up the book and delving into the hollowed-out pages where I had concealed my emergency money. She saw the cash and her face fell.

"Oh no, you don't need to do that. I wasn't asking-"

"-I'm offering, regardless," I said.

"Yeah, but now it sounds like… I was just moaning, it's been a long day. Really, we'll find a way," she said.

I placed the money on the table by the coat stand and reached out to grasp her hands in an attempt to calm her.

"He's been a rock to me too. It would be an honour for me to be there for him," I said.

"I can't take that, that's way too much," she said.

"If you don't take it, I will only come back tonight and push it through the letterbox. So please, save me a trip and accept it, eh?"

Her shoulders relaxed and I caught a flash of relief on her face.

Jayne threw her arms around me.

"Thank you, thank you so much."

Behind her Maggie was shouting something about Jimmy Savile.

"I'll let you go," I said. "Take care. And any word from Thor just give me a shout."

She nodded and disappeared off to see to Maggie.

My exploits at the Clapham Common benches were now not too far from therapeutic counselling sessions with folk stopping by to iron out some of the emotional wrinkles they had acquired during the recent lockdown. I often received the same boost as they sought from our frank but friendly chats.

As I wandered home, fresh from the now weekly meets with Doreen, who still called me Sid. Steve Wooley, the jogger, had left hospital and returned home. His days of running marathons were sadly over.

As I got to my front door, I received a call from Jasmine. It was the first time we had spoken since Christmas.

"Is Iain up with you?" she said.

"No, I haven't seen him since…err, I haven't seen him," I said.

"He got up early and took off. Let me know if he turns up your end," she said.

"He's probably in one of his woodland hideouts," I said.

"Well, if he thinks I'm hunting for him in the bloody woods, he's got another think coming,' she said.

"Maybe I could help out, should I come down?" I said, tentatively.

"No."

"Well, he'll come home when he's hungry, it's what Mum used to say about *me* when I was a boy," I said. She wasn't interested in my attempts to connect on a personal level.

"Just call me if he shows up," she said.

The line went dead. The toxic water from our disastrous Christmas had yet to make its way under the bridge and I was starting to resent her for the way things were playing out.

I called John and he informed me that Fynn and Iain had gone on an adventure.

"I wasn't aware that Iain hadn't told his mum," said John.

"She might not have let him go, if she had known," I said.

"It's half-term so no harm done. I wouldn't be too concerned. If I hear from Fynn I'll tell him Iain needs to phone home," he said.

"With all the madness in the world right now, if you ask me, escaping into the wilderness seems to me like the sensible thing to do," I said.

25. Needles and Haystacks

There was a mounting ton of data online, explicitly showing the death and damage these injections were doing. My experience with Steve Wooley, the jogger who collapsed on the Common, was not unusual. People were quite literally dropping like flies and not all of them were living to tell the tale. Professional footballers, some of the fittest and constantly monitored people on the planet, were collapsing with heart problems.

My articles for the Light Paper now became based around anecdotes from my own life, or things I picked up on my travels, at places like Kim's Tea Rooms. Nothing strikes harder than a human story, especially one free from the usual commercial overtones and self-promotion.

Two days after going AWOL, Iain turned up and received another grounding, although Jasmine did return his phone and he was able to contact me. He said that one night they spent looking up at the stars, from atop a haystack. He said it was a bit like a game, a test they both enjoyed. For their next adventure, he had set a rule that they would make a new bushcraft camp each night from anything they could find in the countryside and move on to a new site the next day.

"Well, you know that one of the reasons we called you Iain, was because your initials would be I.F. And the word '*if*' is always full of possibility. I thought you'd grow up to be an inventor, or an adventurer," I said.

"You just made that up," he said.

We both burst out laughing.

"What if I become a plumber? Or a builder?"

"Noble honest jobs. Anyway, it wouldn't matter what you did, you've always had an inquisitive mind. When we used to go on long journeys to Scotland and Cornwall, I would see your mind whirling as you bombarded me with questions about all kinds of things. I loved those days."

I probed him about the upset he caused by running away.

"I had to do something. Mum was... y'know," he said.

"I know, but you won't get anywhere by antagonising her, believe me," I said.

He agreed not to repeat his secretive early morning exodus and we fell into a wonderful discussion about everything from movies to philosophy. He thought I should stand up to his mother and come to the New Forest and live there permanently.

"London is dying, Dad, all the big cities are," he said.

"It's under attack, that's for sure, but these devils ought to know that if they push Londoners too far, the fight back will be ferocious."

It was great to have a conversation where we were on the same level. I tried to recall a previous time when that may have been the case, but I couldn't think of one. During these past months he had transitioned from boy to man, perhaps a little prematurely, but I was proud of how he responded so intelligently to what was going on in the world. His generation will face more challenges than any have for centuries. Even the dire consequences of living through world wars will be eclipsed by the tyranny heading their way. And, when you consider how many young people are lost to the illusions that have been created for them and instilled by schools, universities, modern literature and popular culture, it may soon become a Nietzschean struggle of survival of the fittest. The most sentient strength being that of the mind to withstand the psychological warfare being raged on every channel and frequency deployed by an enemy that remains invisible to most people.

There was a strange mix of relief and trepidation when the police informed us that the decision on whether to charge Iain had been put back by four months. Pam Sowilo, our solicitor, said it was outrageous and certainly felt like the state flexing its muscles. The government was well aware that those with a legal case hanging over their heads were less likely to cause them any more problems while their fate hung in the balance. The ones that wouldn't be cowed, folk like Thor, would need to be incarcerated.

With spring blowing the winter woes away, and the NHS's inflated case numbers on the wane, the state was forced to relinquish some of its grip. The media declared that we were nearing the end of all restrictions, naming June 1st as 'Freedom Day'. Having dangled the carrot of hope, they still urged people to work from home, wear masks in shops and restrict human contact and most of all, get jabbed. Children were being forced to be tested at school twice weekly, even if they'd shown absolutely no signs of symptoms. These tests returned a mass of false positives that were used to continue their scare tactics. It was a self-fulfilling prophecy of deceit.

My calls continued to hit a brick wall, so I wrote to Jasmine to request a meeting to discuss the Clapham property. People in the know were saying interest rates would be at record levels within the few years, so, with things opening up, it might be the right time to put the house on the market. We needed to make a decision before it financially crippled us.

With Iain's birthday approaching I ordered a water purifier that came in the form of a large straw and various other bits of survival gear. When the parcel arrived, it also came with a small box with 'free gift' printed on it. I didn't recall any mention of a free gift when I ordered his new kit. I opened the box and there in a velvet bag was a penny whistle.

When I was a child, I set my heart on learning the penny whistle. There were two men on our street who played them, often in the form of a whistle duel. My mum went barmy at the sound, but I found it entertaining.

I took the whistle out and gave it some puff. The high-pitched tone I was expecting was usurped by the stifled sound of hot air.

As I unravelled the paper that had been placed inside the whistle, I realised that it was another message from WB, and I now understood that the initials stood for Whistle-blower.

I will raise up a prophet from among countrymen like you, and I will put my song in his mouth, and he shall speak to them all.
PLAY IT LOUD - for breath is the fervour of the soul.
There are Dementors in the health system stealing souls from those they ensnare.

The links brought me directly to the medical establishment's server where documents showed that a policy of using ventilators, where once oxygen had been prescribed, was being stringently enforced. In Italy as many as 80% of patients who were placed on ventilators died. Many people would deteriorate after intubation, but still the practice went on.

I got to work on an article on the scandal. Some digging around of my own, crucial to verify my assumptions, unearthed quotes from frontline health staff.

"They only went into multi-organ failure when we put them on a ventilator," said one doctor. "Something about the ventilators seems to really exacerbate their condition," said another.

Darren Nesbitt at the Light Paper, was so delighted with my article he doubled my money, which made me feel a little fraudulent, as the tip-off virtually handed me the story on a plate. The most important thing was getting the message out and the Light Paper was tripling its circulation with each edition.

I was delighted to receive an invitation to discuss things with Jasmine the following Saturday. I texted to thank her and confirm the date and I instantly felt a shooting pang of anxiety at the thought of our meeting. It was crazy. She was my wife, neither of us had been unfaithful and the circumstances around our split was not of our making, yet, in my mind, this opportunity to have a face-to-face rendezvous had the feel of a make-or-break affair and after our recent lack of communication, I wasn't feeling altogether hopeful.

The days passed with me in the grip of rising apprehension until finally I was standing outside the front door of our quaint little house in the New Forest, except it was Jasmine's home now. My legs turned to jelly as she opened the door and let me in. Using my own key, I considered, may have been regarded as an act of micro-aggression.

Harley attacked me with a slew of cuddles before the doorbell went and he was off out with a playmate that involved a sleepover, reconvened now the iron fist of the government had been so kind as to permit such a thing. The Woodland Warrior was off with Fynn, so it was now just the two of us in the house.

We exchanged small talk but, unfortunately for me, Jasmine spoke in a matter-of-fact kind of way, and it was difficult to gauge the mood behind her shield. I had shared every intimate secret with this woman as we sailed the seas of a pretty comfortable middle-class life together, but now I was reduced to a quivering wreck in her presence, desperate not to make the wrong move. To make things worse, she looked fabulously radiant and, fearing she could read my mind, our personal telepathy had been something we once took for granted, I tried to suppress any carnal desires.

Things started off edgy and went downhill from there. Jasmine had stumped up a bigger share of the deposit for Clapham and wanted that to be part of the settlement in percentage terms as opposed to the exact money she paid. I wasn't there to quibble about money, I was still hanging on to the ragged threads of hope that we could find a way back to where I thought we belonged, but her attitude riled me. Ideally, I wanted to join her and the boys here in the New Forest, even residing in the tiny spare room if required. I braved mentioning it and it was like I had hit the red button and declared all-out nuclear war. She went off like a ballistic missile. I grabbed my emergency bag and headed for the door.

"That's right, run away," she said, as she chased after me, spittle flying from her mouth.

"Said the woman who packed up and ran away from London," I replied.

We were facing off, inches from each other now and my head was spinning, hot flushes of injustice were followed by rage and then shortly replaced by an inappropriate surge of lust. I could sense her breath on my face as she continued to rant at me at how useless a father and husband I was. I responded with equally hurtful discourse and the tit-for-tat was lost to me in the blur of the heaving breaths it took us both to manifest this explosion of stress and tension, neither one of us willing to give an inch. I brushed her arm and for the first-time flesh met flesh. Then something strange happened. My mind was hijacked with the question

'Shall I? shan't I?' I couldn't escape it.

'Shall I? shan't I?'

'Shall I? shan't I?'

'Shall I? shan't I?'

It was intensifying like an orchestra's crescendo, all the while she blasted me with profanity laden invective.

'Shall I? shan't I?'

'Shall I? shan't I?'

'Shall I? shan't I?'

'Shall I? shan't I?'

'Shall I? shan't I?'

'Shall I? shan't I?'

'Shall I? shan't I?' 'Shall…'

I lurched forward and kissed her deeply and she instantly responded by wrapping herself around me and we were lost in an embrace that took us to unimaginable heights of passion. There was no time to breathe, talk or climb the few steps up to the master bedroom. If it was going to happen it would happen by the front door, on the dining table, the living room floor and the sofa.

When the whirlwind was over, we lay there panting, in a state of undress. The room splattered with debris, was no less chaotic than the Clapham break-in.

Jasmine escaped off to the bathroom and showered. Inside I was glowing. The stress and anxiety we just expunged couldn't be matched by a thousand therapy sessions. I was king of my world once more and Jasmine was reanointed as my rightful queen.

When Jasmine returned, immaculately turned out in a tight grey cotton skirt and figure-hugging woollen sweater, I found that, while I was downstairs reassembling the front room, she was upstairs rebuilding her defences. The atmosphere was amicable, but if the fluttering white flag of peace and reconciliation would be flying over this beautiful part of England, I was not duly invited to reside underneath it. For all intents and purposes, we were still at war.

Jasmine made some excuses about going into Dorchester to get some shopping and I could recognise that this was an 'I shan't' moment and cordially cut my losses and exited stage left. When I kissed her goodbye, I was consciously directed to her cheek and not her lips.

I called John and told him I was in Hampshire, whereupon he invited me over to his place. When I got there, he introduced me to his girlfriend, Jill. He made the point of explaining that she was a nurse at the Berkana Hospital in Dorchester, encouraging her to speak freely about the current situation there.

"The public don't know the half of it," she said. "It's hideous. I'm lucky, I'm on the cancer ward, but there are loads of my colleagues… seriously considering jacking it in."

"More people caught the virus in the hospital than arrived with it. Tell 'em, Jill." said John.

"The last place you want to end up right now is hospital," she said.

"It's rife, not just here, right across the country, y'know," said John.

"Yeah, I've got friends in hospitals across the South West, same story everywhere. Last year they released sick patients into care homes," she said.

"It's what killed my dear old mum," I said.

Jill reached out and squeezed my hand.

"It's wicked, so wicked. Every time I question my superiors, I get threatened with the sack," she said.

The conversation moved on to vaccinations and the fact that some countries were now insisting on mandatory jabs for health workers.

"There would be a stampede to the exits," said Jill. "I don't even think half my colleagues have been done. You can imagine the propaganda we get hit with, trying to guilt trip us into getting spiked. The problem for our bosses is that we know the vaccine status of all the sick people we see."

"What would you do if they give you the ultimatum?" I asked.

"I'd rather clean toilets, wash dishes, anything. The only time you should take medicine is when you trust the people endorsing it and believe it will help you. For me, it fails on both accounts," she said.

On my way back to London, I stopped in on Jayne. She was hopeful that Thor would be released on bail when his hearing came up in a months' time.

There was a state of flux in the outside world and one to match in my personal life. With such constant uncertainty it was a struggle to think in terms of future family plans, employment and my long-term abode, so I tried to just live in the moment. If you're fighting anxiety, there needs to be an end point and I just can't see one.

I needed to slow down, take time out of the circus, but how can you slow down when you see a totalitarian monster truck sweeping all before it, heading in your direction?

With money dwindling fast, I secured a job writing critiques of the latest book releases for Literature Review. The money wasn't bad and when Andrew, an old colleague I had once worked with at the Post, said it was under condition that I used a *nom-de-plume*, I was reminded of my current status in the industry.

After a face-to-face meeting with Andrew, to endorse the deal, I went perusing a west end book shop to pick up something for Harley. I really missed reading with him.

As I exited the bookstore, I bumped into Gemma Holgate, a colleague of Jasmine's, heading into the shop. My mind immediately started compiling answers to questions she hadn't asked.

"Oh, Stig. It felt good to be back in the museum, if a little scary," she said.

"Scary?"

"Oh, you know, getting back out there in the world again," she said, as if that was something we hadn't done all our lives.

She kept her mask on and our muffled exchanges really grated. I had no idea what Gemma knew about mine and Jasmine's separation, so I tried to keep the conversation on safe ground.

"The museum opening up again?" I asked.

"Jasmine not tell you? We have got a really amazing show, The Women who drove invention," she said.

"Oh, yeah, I think she mentioned something," I lied.

She skewed her head a little as if to study me.

"Everything ok with you two?" she said.

"Oh, you know," I said, not really answering.

"Well, I hope you get your plumbing sorted out," she said.

"My plumbing?"

"At your house in Clapham."

"Oh yeah. Working on it as we speak," I said.

"She's not going to be able to keep commuting from Hampshire when we go back to full-time."

I nodded.

"I'm picking up a book for Annabel. I don't know if you heard but we had our jabs last week, she's been sick ever since, poor thing," said Gemma.

"I'm sorry to hear that. Give her my best," I said.

Annabel, Gemma, and Jasmine were the three musketeers, tongues as sharp as bayonets and laughter full of mischief. When they were together, you did not want to get caught in the crossfire. They spoke in a shorthand that only they could understand, I often envied their closeness. I imagined that in another era, they might have been marked out as Witches.

I held my tongue on expressing my concerns about Big Pharma. Anything I said would get straight back to Jasmine.

"She's really fed up, but she says at least she knows the vaccine's doing its job," said Gemma.

Annabel was a health obsessive, yoga, jogging and cycling fanatic. If she ever contracted the virus it would probably fly through without leaving so much as a calling card. Yet she took something to protect her from that, that protection incapacitated her for over a week.

Madness really was becoming bigger than Beatlemania.

The book reviews were harder to write than I had expected. The authors were either pandering to a market they had been encouraged to appease or excreting their own prejudices. It was page after page of prose laced with hatred of male archetypes, condemning anything with a whiff of traditional values. I am happy to read voices that contrast with my own world view, but this was a stream of inauthentic cookie-cutter feminist bilge

When it became too much I found myself gravitating to the books I had picked up for Harley.

The Disneyfication of Dickens had rendered him a little passe among the chattering classes, but his prose was a world full of all the colours of life. I was knee deep in the London smog of Oliver Twist, exciting myself by the thoughts of eventually reading it to Harley when, out of the blue, he called.

"Daddy, Daddy," he said.

My imaginations of us reading together burst into life.

"Hiya, little man, I was just thinking about you," I said, contemplating how wonderfully fate had facilitated this connection.

"Daddy, Daddy," he said, his voice suddenly broadcasting a panic to me that I had failed to recognise at first.

"Daddy, it's Mummy, she's not well, she's shaking, really shaky," he said, the alarm in his tone cutting through me like a razor blade.

"Where is she?"

"She's on the floor, but her body is shaking, and she isn't speaking. Daddy I'm scared."

"Ok, Harley. It'll be ok. I need you to be brave," I said.

"Ok Daddy, but get here fastly," he said.

"Where's Iain?"

"I don't know," he replied.

"Have you tried calling him?"

"I don't know his number, Daddy."

"It'll be on Mum's phone."

"I know, Daddy, but it's locked, and I don't know the number code," he said, his fear becoming more acute with every word.

"I'm scared Daddy, she's still shaking, hurry Daddy."

"Okay, stay on the line, I'll call an ambulance."

I phoned 999 on the landline and, as much as this really was a major emergency, after the debacle with Steve Wooley, when they ran through the usual questions, I laid it on as thick as I could, while breaking intermittently to reassure Harley.

"They're on their way, son, okay. Now go and find a pillow to put under Mummy's head and move anything away from her that could cause her any harm, and I'll call Iain."

I threw some things into my emergency bag while I phoned Iain.

"Iain, you need to get home," I said.

"But Dad, we've just made a camp and a rope swing over the river, it's so-"

"-Get home as quick as you can, Mum's having a fit or seizure or something and Harley's there on his own."

I raced to my car and had no choice other than nudge the red Nissan that had boxed me in, triggering its alarm. This heightened my already angst-ridden state.

"Fuck you, tin opener, bubble car bastard," I shouted incoherently.

I didn't have time for the usual inch-by-inch micro-manoeuvrers.

I got to Hampshire in record time and found a distressed Harley being comforted by Iain, their mother now a resident of the Berkana hospital in Dorchester.

As we drove to the hospital, Iain filled me in about what the ambulance crew had said.

At the hospital we were told that Jasmine was in intensive care, and we were not allowed to see her or loiter in the waiting room. Mentally, I was back at St Thomas's hospital in London, reliving the nightmare that was my mother's final hours. I imagined Jasmine would be getting emergency treatment, so it was understandable that we were forbidden to see her right now and so, partly out of consideration for Harley, I didn't put up a fuss.

The problem with believing passionately, some would say obsessively, about anything, is you find yourself viewing things through a narrow prism where everything is connected in some way to that passion. I knew that people all over the world were going through what we were experiencing right now, due to vaccine damage, yet I had no evidence that Jasmine had even been injected and so until I knew otherwise, I had to cling on to anything that staved off that frightening theory.

According to the boys, she had mentioned nothing about being vaccinated.

The hospital said it was unlikely there would be any news until the morning, and they would call if that were to change. I took the boys home and busied myself in the kitchen. I wasn't remotely hungry, but I just needed to do something in an attempt to distract my growing anguish for Jasmine.

26. We should do something

"We should do something, Dad," said Iain.

I gritted my teeth and exhaled. I tried to placate him but just enraged him further in the process.

"They're gonna kill her," said Iain.

"Don't say that," screamed Harley and he took off upstairs into his room.

"Don't speak like that in front of him, he's only eight-years-old for Christ's sake," I said.

"You know it's true though," he replied.

"We don't know that," I said.

"How can you stand there and say that?" he said.

"Just… just…" I trailed off, not knowing what to say.

"I'm going to check on Harley."

I could hear his sobs as I neared his bedroom. He said he wanted his Mummy and that set him off again. I eventually coaxed him downstairs for a dinner than none of us wanted and all of us barely touched. Iain apologised to Harley, and I caught a glimpse of the tender side of him that had been mostly hidden behind the façade of teenage bluster these last few years.

When it was Harley's bedtime, I read a handful of stories that neither of us absorbed, the words just disappearing into nothingness as soon as they left my lips.

We were all treading water until the weight of our eyelids got the better of us and, one by one, we drifted off into a temporary state of sleep, one ear always open for the sound of a ringtone that would herald fresh news of Jasmine.

In the morning I contacted the hospital. They confirmed that she experienced a pretty stable night, and a doctor would call with more details. I was reminded that due to virus regulations we would still be prevented from seeing her.

The doctor phoned and said that although Jasmine was stable, she was still in a critical condition and was having some breathing problems.

"We think the non-epileptic seizures will respond well to the treatment," he said.

"Is she talking?" I asked.

"There's been no verbal response at this point," he said. The only time I ever knew of her going to a hospital was when she was pregnant.

"She is also some paralysed down her right side. The specialists will be assessing her tomorrow, so we'll have to wait and see what they have to say," he said.

Inside my head I was screaming 'No More.' They were deconstructing the most wonderful human being I had ever known. The only woman I had ever truly loved. The person who gifted me two little angels. I desperately wanted it all to stop.

The doctor went through a list of questions in search of a probable cause for her condition but there were no threads he could join up. Jasmine had been pretty lucky on the health front and I wasn't aware of any hereditary illnesses. She had been the picture of good health and now she had been reduced to this.

He said it was a mystery, but that they would do their best to work it out.

"Is it," I took a deep breath in anticipation of a negative reaction. "Is it vaccine damage?" I said, hoping he would inform me that she hadn't been injected.

"We're not thinking in terms of vaccines. This is far more serious than we would expect from any adverse reaction to vaccination," he said.

"Well, I've read about all kinds of horrendous injuries they've caused," I said.

"Mr Fisher, they wouldn't run a vaccine programme if it wasn't safe," he said.

I could sense that I was stepping into territory he was keen not to explore.

"She was vaccinated, though wasn't she?" I asked.

"Yes, but like I say, we don't think that has any relevance to her current condition," he said.

I was too numb to argue. I wanted so badly to see her, to hold her hand and tell her it was all going to be ok.

Asking if I could visit her, he parroted what I had already been told about their pandemic protocol. Inside I was petrified that I would lose my wife almost exactly a year after my Mum was stolen from us.

After speaking to Fynn, Iain said that Jill would find out how his mother was. Iain was unsurprisingly agitated and, when Harley went to bed at night, he repeated his theory to me that they would kill her, even quoting an article I had written about ventilators.

"You need to be more like Thor," said Iain, goading me. "He *saved* his mum."

"His mother was in a care home, not a hospital," I replied. Although the thought was at the forefront of my mind that we would get her out of there at the earliest opportunity.

Every day I checked, every day they told me there was no improvement and she still hadn't spoken.

Unfortunately, the human mind discovers patterns and acclimatises to its daily predicament. This was fast becoming our new normal. Clogging pain and biting anxiety, repeated groundhog-style each day. I felt helpless and utterly feeble.

On the sixth day, John's girlfriend, Jill, was able to gain some information from her friend in the ICU. It wasn't good news.

"They put her on a ventilator. My friend Sarah, in ICU, has complained to her superiors, but the protocol has been enforced from above. I'm sorry, I wish I had better news," said Jill.

The rest of what she had to say melted into the words of the article I wrote on ventilators that Iain had quoited from the Light Paper.

I had powered down, my battery critically low, fighting the stark realities of contemplating life without Jasmine. My children would be motherless. Like all couples, we had endured our highs and lows and we may have Yo-yoed a great deal lately, but I always felt that we were one bounce away from getting back on track.

The eighth day was the worst. It was Iain's birthday. I had no idea how to cope with that. Under the circumstances, he didn't want a fuss, but it was an important distraction for Harley. When he blew out the candles on the cake, we all knew what he wished for. We wished for it with all our hearts too.

I successfully avoided the TV news but, when I was travelling back from an essential food run, I caught a fragment of the radio newscaster revealing that the government were considering vaccine passports. The very next item on the show was about a scientific study proclaiming that you were just as likely to catch the virus and pass it on whether you had been jabbed or not. The hypocrisy was astronomical, but I was in no doubt that it would take the usual course and fly over most people's heads.

I received a message from Jayne informing me that Thor was refused bail and would remain in Wormwood Scrubs for the foreseeable future. The sky was falling.

Jamie, Harley's friend from school, called around and asked if he wanted to go with them to their house for the afternoon. I didn't think so, but he surprised me when he said he would. I guess a boy of eight can only hold his breath for so long before he needed come up for air.

Jamie's mother was able to negotiate Harley's release with just the right amount of sympathy and compassion, for which I was extremely grateful.

He climbed in the car and they all affixed their virtue masks and drove off.

As I turned to go in, Iain just exploded.

He gathered up my collars and yelled in my face. "Do something, Dad. Why don't you bloody do something,"

"What do you expect me to do, huh?" I yelled back, breaking free from his grip.

"The next time we see my Mum she'll be in a coffin, if you don't do something," he ranted.

I wasn't a superhero like Thor. I was an out of work journalist squeezing my eyes shut for fear of opening them and finding myself staring down the barrel of a world devoid of hope. His words crashed into me like a wrecking ball. I was broken and this was just another part of myself crumbling helplessly into a black sea of pain.

"If you really meant one word of what you said to those people in Trafalgar Square" he said. "You would get off your arse and go rescue her."

27. Action Stations

Jill was there as promised, her foot keeping the staff entrance ajar. It was a job to keep calm and I wasn't sure whether it was the thought of getting caught or my anguish at what I would feel when I saw Jasmine. Either way, the wheels were in motion, there was no turning back.

As we approached the door, kitted out in masks and doctor's white coats, I took a deep breath.

"Second floor, half-way along on the left," said Jill quietly. "You'll see the signs."

"Thanks, Jill. I really appreciate this," I said.

"Be confident and be quick," she said.

We took off along the corridor and when Iain told me to slow down, I tried hard to calm myself. Whenever someone approached, I avoided their eyeline busying my gaze on the NHS clipboard Jill had availed me with.

On the second floor, Iain grabbed a wheelchair and positioned it a few yards from the ICU doors.

I buzzed and waited.

"ICU," said a Scottish voice.

"Doctor Taylor, come to check on a patient," I said.

My heart was in my mouth as I sensed a hesitation.

"Your pass not working?"

"A patient threw up on it this afternoon, hasn't been the same since," I said.

"Okay, come in. You know the protocol, fresh gown and mask at the door."

"Yes, of course," I said.

The buzzer sounded to unlock the door.

"Wait here and try not to be too conspicuous," I whispered to Iain.

Inside, I donned the relevant PPE and headed for the nurse's station.

The noise of the place was a mix of the artificial and human. Bleeps and mechanical machinations competed with awful sounding breathing, coughing and snoring.

"Can you tell me where I can find," I looked down at my clipboard. "Patient 200324 Jasmine Fisher?"

"Fisher's in IC6," said a nurse, a post box sized space around her eyes was all I could see of her face. I guessed that she was Asian or perhaps South American.

"Thanks," I said.

Even though my nerves were hidden behind this bright blue paper disguise I could see that my presence wasn't without some suspicion. Jill told me to just bluff it and be confident as I was masquerading as a doctor of a much higher rank than the nursing staff I would encounter in the unit at this time of night.

"What's the purpose of… I mean it's a wee bit-," said the Scottish nurse questioningly.

"-Anomalies in her bloods. She may be able to help us isolate the virus in a way that could be helpful in terms of research. And yes," I said in a commanding tone. "It's been a long day. Thank goodness for coffee beans, that's all I can say."

"Would you like one?" she said.

"Maybe afterwards, thanks." I said.

She seemed to buy it and I wasn't going to waste another moment risking being discovered.

Jasmine's bay was conveniently positioned near the exit. Through the Perspex glass I could see her chest moving up and down, her beautiful face obscured and imprisoned in an ugly big mask, a tube jutting out of it like she was the prey of a plasticated octopus.

Once inside her bubble, I just stood there, looking at her and I was brought back to the moment my dad passed away. Her face, just like his, was missing something. The life had been sucked out of her. She was more poorly than I had imagined. Her eyes stared gauntly at the ceiling, devoid of any kind of acknowledgment that I was there.

If the eyes truly were the window to the soul, then these windows revealed nothing but a void where once the vivacious carefree spirit of a beautiful human being had danced across them.

What should I do? I had researched how to disengage a patient from a ventilator, but this wasn't a patient, this was my Jasmine. I genuinely believed the treatment they were prescribing was going to kill her, but faced with the bleeping machines, with all the swirling emotions spinning in my head, I had to admit I had no idea what I was doing. I was completely out of my depth. I felt tears crawl down my cheeks and stick to my paper mask.

"You're coming home, honey. Love will make you better," I whispered.

I switched the machine off to see if she could breathe unaided and she coughed and spluttered but still her eyes remained in a glazed-over state.

Behind me I heard a voice.

"Switch that back on, now!" shouted the Asian nurse.

I stood frozen by the dark reality of the situation.

"What do you think you are you doing?" cursed the nurse.

The nurse charged over and restarted the machine.

"Who even are you?" She demanded.

"I'm her husband," I said.

I stood staring at Jasmine, paralysed in a fog of heartbreak, the clipboard tumbling from my hands, clanging on the floor.

"Intruder in ICU 6. Immediate assistance," she spoke into an intercom by the bed and a red light started flashing.

I threw my arms around Jasmine and buried my face in her bedsheets.

"I love you," I murmured.

"If you disconnect her, you will kill her. She is extremely ill. Don't you understand that?"

The Scottish nurse rushed in and dragged me away from the bed. The room was now spinning and when the nurse spoke, her muffled voice was transmitted to my ears, as if under water.

She pointed to the door.

"You need to leave. Right now."

I held my hands up in surrender, I don't know why, I guess I wanted them to understand that I was no risk to their safety.

"Call off security," said the Scottish nurse.

"but we must... it's protocol," said the Asian nurse.

"Call them off. I don't want an inquiry," said the Scottish nurse, imposing her authority.

"But the-"

"-Just do it," insisted the Scottish nurse.

Her colleague conversed with the intercom as I was led out of the Intensive care unit.

"I'm sorry you have been prevented from seeing your wife," said the Scottish nurse firmly. "But this is not the way to do it. There are some very sick people in here and we can't afford for their health to be compromised by such a dangerous stunt like that," she said.

She was right of course. It dawned on me that I had done something so incredibly reckless.

I apologised and she quickly returned to the ward, ensuring the door was firmly shut behind her.

I leant on the wall. All reality temporarily suspended.

"Dad," called Iain, snapping me out of it.

I looked around at him.

"Where's Mum?" He said.

I shook my head. He needed to get out quick. He was half-way along the corridor, next to a vending machine. We had a quick exchange as I passed him.

"Where's Mum?" he said with more urgency.

"She's not getting out. Just go," I said.

"But-"

"-Get out of here," I said.

I pulled off my PPE as I rushed for the lifts while Iain took the stairs.

While I pressed the button and prayed it would arrive swiftly, I spotted a beefy security guard racing towards me. He was older than me, but his confident and menacing manner told me that he was probably ex-military. Before I knew it, he had me in an arm lock, my face pressed up against the wall.

"You'll go to prison for this, you sick bastard," he said, clearly enjoying the confrontation.

"Get the fuck off me, you prick," I said grimacing through the pain.

The lift opened and Jill appeared, rushing to my aid.

"Let him go, Jack. He's not an intruder, there was a misunderstanding in ICU," said Jill.

She prized me away from this giant lump of muscle.

"I've just spoken to Shona. I'll get ICU to fill you in. Let's keep this under wraps, eh? Don't want Doctor Taylor putting a complaint in," said Jill.

"Okay Babe, if you're sure," he said.

She bundled me into the opening lift. As soon as the doors closed, she confronted me.

"What the bloody hell happened in there?" she said.

"I… I tried to rescue her," I said.

"What the hell? You said you just wanted to see her," she said.

"I'm sorry. I just… her eyes."

The lift arrived at the basement and the doors sprang open.

"Right, give me your coat and get out of here and exit the way you came," said Jill. "And hope to hell that I can go back up and smooth this out with ICU. For both our sakes."

28. Why?

During the following four days, I spoke to the hospital, and nothing was mentioned about our ill-advised rescue bid, so I assumed Jill had found a way to make the incident disappear. I didn't dare call John and ask how Jill had saved the day, imagining how livid she must have been. I couldn't face up to that right now.

When the hospital finally agreed that we could visit Jasmine, I knew that it could only mean one thing. She had irreversibly deteriorated. We were being permitted to say our last goodbyes.

I went to town and got my hair cut, regretting it half-way through due to the colossal effort it took to communicate with the barber. They had only been open a week or so and transformed their shop into a cross between an operating theatre and an abattoir. There were plastic curtains, marked off areas and everyone was in masks. All this madness for a disease with a survival rate of well over 99%.

We parked up and before entering the hospital I grouped us together for a hug.

"Take a deep breath and let's be strong for Mum, eh?" I said, as much for myself as for them.

My words choked me instantly. I could see that it hit them too as they nodded instead of responding verbally. I was under no illusions, it would be like attending a funeral, yet we were visiting the dead that hadn't yet passed away.

Inside we were dressed like plastic sheeted spacemen. No gifts were allowed, and we weren't permitted any physical contact. If you could devise a method of destroying the human spirit, then this was it. Saying goodbye to the one you love while treating them like they were rotting garbage in a plastic bin bag. I now wholeheartedly regretted bringing Harley. This wasn't the natural process of life, illness and death. Putting aside the premature nature of Jasmine's demise, this was a circus of Luciferin proportions.

We stood by her bed and it took all my strength to speak.

"Just tell her you love her," I said.

It was traumatic, particularly for little Harley. He brought a teddy bear that Jasmine gave him a few years back. It was a monkey holding a banana they had christened *Chompy*. It was an icon of his childhood that he knew represented happy times and it was his way of conveying that happiness to his dying mother.

Iain had been at loggerheads with his mum over much of the last year and I sensed a feeling of guilt hanging over him. He too brought something, a small framed picture of the pair of them laughing. I took the photo in a restaurant in Rome where my attempt at conversing in Italian had sent them into fits of laughter. When the waitress asked if we were finished, I meant to say 'coronamento', Italian for *all finished*, but instead confused her by responding with the word 'Cavolo' which is the Italian word meaning 'Cabbage'.

I had seen Jasmine's gaunt face and vacant eyes. I had seen her strapped up to that machine, both at the time of our abortive raid and in my nightmares ever since. After today, I was in no doubts that this bleak and harrowing vision would haunt our children in the dead of night too.

"She can hear you. She knows you are here," I said. There was a silent pause so loud I thought it would blow my ears out.

"Mum, I love you with all my heart," said Iain.

His words triggered Harley, who instinctively reached out and hugged his mother. I briefly turned to see if the nurse was going to intervene. You would have required a heart of arctic temperatures to prevent that little boy's gesture of tenderness.

"Mummy, get better. Get better, I love you. Chompy loves you too, Mummy," he said.

Being smashed, square on, with an enormous sledgehammer would have been a softer blow than that little boy's words and I could sense the tears welling up in the nurse's eyes as she swiftly turned her head away.

I left with one boy in each hand. I squeezed their hands tight until we were free of the brutal claustrophobia of the hospital and its sanitised aroma and stale air.

"You were so brave, I'm really proud of you both," I repeated as we headed for the car, tears streaming down our faces.

Like a song of heavenly purity and innocence slashing at the darkness, Harley's little voice issued a sound that absolutely floored me.

"What will happen to Mummy?" he said.

I exchanged fleeting looks with Iain, and I will be forever grateful for his intervention as I found myself devoid of the words to respond.

"They are doing their best, Harley." He pulled his gaze from his younger brother and focused on the hospital building. "They're doing their best."

I pondered the point of life. With a day like today it was hard to even imagine a tomorrow. I still had my precious boys, part of a daisy chain of commitment to our existence that stretched back to the days of Gods and Kings. How far forward would it reach now the devils of destruction had taken over, poisoning us out of existence? A cult of darkness had twisted everything natural and healthy into a vile, meaningless emptiness.

That evening, when I saw the hospital number flashing on the display of my mobile phone, I took a long and deep breath and exhaled before answering it.

I knew it was over.

She was gone.

She would become a statistic, propping up the lie that she died from the virus. They would hide the reality, that her death was caused by a dangerous vaccine foisted on her with the aid of a media as guilty as those who dreamed up this hellish scheme.

In the end, she heard the voices of her beloved children and then slipped away into the shadows of time.

Printed in Great Britain
by Amazon